Also by J.T. Lundy:

Happy Utopia Day, Joe McCarthy

Saving Grapes

Little Joe McCarthy,

A NOVEL

King of America

J.T. Lundy

Green Light

Published by Green Light Books
Naperville, IL

ISBN 13: 978-0-9960708-0-5
ISBN 10: 099607080X

Library of Congress Control Number: 2016901506

Issued also as an ebook.

Design and composition by Green Light Books
Cover design by Green Light Books

For Renée, Calvin, Cooper, and Colin

Old Faithful

SCOTTY HAS HIS feet up on the RV's dashboard as I drive. He slouches in the passenger seat, his fingers tapping furiously away at a game on my wife Karen's iPhone. He looks up. "Is Yellowstone dangerous, Dad?"

I smile at him. "Perfectly safe, son."

"Do you think we'll see a bear?"

"We might. But don't worry, buddy. We're going to have a great time in Yellowstone. You'll see."

"Can we see Old Faithful first?" Scotty makes a geyser-like explosion sound.

"Sure, sport. It's your birthday. You call the shots today."

Karen sits on a tan vinyl swivel seat behind Scotty. She closes her book, puts her hand on his shoulder, and looks at him with a forlorn happiness. "Eleven years old. I can't believe the time has gone by so fast. It seems like yesterday when we brought you home from the hospital, walked through the front door—"

"And Dad yelled at Grandpa Archie for filling the house with balloons." Scotty laughs. "You tell the same story every year."

Karen rubs Scotty's head playfully. "That's not the main point of the story."

"It's the funny part," Scotty says.

"Balloons just seem dangerous for babies," I say, looking into the rearview mirror at the brown mosaic décor of the 1982 Winnebago I'd borrowed from Archie, my best pal from my job at the US Customs Service. Archie had loaned us the RV to drive from Las Vegas, where my last and only spy mission had ended, and where Archie was enjoying his honeymoon with my mother-in-law. Archie had recently married Karen's mom, to the delight of everyone but me. Archie is a good guy and all, but he has an irritating way of bumbling into my business. "Grandpa Archie—very funny," I say.

"Well, he is my grandpa now."

"Archie told Scotty to call him Grandpa," Karen says. "You better get used to it, Chris. Archie is your father-in-law now."

A father-in-law who's a year younger than me. I don't think I'll ever get used to Archie being a member of the family, but I remain silent and let Karen and Scotty enjoy teasing me. In my peripheral vision I see them smile conspiratorially at each other.

My name's Chris Thompson. Officially, I work for the United States Customs Service in the Washington DC office. Unofficially—for the past few weeks, anyway—I have been working undercover as the President of the United States' personal spy. Originally I thought this would be the coolest thing (I've always wanted to be like James Bond and work for the CIA), but after nearly being killed by a college campus cop turned border patrol commandant, Apache helicopters, and an old Fat Boy nuclear bomb, I now yearn to get back to my old predictable paper-pushing desk job.

The president had pulled me out of that job in order to send me on a cross-country spy mission that helped save the United States from a resurgent McCarthyism and the totalitarian regime of the Big Mac Party. Only I and a few others know that the president, whom Big Mac's leader Vance Slater had drugged with a chemical called Macwacky, is completely innocent of any of that regime's crimes.

One week ago the mission ended, and the president has given me a month off. Scotty, Karen, and I are heading back from Las Vegas at a leisurely pace, and we plan to see all the sights. On the president's recommendation, I've turned my cell phone off and we have been "off the grid," enjoying ourselves as a family, thankful to be alive, safe, and together again.

President Wright granting me this leave was a godsend. I'll always be grateful for all that he has done for me. I sure hope he survives the political fallout from Big Mac.

We enter Yellowstone through the south gate and motor toward Old Faithful along a rolling, curvy road. Tall, slender, lodgepole pines create a flickering green wall on both sides of us as we pass.

I pull the Winnebago into the Old Faithful parking lot.

Karen and I hold hands as we follow Scotty over to the geyser. Scotty walks around the perimeter, giddy with anticipation. I sit with Karen on a bench. She puts her hand on my leg and rests her head on my shoulder. The past week has been good for us—good for us as a couple, and good for us as a family. It's great to be together again, safe, without stress or worry. And to think that we have three weeks left before we have to return to Washington, DC.

"Dad! Mom!" Scotty races toward us. He points at a turbulent, gushing pot of steam. "Look."

Karen and I stand up. Old Faithful shoots hot steam high into the blue sky. A mild mist that smells like sulfur dampens our skin.

Cheers and ahs go up from the crowd surrounding the geyser. There are old couples, student tour groups, and young families, all looking up at the whitewater tower. Park rangers mill about, explaining the science and history behind the phenomenon we are seeing.

I notice a thin, sharp-looking ranger watching us from the opposite side. He stands ramrod erect, and his green ranger's uniform and tan hat fit perfectly. He has a mustache and small goatee. As soon as I notice him, he looks away and starts talking to a couple of backpackers. Scotty is jumping up and down, raising his fists into the air like Rocky, yelling at Old Faithful. "Whooh!" I turn around and see the Yellowstone lodge. Maybe the ranger was looking at something there, or perhaps he just found Scotty entertaining. I have to relax. I'm still too keyed up and paranoid from the mission.

Old Faithful simmers down, and we return to the Winnebago and drive over to the Fishing Bridge campground to set up our spot. I plan to do nothing but relax and celebrate

Scotty's birthday for the rest of the day.

It's evening, and a sleepy golden sunlight slowly retreats through the pines. Swarms of mosquitoes have driven us inside. Scotty is in the back bedroom, lying on our bed and watching *Skyfall* on DVD. Karen is at the kitchen counter spreading chocolate frosting over the yellow cake she has managed to bake in the RV's tiny oven. The cake's buttery aroma spreads throughout our little home. I step up behind Karen and nuzzle her neck.

"No, you can't have any frosting," she says.

I put my hands around her waist and gently press against her. "I was thinking about more than just a little frosting." I rock our hips together. "How about a little twerk?"

"I'm too old to twerk."

I pull away from her. "Oh, I'm sorry, ma'am. I thought you were Karen Thompson, my young, hot wife."

"Ha." Karen turns around and sticks a finger globbed with chocolate into my mouth. I suck the chocolate off seductively, and she giggles. She kisses my neck, turns me around, and smacks me on the butt. "Go get Scotty. It's time for the birthday party."

Scotty doesn't have to be told twice. He bounds through the kitchen and sits in a booth at the dining table where Karen has set up a pile of presents. "Can I?" Karen and I smile and nod, and Scotty tears into his presents.

Karen lights the candles and places the cake in front of Scotty. I hear a throaty *tut, tut, tut, tut*, like someone has hooked up an outside generator. The noise gets louder, and the sound of a helicopter flies overhead. I flinch. I haven't heard or seen a helicopter since Las Vegas, and this copter is loud, like a powerful military helicopter. Maybe the rangers have a helicopter, or maybe it's a firefighting helicopter. But then again, Yellowstone has a policy of letting fires burn.

The helicopter passes, and then Karen and I start to sing "Happy Birthday." We sit down across from Scotty. I'm holding the video camera, so I have to lean back a little to frame both him and the cake. "Make a wish," Karen says. Scotty closes his eyes tight and concentrates. He opens them and blows out the eleven candles. Karen and I cheer. I set the camera down, and we all hold hands. We raise our arms and hands together and then let go, throwing our hands and fingers toward the sky. "Wish!" we shout, propelling Scotty's wish to the cosmos, a family birthday tradition.

There's a knock on the door. We all look at each other and shrug. I open the RV door and see a ranger standing before me.

"Good evening," he says.

"Good evening. Is everything all right?"

"Nothing to be alarmed about." He looks past me into the RV, and his gaze settles on Karen and Scotty. He tips his hat to them. "Good evening."

"Good evening," Karen says.

It's all rather awkward. The ranger seems more interested in looking at us than talking to us. He has a skinny frame, but the muscles in his arms are taut, and he seems tough. His uniform looks brand-new. An image of the ranger that was watching us at Old Faithful flashes in my mind. The ranger before me doesn't have a goatee, but the two rangers are eerily similar somehow.

"There are reports of a female grizzly with two cubs in the

area. We suggest you stay inside for the rest of the night."

"Cool," Scotty says. He puts his hands on the window and starts scanning the woods.

There's a tattoo on the ranger's neck, partly covered by his collar. It starts with a distinct B, and then I can't make out the rest. There's an N, or an M, or maybe an R.

"Will do," I say. "Thank you, sir."

The ranger nods and walks away.

I quickly close the door.

Karen passes out pieces of cake on small red paper plates. "Cake, Scotty. You can look for bears later."

I open the door back up. "I'll be back in a minute."

"Dad."

"Chris, what are you doing? Stay inside."

I step outside. "Just a sec."

"Chris." I look back. Karen holds a piece of cake tantalizingly toward me. "Cake."

I hold up one finger. "One minute."

I close the door and scurry around the RV. That tattoo might have read BM, which could mean Big Mac. There could still be some loyalists out there, and I would be their number one target. Why have I been so complacent? I pick up all of our folding chairs and slide them into the storage compartment. I unhook the water, sewage, and electric, and then I remove the tire blocks.

I enter the RV and head back to the bedroom. I grab my keys from the nightstand drawer and turn to go to the front. Karen stands before me. "What is going on?"

"Put away the loose things. We're leaving." I brush past her and walk to the driver's seat.

Karen follows. "Are you afraid of the bear?"

"Not just a bear—a grizzly bear with two cubs. But that's not it. I'm not afraid."

"Dad's not afraid."

I put the key into the ignition and start the old Winnebago.

Karen stands over my shoulder. "We are perfectly safe from any kind of bear inside the RV."

I turn on the headlights and step on the gas. "I said I'm not afraid." I tear out of the campground a little too fast. Karen falters and grabs a cupboard to balance.

"Dad's not afraid. Are you, Dad?"

I pull out onto the asphalt road and our ride smooths out. "It's those rangers that have got me nervous."

Karen sits in the passenger seat. "There was only one ranger."

"You didn't see him, but there was another ranger checking us out at Old Faithful."

"Checking us out?"

"Looking at us a little too long, just like this ranger did."

"He did look at us weird, Mom."

"Military types—both of them," I say.

Karen buckles her seat belt, resigned that we have left. "I just don't understand."

"Did you hear that helicopter that flew over? This is Yellowstone. I'd say it's pretty rare for a helicopter to fly over a campground at night." I look in the rearview mirror. Nobody is following us. "Scotty. Check out the sky. Do any helicopters or airplanes appear to be following us?"

"Ridiculous," Karen says. Still, she looks out her window and checks the sky. "All clear on my side, Captain," she says sarcastically.

"That ranger had a tattoo," I add. "It might have been a B

and an M."

"Bowel Movement." Scotty cracks up. "What dork would get a BM tattoo?"

"Exactly, right, Scotty. See, Karen? It could be Big Mac."

"Or Bill's Motors, or Big Man, or anything," Karen says.

"Or Butt Muncher." Scotty laughs, but Karen shoots him a stern look. "The sky is clear on my side," he snaps.

I pull off the main road onto a gravel road that looks little used.

"Now what?" Karen says.

"I think it will be safer in the backcountry."

"Safer from what?" Karen has an edge in her voice, and I can tell she's becoming angry.

"I don't know. Okay? I don't know. But something is not right, and it's been my experience that being on the move works best in these situations."

"Dad's a spy, Mom. He should know."

"He's a United States customs officer who went on a two-week harebrained trip." The RV is vibrating and rattling fiercely from the gravel road, and Karen looks more frantic the farther we go. "What situation? There is no situation. You're imagining things, Chris. Please. Can we turn back?"

The headlights shine on a small, open clearing. I pull the Winnebago off into the two-foot-long grass and park. "This should do us."

"We have no hookups," Karen says.

I turn the ignition off and pat the steering wheel. "It's an RV. We have a generator for electricity, full tanks of gas and water, and an empty sewage tank. We're good for a few days."

"A few days. This is the backcountry. There's grizzly bears out here."

I look at her smugly. "As you said, we're perfectly safe from grizzly bears inside the RV."

Scotty laughs. "Yeah, Mom. You did say that."

"Don't you two gang up on me."

Scotty walks to the front and puts his arm around Karen. "It's all right, Mom. Dad knows what he's doing."

The morning is crisp and cool. A cloud has yet to appear in the sky, and the sunshine makes everything seem safe. I stand outside in the tall, wet grass. Birds are chirping, and I hear running water from what must be a nearby stream or river. Perhaps I did overreact yesterday. Everything seems so peaceful, so safe.

The RV door opens, and Scotty jumps out, ready to go. I can see Karen sitting on the couch reading a book. She's still in her flannel pajamas, and she has headphones on.

"Sure you don't want to explore with us?" I say.

Karen rocks her head side to side with the music, oblivious to what I have said.

"She's cranking to Eminem," Scotty says. "Mom doesn't hear anything else when she listens to Eminem."

"Eminem?"

Scotty laughs somewhat sheepishly. He tilts his head and shrugs his shoulders. "She started playing Eminem after she discovered you went to that dance bar where the girls are naked."

"That club was part of my mission."

"We knew that, but Mom said she still needed a way to get her anger out."

I shut the RV door. "Let's check this place out."

Scotty and I walk toward the rushing water sound. We reach a bluff and see a tranquil pond that feeds a slow-moving river. On the back side of the pond is a white rock wall. A ten-foot-wide foamy waterfall cascades down the wall from a high cliff.

"Cool," Scotty says.

"Yeah. Really cool," I say.

"Dad?"

"What?"

"Can I ask you a question?"

"Yeah, sure." I take a deep breath of the fresh pine-scented air. "What's your question?"

Scotty has a serious look on his face, like he has been pondering something for a while. "Do you like looking at naked girls?"

Scotty and I have had the birds and bees talk, and we attended a sex education presentation at his school, but both discussions had been mostly scientific. "Um, well, you see, Scotty." A movement catches my eye, and I see a moose with magnificent antlers dip its mouth into the water on the other side of the bank. I motion to Scotty to keep quiet and then point to the moose. We stay silent, smile at each other, and watch the moose. Several minutes go by. The moose looks up and settles his gaze on us. He sizes us up and then turns around and walks back into the forest.

"Cool, yo." Scotty walks down the bluff to the water and I follow. He picks up rocks and inspects them. "Do girls like looking at naked boys?"

A faint helicopter motor in the far distance disrupts the area's peaceful, natural sounds. "Maybe. I don't think as much though."

He throws a rock into the water. It skips twice. "It just seems weird. Do you think I'll want to go and watch naked girls dance?"

I put my hand on his shoulder. "Don't worry about it too much, son. You'll figure these things out soon enough. But I definitely don't recommend hanging out in strip clubs."

The helicopter sounds closer. I see it appear over the treetops, perhaps a half mile away. I can't believe there are so many helicopters in Yellowstone. I'd think people would complain about the noise pollution.

Two red dots, like laser pointers, flash next to the helicopter and then disappear. On instinct, I crouch close to the ground, pulling Scotty down with me.

"What's wrong, Dad?"

"Probably nothing. Just being safe."

Scotty watches the helicopter, excited like we're playing a game, feeling important. He's exactly like I was when I started this spy business last month. I know better now.

Two flying silver dots dart across my eyes.

Scotty sees them, too. "Bees." he says.

The small, cylindrical objects, each about the size of an unshelled peanut, circle around us. Each has a tiny, illuminated red dot on its front end. Although we can't see the helicopter, it must be close because the sound of its motor is turning into a roar.

"Move." I grab Scotty's hand and run with him along the bank. The peanut-like drones follow, hovering four feet above us.

I look at Scotty and nod toward the water. "We have to go under. Ready? Dive."

We both take a step and dive underwater. I grab Scotty's hand, and we swim toward the center. We pop our heads out of the water as carefully and quietly as we can, and we take deep breaths. The water is bitingly cold. I wish that was our only worry. The two drones circle searchingly twenty feet away, at the place where we disappeared under the water. A throaty whup-whup-whup sound deafens us. The helicopter appears from over the cliff, shooting a burst of air down on us, rippling the water.

"Under!" I shout.

Scotty and I submerge again. I grab his hand and swim toward the rolling bubbles where the waterfall collides into the pond. The coolness of the water quickly warms to my skin as I swim as hard as I can. The water is pure and translucent, and I can see the rocky ground below us. Clusters of underwater seaweed-like plants seem to wave at us, wiggling from our turbulence. Scotty and I are probably easy to spot through the clear water, too. We have to get to the falls where we can hide.

My legs ache. My lungs burn. I hope Scotty can handle staying underwater so long. We reach the falls, kick through the roiling water, and then shoot up, gasping for air, hidden behind the waterfall. We grab on to the rock wall and are able to find small ledges under the water to stand on. The crashing sound of the falls is all we can hear now.

What were those little drones? Were they cameras? Perhaps they were even weapons. Is Big Mac back in power? Or is this some kind of new threat from some other secret group trying to take over America? Or maybe it's a foreign power, like the Canadians. Everyone's been worried about them lately.

If the drones are after me, though, then they must have something to do with Big Mac, or at least some subsidiary of them. I doubt they're back in power—supposedly the leaders were all going to be rounded up and arrested. The authorities got Vance Slater and Chief Justice Lancaster; I saw both of them carried away myself. One thing is for sure, though: I don't want Karen and Scotty to be harmed because of me. I need to make sure they are safe somewhere and then figure out what is going on.

It is dim behind the falls, but some sunlight filters in and we can see. Scotty looks scared and bewildered. I put my arm around him. "We should be safe here."

He nods and seems to gather strength. His eyes open wide. "What about Mom?"

Damn. I selfishly forgot all about Karen. I stick my face slowly into the falls until I can see the other side. Hopefully I'm still hidden.

There is no sign of the minidrones, but the helicopter is just behind the embankment on the other side. It is hovering over the grassy knoll where the RV is parked. Shit.

I pull my head back behind the falls. Scotty looks at me hopefully. "I'll go get Mom," I tell him. "You stay here. If I don't come back within fifteen minutes, then come out."

Scotty's lips quiver, and he's about to cry. I put my hand to his face. "I might have to be a spy again, son." I touch my temple twice quickly and then point at Scotty. He touches his temple twice and points at me.

"We'll be all right," I say. "But you have to be strong." I kiss his forehead. "I love you, Scotty."

"I love you, Dad. Go save Mom." He pushes me away.

Little Joe

MY NAME IS Joe. I like to watch the National Geographic channel, play video games, and learn about the world on the internet. When I get mad, I swear.

I just had my twelfth birthday, and a lot of people I didn't know came to my party. I don't have any friends. People say they are my friends, but they are all adults. I don't know anyone twelve years old. I know a lot of doctors and nurses and generals and other important people, like politicians.

Sometimes someone takes me to a park. Once, when I was nine, I played with a boy next to me on a swing. We pretended to be fighter airplanes, but then they made me leave. Mostly I stay inside and watch TV and play video games. I'm not officially allowed to go on the Internet until I complete my high school course and mature, but I haven't even started my high school course yet. I can't wait that long. I sneak on the Internet every chance I get.

I have a destiny, they say. If that's true, then why do I have to do all this crap? Why do they test me so much? Every day they make me study. Every day they test my intelligence. Every day they poke me with a needle or do something else to see if I'm healthy. Someday I'll get a big needle and poke them.

I like watching what's outside on National Geographic. My favorites are the mountains. I've never seen a real mountain. I like watching about the wolves in Yellowstone. Some people don't like wolves, but I think they are really nice. They have real families and take care of each other.

General McGuffin is nice to me. I've known him forever. Sometimes I like to think that he is my dad. I call him Papa sometimes. I wish he was my dad, but if I say anything like that everyone gets all funny. "No, no," they say. "You are special. You are—" I don't want to talk about it. You don't know me yet. You wouldn't understand either.

Total Immersion

I DIVE UNDER the waterfall and swim as far as my breath will take me. I emerge and see the helicopter still hovering directly over the RV. It's a Super Stallion, the largest US military helicopter. Four long straps are hanging out of it. Two men are sliding down one of the straps.

I swim as fast as I can to the shore, climb the embankment, and run toward the RV.

Karen stands in the kitchen window. She still has the earphones on, and she's bebopping back and forth and singing. She has a knife and is spreading peanut butter from a jar onto a piece of bread that she holds in one hand.

"Karen!"

I'm almost there. The men take the four straps from the helicopter, connect them to two straps underneath the RV, and then climb on top. The helicopter begins to rise, pulling the straps taut, and the RV slowly lifts into the air. Karen continues to dance, sing, and spread peanut butter.

"Karen!" I run and jump at the floating RV. I'm just able to grab onto its rear bumper. If I work at it, I think I can pull myself up to the back ladder that leads up to the roof. I sway and try to pull myself onto the bumper.

The RV is twenty feet off the ground. The helicopter and RV slowly rotate, and the waterfall comes into view. I imagine Scotty behind the waterfall, patiently waiting, cold, afraid. Karen's in obvious danger, but Scotty is just a kid, alone in the wild. I drop my leg, hang from the bumper, and then let go.

I hit the ground feet first and then fall hard onto my left side. I look up and watch the helicopter and RV lift higher into the sky. They hover over the cliff and waterfall, and then they float away.

I'm breathing heavily, starting to panic. Okay, okay. Someone has kidnapped my wife. Did they mean to? Maybe they just wanted the RV. No, that's ridiculous—they wanted me. I shouldn't have hid in the falls like a coward. But I was protecting Scotty. What do I need to do now? I need to make a plan. Okay, okay. I have to get Scotty and get back to civilization. I should contact the president, or Derek—probably Derek first. He's reliable. He'll be able to see clearly what's happening here.

I stand up and quickly gather my bearings. I run back to the pond and swim to the waterfall, and then through to Scotty. He's clutching the rock wall.

"I don't like waterfalls," he says, shivering with cold. "I was scared."

"I don't like waterfalls either." I put his arms around my neck. "No more waterfalls. Let's get out of here."

Scotty holds on to me and we swim to the shore. We stand on the bank, our clothes soaked and dripping. I wrap Scotty in my arms and try to calm his shivers.

"What happened? Where's Mom?"

"That monstrous helicopter. It, it—"

"What, Dad, what?"

"It snatched the RV and flew off."

He looks at me confidently, certain that somehow I have found a way to save his mother. "And Mom?"

"I'm sorry, Scotty. She was in the RV making PB&Js when they took it."

Scotty squirms out of my arms and runs up the bluff to see for himself. I follow him, and we walk around inspecting the depressions in the grass where the RV was, hoping for a clue.

I put my hand on Scotty's back. "Let's go find help."

He spins away from my touch. "How could you let this happen? Why didn't you stop them?"

"I'm sorry, buddy. I was too late. They had a helicopter and trained men."

He clenches his fists and his face turns red. Tears swell in his eyes. "I thought you were a super-spy. You fought an army of men and saved the whole country. A helicopter and a few guys should've been easy."

I try to reply, but he looks so disappointed in me that it takes my breath away. I failed him, and it kills me.

A few moments go by as Scotty comes to terms with my limitations.

"So what about Mom?" he says.

"I need you to be strong, and I'll need your help, but we'll find her." I look at him as if there is no doubt, because that's truly how I feel. "Whatever it takes. We will find her."

Scotty purses his lips and nods, accepting our mission. "What should we do?"

I look around searching for something, anything, that will help us, but we are alone.

"Dad. What are we going to do?"

I start walking. "We're going to get out of Yellowstone and find Derek."

"Cannonball? I get to meet him?"

I wonder if people are after Derek, too? I can't think of that now. It doesn't matter. If Big Mac is back, we're going to need each other no matter what. Derek and I operate better as a team. Okay, I suppose we're kind of blundering idiots, but we get the job done somehow.

"Yes. Derek the Cannonball," I say to Scotty. "Come on, now. We have to hurry."

We walk down the empty gravel road we had driven last night. "Do you think Big Mac took Mom?" Scotty asks.

I don't say anything.

"Do you think Big Mac is back in power?"

I had turned my cell phone off, and we had ignored the outside world for a week; no radio, TV, or newspapers. When we left the FBI was supposed to be rounding up the leaders of the Big Mac Party, but anything could have happened since then.

I hear a car engine and voices, and a camper trailer whizzes by. We're near the main road. "We're about to find out," I say.

At the end of the gravel road, there are two ranger SUVs parked with yellow lights flashing. Orange barricades block the intersection with the main road.

"Hey. You two," a ranger calls to us. "This area is closed. You shouldn't be in here."

Two rangers stand with arms folded.

I stop and hold Scotty protectively. We really look like a

mess.

"You two all right?" one asks. He's in his sixties and has a protruding belly. If he's working for Big Mac or whomever, he's not their best. The other ranger is in better shape, but both of them wear uniforms that look like they weren't bought just today. These two are real park service rangers, I conclude. Still, I need to be safe.

"Stay here," I say to Scotty, and I walk up to the rangers. "We could use some help."

"It looks like it," one ranger says.

The rangers are friendly. I've no choice but to trust them. They put us into the back of an SUV and drive us to a ranger station. It's a small log cabin. Inside, it's dark and rustic. Small, dusty mullioned windows cast faint squares of light on a few old desks and chairs.

They give us blankets and hot chocolate. An old ranger with cropped gray hair paces back and forth before us as I tell him our story. He does not look impressed.

"I first became suspicious when I saw a ranger watching us at Old Faithful."

"Watching you?" The old ranger looks angry and doesn't seem to trust me.

"Yeah, watching us—like he had us under surveillance." I touch my chin. "He had a small goatee."

"None of my rangers have goatees."

"You see? There you go. It's suspicious." I look to a younger ranger who sits at a desk to the side of us, observing. "It's suspicious, right?" I look back at the old ranger. "And why exactly was that road closed down?"

The old ranger stops pacing in front of me. He bends over, puts his hands on his knees, and thrusts his face in front of mine. His breath smells like coffee. "Your wife disappearing—being carried off in an RV by a helicopter, you said?" He says the words very methodically. "That's suspicious."

I constrain my voice and speak slowly. "Who ordered the road closed?"

The ranger stands up. "We did. There are bears in the area." He looks at Scotty. "Did you see your mother carried off in an RV by a helicopter?"

"I saw a helicopter," Scotty says.

"Sir?" The young ranger has his finger in the air as if to make a point. "There were no bears in the area. We didn't actually order the road closed."

"What? I thought that's what Hank said."

The young ranger shakes his head. "Hank was just assuming. That road was closed by an order from the Pentagon in DC."

A thundering roar passes over us, rattling the wooden ranger station.

The old ranger looks at the ceiling with irritation. "I don't know what the hell is going on." He looks at me. "But you're not going anywhere. I'm calling the state police."

If the state police know I'm here, they might inadvertently alert Big Mac. I need to distract these rangers until I can figure out a way to get out of here without calling attention to ourselves.

"Why don't we talk this through before the police get involved?" I ask. "We've done nothing wrong. I'd like to talk to your superior."

"The kid's done nothing wrong. I'm convinced of that," the ranger barks. "You, on the other hand, are missing your wife, and I'd like to know why."

"I'd still like to talk to your superior."

"I am the superior here. I only report to Washington DC."

"Me, too." I know exactly what I need to do. "I'd like to make a phone call."

"We don't give phone calls. We're not a jail."

"Then let us go," Scotty says.

The ranger considers. "Whom do you want to call?"

I reach into my back pocket and pull out my wallet. "My good ranger, I am going to call your boss and mine."

"I told you. I'm the only boss around here."

With dramatic flair, I pull out my tri-Delta ID card with the number for the presidential hotline. "If you'll dial this number for me," I tell the young ranger at the desk, "we will be connected to the president of the United States."

The young ranger smiles.

The old ranger slaps his thigh. "Ha. You really are a nut."

Scotty stands up, ready to defend me. "My dad does know the president."

"Well, let's call him then," the old ranger says. "What's the number?"

"It's 1–888—" I look down at the card. It is damp and limp from being soaked during my pond swim. The numbers and words are blurred beyond recognition. "Um."

"What's that?"

"I can't read the number."

The ranger shakes his head and grimaces. "Mister, I can see you have your problems, but they're not mine. Just hang tight until the state police get here."

"Where do you think Mom is, Dad?"

The rangers watch me closely for my reaction. She could be anywhere. McCarthy started that secret nuclear bunker in Nevada for the 1950s Emergence repopulation program that was the cause of the Big Mac uprising. There could be secret bases or hideouts all over the country. "I really don't know, Scotty."

"The longer we're here, the farther away she's getting," Scotty says.

He's right, and I really don't want to deal with the state police. We have to get out of here.

"Why don't we go, Dad? We're not under arrest."

I stand up. "My son's right. You can't hold us."

The old ranger looks up. "I suppose you're right, but you're on foot, and there's no law against my rangers following you on their four-wheelers. Yellowstone's a big place, and you're not going to go anywhere we won't know about. Make it easy on both of us and just sit tight, will you?"

"Not a chance. Come on, Scotty."

Scotty jumps up, and we walk toward the station door. Right as we reach it, it bangs open. A man in an Air Force jumpsuit stands in the doorway. He has short black hair that spikes in the center. He takes off his fighter jock sunglasses and slides them into a zipper pocket.

It's Fixer. Or at least someone who looks exactly like Fixer, the crazy secret government operative who claimed that he was the best pilot in the world—and whom I saw die after a botched parachute landing.

Fixer brushes by me and Scotty without noticing either of us. He stands directly in front of the old ranger. "You don't need to know who I am, but I'm going to need your help."

The ranger stares at Fixer, dumbfounded.

Fixer holds up an iPhone. Scotty and I step around him to see. The screen comes to life and President Wright's face appears, the distinctive bump in his nose looking more prominent on the small screen. He's supposedly off the Macwacky hallucinogens, but he still has a slightly crazy gleam in his eye. "Hello, ranger. . ."

"Zens," the ranger says, squinting his eyes at the president's image like he's trying to verify that this is all real.

"Right-oh, Ranger Zens," the president says. "You don't need to know who this man is, other than that he is under orders from the president of the—er, me!—to extract a secret agent, one Chris Thompson, and his family, whom we believe to be vacationing in the area. We are going to need your help."

The ranger still looks bewildered. After a moment, he seems to get an idea and looks at me. "Are you Chris Thompson?"

Fixer turns to look at me, holding the iPhone so that the president can see as well. A huge smile spreads across Fixer's face. "Giorgio."

"Thompson," the president growls. "Where the hell you been? Why don't you answer your phone?"

"You told me to turn it off and enjoy my vacation," I say.

The president points at me. "Stick with Fixer, Thompson. I'll see you soon." The screen goes blank.

Fixer slaps me on the shoulder. "Giorgio." He looks to Scotty. "And you must be little Giorgio."

"I'm Scotty."

"Do you want to fly in a cool plane, Scotty?"

Scotty looks to me. The last time I saw Fixer he was dead: no heartbeat, blue in the face dead. I don't know what to think.

"Come on, Giorgio. What else are you going to do?"

"Why do you call him Giorgio?" Scotty asks.

"Everyone needs a code name," Fixer says.

Scotty is becoming more interested. "Spy stuff," he says with admiration.

Fixer is right. The president ordered me, so even if I believe that Fixer is supposed to be dead—and if not dead, at least idiotically dangerous; I mean the guy is a daredevil maniac—I guess we have to go with him.

"You want a code name?"

"Yes." Scotty says.

"Okay," Fixer says. "How about Tuff?"

"Tuff?"

Fixer clenches his fist and flexes his biceps. "You can be the tough guy in this operation."

Scotty clenches both his fists. "Yeah. I can bring the cannons."

Fixer pats Scotty on the back and punches me hard in the shoulder.

"Ow." I massage my upper arm.

Fixer stands toe-to-toe with me. He puts his face an inch from mine and becomes serious. "You left me for dead," he hisses.

"But, but—you were dead." I look around at the rangers and Scotty. "I assure you. He was dead. I don't understand."

Fixer smiles broadly. "I'm just messing with you, Giorgio." He gives me a long, affectionate hug. "It's good to see you." He turns and walks toward the door. "Let's go."

Scotty and I look at each other and then follow. The rangers have watched our interaction with Fixer with wary eyes. They don't say a word as we walk out of the station. I think they're happy they won't have to deal with any of us.

We walk on a path through the woods behind the ranger station. Fixer is whistling the Marines' Hymn.

I quicken my pace so that I'm walking evenly with Fixer. "I still don't understand. You were definitely dead."

"I told you, the government has figured out the key to everlasting life." He continues whistling as we walk.

"Please stop whistling."

Fixer looks at me like, what's the big deal? But at least he stops whistling.

"That everlasting government life stuff was a bunch of crap," I insist. "Those young people in the shelter were brainwashed by Big Mac into believing they were destined for their utopia. Instead they were unwitting instruments of evil until their time was up, and then Big Mac killed them."

Scotty pulls on my arm. "Is that what they're going to do to Mom?"

Whoever took the RV most likely just wanted me. Karen could be of no help to them. "No. I don't think they'll do anything to Mom."

Fixer stops walking. "The Emergence program was fucked up." He slaps me on the shoulder. "You did well, Giorgio."

"I was interviewed on national TV. I think you can call me Chris, you know?"

Fixer just smiles at me like I've said something stupid.

Scotty shouts at both of us. "What are we doing? We have to save Mom."

"Someone in a helicopter hauled our RV away with my wife

inside," I explain.

"That's why I'm here," Fixer says. "I was trying to stop Big Mac from kidnapping you, Giorgio."

So it was Big Mac. "Has Big Mac taken over again?" I ask.

"No. But they're still a force."

"Isn't Slater in jail? Is the president in charge? Where would they take Karen? Where's Big Mac operating from?"

"Why are we talking so much?" Scotty says. "We have to chase that helicopter that has Mom."

"Tuff's right. We're talking too much. Time to move," Fixer says.

"Mr. Fixer, you said you had a plane?" Scotty says eagerly.

Fixer's whole face lights up. "Oh, do I have a plane." He runs ahead of us. "Come on, Tuff. I'll show you."

After a hundred yards, Fixer stops. Scotty and I catch up. We are at the edge of a clearing. Before us is a V-22 Osprey, a military airplane with two giant propeller engines that can rotate so that the plane can take off and land vertically.

Fixer runs into the plane through a side bay door.

Scotty and I walk closer to the plane and then stop. "This Fixer guy is a crazy pilot. I mean, crazy, crazy." I think about Fixer putting that old DC-10 into a pilotless dive just to experience weightlessness. "I think we need a different plan."

Scotty looks exasperated with me. "What other plan? The president sent Fixer. That ranger will send us to the state police." Scotty looks at me like it's all so obvious. "Fixer has a plane. We've got nothing else, Dad."

A propeller starts to turn. The engine comes to life with a throaty drone. The second engine joins the party. Fixer appears in the doorway and waves us in.

I stand frozen.

"Dad!" Scotty screams through the deafening propeller noise. "Dad! Are you scared?" He looks at me as if the possibility doesn't make any sense.

Yes. I am scared. I'm scared to ride in a plane with Fixer, someone whom I saw die. This must be a bad dream. Scotty is looking at me beseechingly, finding his mother the only thing on his mind. I grab his hand. "Let's go." We run for the plane. Fixer guides us in and shuts the door.

Fixer walks toward the cockpit. He turns and waves Scotty forward. "Come on, Tuff. You can be copilot."

Before I can object, Scotty scampers excitedly after Fixer into the cockpit.

Green canvas seats with their backs to the fuselage line the empty cabin. The plane is designed for carrying cargo. I take a seat and strap myself in.

The engines become louder, and I feel the plane lift straight up like a helicopter. After a minute, our ascent angles like a regular plane taking off. We reach altitude and level off. Everything has gone smoothly, and I relax.

Big Mac is not dead. The last I heard, Vance Slater, Big Mac's leader and the White House chief of staff who had drugged the president and taken over the country, was in custody. So was Supreme Court Chief Justice Timothy Lancaster, another Big Mac party leader and Joe McCarthy disciple. So who else could be controlling the Big Mac party? And how did they have enough power and resources to obtain a Super Stallion helicopter? Perhaps it was Preacher or someone else from Star, Utah, that town of McCarthy-worshipping zealots? I have to think this through.

Fixer appears in the cabin. My heart leaps for a second, but the plane is flying normally and I realize it is on autopilot. Still, though, Fixer makes me nervous. I stand up and walk toward Fixer. "No drinking beer on this flight."

Fixer looks at me, appalled that I could have said something so outrageous. "What? With a kid on board? Come on, Giorgio. I have standards." He looks around. "But if we can keep it quiet, I have something to calm your nerves." He reaches inside a pocket and pulls out a small silver flask. He holds the flask out to me.

"No."

"Suit yourself." Fixer takes a swig. "Kentucky bourbon— smooth."

"You're a maniac. Give me that." I grab for the flask, but Fixer dodges past me and runs farther into the cabin. He jumps up onto a seat. He takes a long swig and then shakes his head rapidly back and forth. "Woohee."

I take a step toward him. My fists are clenched, and I feel the tendons in my neck popping taut against my skin.

Fixer holds up a hand. "Okay, okay." He puts the cap back on the flask and slides it back into his pocket. "I forgot how much of a frightened prude you were, Giorgio."

I'm still angry. "How come you're alive? Tell me now. I want answers, not bullshit."

"You left the transponder on me, and the best medevac team we have showed up and revived me."

"I swear to God you were dead. You had no heartbeat."

"Wrong-oh, my friend." He jumps down from the seat. "I had a heartbeat. It was just very slow." With an open hand, he pats his chest in a slow-motion heartbeat rhythm.

"I would've felt that. Ninjenna was there, too. She confirmed that you were dead."

"You wouldn't have felt the heartbeat."

"I didn't feel it. That's what I said."

"I'm going to trust you with a secret, Giorgio." Fixer twists his arms in front of me like slithering snakes. He lowers his voice. "I was trained by a master yogi in Puducherry, India." He closes his eyes and places his palms together in namaste fashion. After a minute, he whispers something.

"What?"

"Feel my heart."

I touch his chest and don't feel a thing.

Fixer slumps into a seat and then lies down on his back.

"Fixer." I put my ear to his chest and listen for fifteen seconds. Nothing. "Fixer." I slap his face and then put both hands in the middle of his chest and prepare to pump.

Fixer smiles and his eyes open. He sits up slowly and then shakes his whole body in a giant shiver. "Whooh." He pokes me in the chest. "Got you again."

"What the hell was that?"

"I was in a state of samadhi—a state of deep meditation where my heart beats so slowly that its pulse is imperceptible." He stands up. "And that's how I die and then come back to life. I do it all the time."

"But why?"

"Why are you so dense? That's the real question, Giorgio." Fixer's eyes widen and he looks at me, like really? "You see, whenever I'm hurt, or caught in a trap, or about to be killed, I slow my heart and 'die.' You wouldn't believe all the trouble it's gotten me out of."

The plane suddenly banks to the left. It straightens out and then banks harder to the right.

"Scotty!"

Fixer sprints toward the cockpit. I run after him. The plane starts diving. At the cockpit door, Fixer stops and turns around. I nearly collide with him. For some reason, it looks like he is blocking the door. "We can't go in there."

The plane's dive becomes steeper, and it feels like we're picking up speed.

"What the hell are you doing? Get in there and control this plane."

Fixer looks relaxed. He is a true lunatic, just as I was afraid of. "He's got to learn on his own. It's the best way."

"Who? What?"

"Your son, Tuff. He's learning to fly. I gave him some maneuvers to perform."

"You maniac. Get out of my way." I try to charge through Fixer, but he has anticipated my move; he dives low and tackles me at the knees. We wrestle around on the ground until we both have each other twisted so that neither of us can move.

"You're a psycho," I tell him. "You're going to kill us all."

The plane pulls out of its dive and levels off, pressing us into the floor.

"Relax, Giorgio. He's got this baby, no problem. See?"

The plane starts a steep ascent.

"I'm going to kill you," I say.

Fixer and I wrestle around some more, but neither of us can gain the upper hand, which is a victory for Fixer and whatever death wish game he is playing.

"Total immersion. It's how I learned to fly. It's the best way. Haven't you ever taken a foreign language?"

I flip Fixer over and put my knee into his stomach. "Speaking a foreign language can't kill you."

"Yes it can," Fixer says. "You'd be surprised. I was undercover with the Zulu tribe once, and—"

"Shut up." I push off Fixer and try to stand up, but the plane goes vertical, and I fall forward and tumble down into the cabin.

The plane has stopped climbing.

"He's stalled it," Fixer says.

The plane feels like it is falling back over itself. I have my feet against the fuselage, and I am holding on to a loose seat belt strap. We are falling and spinning. Fixer climbs along the seats toward the cockpit. "He needs help," Fixer says.

"No shit." I try to make it toward the cockpit, but the spinning plane slams me into a side seat. I try to get up but the force is too strong. I can't even lift my head. My chin is pushing toward my chest, and I'm stuck in a fetal position. I'm disoriented and feel ill. I curse myself for ever getting into a plane again with Fixer. This is it. We're going to die. I'm sorry, Karen. I've failed you.

The plane feels like it is diving straight down like a missile. I see Fixer fall into the cockpit. The propellers are whining. The air hisses all around like a scream. By pushing with my legs, I'm able to slide down toward the cockpit. It feels like we might be pulling out of the dive, and then the g-forces smash me into the floor. The noise of the propellers returns to a deep, pleasant-sounding growl.

I try to stand up, and as I do, I puke everywhere.

The plane has leveled off and is flying normally. I step into the cockpit. Fixer and Scotty each sit in a pilot seat. They look around and smile like nothing has happened, like they are bored.

Fixer looks me over. "Aw, Giorgio. You got sick again? Man, you are just not made for flying."

"Not made for flying with you. You should never be

allowed passengers. You almost killed us."

Scotty smiles at me and looks as if he couldn't be happier. "I can fly now, Dad."

I point at Scotty. "No you can't. That was not flying. That, that was—"

"Perfectly safe," Fixer says. "We had plenty of altitude to make any kind of mistake."

I speak through gritted teeth. "Please just land us at the nearest airport."

"Okay, okay." Fixer motions for me to leave the cockpit. "There are towels in that cabinet around the corner. Go clean yourself off."

I look at Scotty and motion with my thumb out the cockpit door. "Take a seat in the back, Red Baron."

"Aw, Dad, when am I ever going to get this chance again?"

"Let him stay, Giorgio." Fixer motions his hand like he's smoothing out a bed sheet. "Autopilot the rest of the way. I promise."

Fine. Whatever. After cleaning up, I go to the back and plop into a seat. I'm exhausted. I lean my head back and close my eyes.

I doze, fading in and out of sleep for I don't know how long. When I wake up, I see Fixer standing before me, as if in a dreamy vision. He's got his head back and is guzzling bourbon out of the flask.

I jump up, fully awake. "What are you doing?"

Fixer nonchalantly tosses the empty flask onto the floor.

"You idiot. You're drunk. You're breaking the number one

rule for flying airplanes—don't drink and fly."

Fixer wipes his mouth. When he speaks his words are slurred. "I'm not a drinker."

"You certainly fooled me. All I ever see you do is drink, fly, and crash airplanes."

Fixer does a little hop, like he is practicing. "Oh, I only drink when I'm going to jump. I tried not to let it show before, but I get very nervous when I jump. Especially after what happened last time."

I notice the straps that crisscross over Fixer's torso.

"Get back in that cockpit and land this plane," I tell him.

He turns around, walks to the wall, and pulls on a lever. On his back is a parachute.

I run over to him, and as I do so, the back hatchway opens. Cold air fills the cabin.

"I trained your son. No worries. He can land this baby."

I scream at Fixer through the air and propeller noise, and I grab on to his parachute straps, ready to drag him if necessary. But Fixer kicks me in the nuts, and I go down.

"Sorry, Giorgio. I have to keep a low profile. I'm no longer alive. Good luck."

With that, Fixer runs and jumps out the back of the plane. He disappears into the twilight.

First, I use the lever to close the back hatchway. Then, I race into the cockpit. Scotty sits attentively, watching the plane fly itself. I sit in the captain's seat next to him. "No more funny stuff," I say. "Fixer's gone."

His face lights up. "I can fly this thing, really, Dad."

I try to think of a way out of this mess. "Let's figure out how to get this radio working. We need to call a mayday or something."

"I've already been talking to air traffic control." Scotty puts on a microphone headset. "There's no need for a mayday. The autopilot will take us all the way to Andrews Air Force Base. It can even land the plane."

"Thank God." I lean back in the seat and my stress level diminishes ever so slightly.

Scotty points at switches and taps video displays. "This is the airspeed indicator. That's the altimeter."

I'm impressed and proud of Scotty. He really has picked up on how to fly this plane, something I would have never been able to do. He's so calm, too, so confident. I hate to say it, but he'd probably make a good spy someday. I hope that never happens.

"These adjust the flaps." Scotty reaches for the controls.

"Stop it."

"Geez, you're nervous, Dad."

I reach over and grab his wrist. "A big part of completing a successful mission is being careful and safe," I say sternly. "How are we going to save Mom if something happens to us?"

Scotty's smile disappears, and his giddiness leaves him. He pulls his hands away from the instruments and slides back into the seat, like he does this every day.

I put my microphone headset on and call out to whoever is listening. I talk to a controller and a pilot who are monitoring us. They assure me that they will guide us in and that we will not have to do a thing.

Scotty and I are quiet, each in our own thoughts. I think about Karen and how frightened she probably is. She never wanted me to be a spy. She just wanted our normal life back again.

"Do you think Mom is all right?"

I try to sound as confident as I can. "Whoever took the RV just wanted me. You know that, right? I'm sure they'll let Mom go right away soon as they figure it out."

Scotty laughs a little. "I bet she gives whoever took her a real yelling."

I laugh.

We fly uneventfully for an hour. The plane begins to descend. The controller announces that we will be on the ground within ten minutes. I sure hope President Wright is still off the Macwacky and thinking clearly. Will he have a plan? Does he have someone trustworthy to advise him? I think back to being in the shelter and all the communicating the chosen ones were doing with Big Mac followers. Big Mac could be anywhere, working in important posts, ready to emerge when needed.

If Big Mac is back, and the president is somehow relying on me again, the country is in deep trouble.

It's dark out now. The lights of DC and Maryland outline the land against the dark patches of Chesapeake Bay and the Atlantic Ocean beyond. We turn slightly and descend directly toward the runway. Flashing lights from fire trucks and other emergency vehicles light up both sides of the runway.

"Thirty seconds," someone in our headphones says.

And then an alarm sounds. An electronic emergency voice fills the cabin. "Pull up. Pull up."

Talibanny-Buster

THE EMERGENCY VOICE continues to call, "Pull up. Pull up."

We are dropping fast, five hundred yards short of the runway and in danger of crashing into some sort of Air Force building.

Scotty pulls back on the yoke with two hands. "Power, power," screams a voice in our headphones. I reach for what I think is the throttle, but Scotty is way ahead of me. He pushes the throttle forward and the plane surges, holding its altitude. We clear the building and are over the runway.

"Power back," the voice in our headphones yells. Scotty pulls the throttle back, and we glide toward the runway.

The plane yaws to the right.

"I can't reach the pedals to control the tail," Scotty says. "Push the left foot pedal down hard, Dad."

I push the left foot pedal down, and we straighten out.

"Hold them straight now," Scotty says.

We are about to touch down. Scotty pulls back on the yoke, and then pushes the throttles all the way back. The back wheels hit, and then the front—smooth. "You have to steer now, Dad."

I grab the yoke and try to hold the plane steady down the center of the runway.

"That doesn't do anything," Scotty yells at me. "Your foot pedals control the steering."

I put pressure on the pedals evenly. They are vibrating, and I try to hold them straight. We are ten feet from the center line, but the runway is wide and we have plenty of room. I try to hold us straight.

"Brakes, Dad!"

The end of the runway is close. If we keep our current speed, we'll smash right into an airplane hangar. "Where are they?" I ask my son frantically.

"The tips of the pedals," Scotty says.

I lift my feet and push with my toes into two metal tabs on top of the pedals. The brakes tug at the wheels. The hangar approaches. I push harder.

Scotty kills the engines.

I push too far with my right foot, and the plane veers to the right. The left wing smashes into the hangar door, caving it. The plane comes to a stop. Emergency vehicles with their lights flashing race toward us.

Scotty and I smile at each other. We fist bump. The kid has talent, I must admit. "You really can fly. I can't believe Fixer was able to teach you so quickly."

"Well, I do play a lot of Xbox."

We exit the cockpit and open the side cabin door. A small contingent of firemen and paramedics help us down the short steps. The night air is warm and humid and smells like jet fuel. Sirens wail as two police cars escorting a limousine pull up next to us. The limousine doors open, and two Secret Service men get out. One of the men flashes a badge.

"Chris Thompson?"

"That's me." I touch my pockets. "I'm sorry I don't have any ID."

"That's all right. I recognize you from last time." He motions toward the limousine. "Shall we?"

The other Secret Service man opens the back limousine door. Scotty tugs on my arm. He looks nervous. "Me, too?"

I look at the first agent. "I'm not going anywhere without my son."

The agent looks confused. "Just a moment." He pulls out his cell phone and walks away to talk. He returns with an apologetic look on his face. "I'm sorry, the president is uncomfortable with children in the White House."

I take a step toward the agent. My eyes squint in anger. "You tell the president I rode in a car with his whiny daughter all night long. I'm not going anywhere without my son."

The agent returns to his cell phone. After a minute he puts the phone away, motions to the car again, and says, "Right this way if you please, Mr. Thompson and son."

"I'll be good," Scotty says. "I won't say a word in the White House."

Scotty and I slide into the limousine. The leather seats are cool. The first agent sits across from us. The other agent drives.

"Sweet," Scotty says. He presses buttons, and the glass divider goes up. The agent gives Scotty a stern look. Scotty slumps down in his seat. "Sorry."

With the police escort, it only takes twenty minutes to arrive at the White House. We pull into an underground parking lot. Someone opens our door, and the president is there waiting for us with some people I don't recognize.

"Thompson." The president reaches into the limousine and pulls me out by the hand. He gives me an uncomfortable hug, pressing his head against my chest. "You did it, Thompson. You saved the country, and though we're not out of the woods yet, at least you've given us some breathing room."

There is no security gauntlet to pass through like last time I visited the White House. I guess I'm trusted now. "What's going on? I thought Slater and his cronies were arrested."

The president ignores me and goes right for Scotty. "Hey, little buddy." He rubs Scotty's hair. "I just love kids. I'm sure your dad told you that."

Scotty smiles and looks overwhelmed from meeting the president, the same way I was when I first walked into the White House last month.

"Pretty cool your dad is a super-spy now, huh?"

"Super cool," Scotty says.

"You want to see something else super cool?" the president asks.

"Sure, okay," Scotty says. His face suddenly lights up, as if he has figured out a riddle. He looks at me and then to the president. "Is my mom here?"

I feel like a schmuck for not thinking to ask the same thing. "Yes. Is my wife, Karen, here?"

The president's face becomes solemn for a brief moment. "No, I'm sorry." He turns and walks away and mumbles something.

A black-haired man in his late twenties walks to the president's side. He turns to look at me. "He said that we can talk about your wife when we are in a more secure environment." The man's eye twitches behind his square-rimmed glasses, betraying his nervousness. Is this guy some aide to the president? He's so young, but still, he carries himself like a trusted advisor, walking close, leaning in to the president, talking confidentially. Has this guy replaced Slater as the new chief of staff? Where'd he come from? Can he be trusted?

We enter an elevator guarded by marines.

"Only Brandon and Shawna," the president says.

A Secret Service guard is about to object. The president holds up his hand. "Brandon and Shawna only. None of us would be here if it wasn't for this man." The president touches me on the shoulder. "I trust Chris Thompson with my life." Then the president holds up his fists toward Scotty, like he is about to box. "And I think I can handle this guy."

Scotty puts up his dukes and does some shadowboxing.

The president laughs. "I like this kid."

The Secret Service agent is not happy. "There's another individual below."

"I know, I know." The president shoos the secret service agents away. "I trust him too. You guys need to relax a little."

The young, skinny advisor with glasses, who must be Brandon, steps into the elevator. A short, stocky African-American woman follows him. She wears a black suit and has a dark-brown leather briefcase handcuffed to her wrist.

"Shawna has over one thousand nukes ready to go." The president laughs. "Lock and load. Can't go anywhere without Shawna."

The president presses a button, the doors close, and we descend. After a while, the doors open and we walk down a short, brightly lit hallway. Everyone is silent except for the president, who is whistling. He opens a door at the end of the hallway and leads us into a room. The room is long and rectangular. An elliptical boardroom table is surrounded by powerful leather chairs. Flat-screen monitors cover the walls. There are two other doors that are open to what look like small conference rooms.

"Hello?" a voice calls from one of the small rooms. A bald man with a smooth brown head peers out of the doorway. It's Derek—Cannonball—the former marine turned bartender and guard for the Emergence program who sided with me against Big Mac when it counted most. Derek and I faced life and death together, and I've never felt closer to any other friend in my life.

"Derek," I say.

Derek walks toward me, his arms open wide. "Chris, the liaison, Thompson."

Derek and I hug. It's good to see him. Then I take a step back. "I'm sorry. I forgot about your arm. Are you all right?"

Derek lightly rubs his left upper arm, where he got shot when we stormed Big Mac's Emergence headquarters. "Still a little sore. I've got your back, though, don't worry."

"What've you been up to?"

"Spent a couple of weeks down in Cabo, unwinding, trying to forget Big Mac ever existed."

"You take your lady? I'm sorry, what was her name again?"

Derek looks to the ground. "Yeah, she was there."

I wait for him to say more, but the president interrupts. "Shall we sit and get started?"

Snapping out of his mood, Derek shakes Scotty's hand. "You must be Scotty. I've heard a lot about you."

"Cannonball," Scotty says.

"Now, Scotty—it's Mr. Allen, please."

Derek smiles. "With my friends, Cannonball is perfectly fine."

Scotty is impressed. "I heard you're tough."

Derek nods his head assuredly. "That's right, little man, that's right."

The president is sitting at the head of the table. Brandon sits to his right. Shawna reads a magazine in one of the conference rooms.

"Please," the president says. "Can we start?"

Derek and I sit across from the president and Brandon. The president seems sure of himself and very presidential, not at all like he was when he broke down in front of me in the ASU jail.

Scotty timidly walks up to the president. "We have to find my mom."

"Will do, son, will do." The president says with confidence.

Scotty looks as if he's about to object, but remains silent.

"The problem, gentlemen"—the president slaps his hands on the table—"is that Big Mac is still alive."

The flat-screen monitors are all off, and it is eerily silent. This must be the quietest presidential crisis ever.

"But Slater is in jail," Derek says.

"The vice president is the problem," the president says.

"And General McGuffin," Brandon says.

"I don't understand," I say. "Aren't they in jail, too?"

"We can't find them," the president yells to the ceiling. He looks around, slightly paranoid. "They're among us somewhere, controlling Big Mac, conspiring against me. They're traitors in the first degree."

"But . . . but we saw them on TV. They supported the Big Mac takeover." I look at Derek. "We saw them, right? Everybody saw them."

"Not Vice President Carlson," Brandon says. "He wasn't with the coup group. They just claimed they had his support."

"McGuffin was there," Derek says. "He was one of the leaders."

"McGuffin, McGuffin, McGuffin." The president looks at Brandon with irritation. "We have the best spies in the world, and we can't find him."

"McGuffin has too many political allies," Brandon says. "We tore off Big Mac's head, but the rest of the organization had already been activated. Everything happened so quickly. It was chaotic—we couldn't catch them all."

"But you're still in control, right?" I say.

"I don't feel like I'm in control," the president says, like he is out of control.

"Barely," Brandon says. "As I said, it's chaotic. We can't tell who's for Big Mac and who isn't. McGuffin is operating from somewhere, directing a smear campaign against the president. We think that many in the House and Senate will do his bidding."

The president shakes his fists toward Brandon. "We have to find McGuffin and Carlson. Keep chopping at the leadership. It's the only way to blight the menace."

"The Pentagon," Scotty says. "The ranger in Yellowstone said they received an order from the Pentagon to close the road we were traveling on."

I look at Scotty. Why didn't I think of that? "He's right. They could be in the Pentagon."

"Our people are searching the Pentagon," Brandon says.

"The Pentagon is just so damn big," the president says irritably. "We're boring the kid. Why don't you go play somewhere?"

"Okay," Scotty says. He stands up and starts meandering around the room.

"It's difficult," Brandon says. "They could be anywhere, really."

We sit in silence for a moment, contemplating the idea that Big Mac may have infiltrated the government. Who is loyal and who is not?

"And now I've got this damn impeachment trial," the president says. "That's how they want to take over—impeach me."

"Impeachment trial?" I say.

"Why do you think you are here, Thompson? What do you think this is all about?"

"My wife was kidnapped—wife-napped, whatever. That's what I thought this was all about. I'm trying to find Karen." I look around at everybody. Shouldn't it be obvious?

"McGuffin probably has her," Brandon says. "He wanted to capture Mr. Thompson, but he got his wife instead."

"Genius," the president says. "That's spot-on, Brandon. But the joke is on McGuffin, because we have Thompson, our star witness who is going to save my ass from impeachment."

Brandon looks uneasy, like he's on the losing side. He takes a breath and looks at Derek and me. "You two are our star witnesses for Slater's treasonous actions. Especially you, Mr. Thompson. If you can help us prove that the president was an innocent bystander during Big Mac's takeover, he just might be able to escape impeachment, and then he can send Slater off to Guantánamo or someplace, and we can go after the rest of Big Mac with renewed power."

A high-pitched alarm sounds from one of the side rooms. The president pushes his chair back and stands up. "My Talibanny-buster." He rushes into a side conference room that evidently Scotty has gone into. "Easy there, Maverick."

The rest of us file into the room. Scotty is sitting in the leather fighter pilot's seat of what looks like a video arcade machine. He is pushing a joystick around between his legs. The large video screen in front of him shows images of a desert landscape, as if he's flying over it. A large target finder is in the center of the screen, surrounded by myriad attack support displays.

The president gently helps Scotty out of the machine and then takes a position in the seat. "You didn't shoot anything, did you?"

"No, sir. I was just flying, like Mr. Fixer showed me."

"Fixer, nuthin'." The president moves the joystick, and the video feed on the screen spins upside down and starts diving toward the ground. "This ain't just one of those reality games. This is as real as it gets. The boys and girls at the CIA gave me my own personal drone for shooting Talibanny, Al-qaider, and Icey terrorists."

As the drone approaches the ground, buildings come into view. People are milling about, seemingly unaware of the danger flying above them. On the screen, green circles surround each person. In a field away from the buildings, a red X pops up over what appears to be a farmworker.

"There's one." The president points at the red X. "It's a terrorist."

We all lean in to take a closer look.

"How can you be sure?" Derek asks.

"Because that's what the red X means," the president says with frustration. He flies the drone straight toward the person in the field. "We'll blow him sky high." The president looks around. "Who wants to take the shot?" He points at Scotty. "How about you, Maverick? Are you really Top Gun?"

"I don't think that's a good idea," I say.

"Just press the red button here," the president says.

Scotty shakes his head slightly. "Nah, you better do it."

The drone is bearing down on the person. Everyone in the room is tense except for the president. "Say good night, Tali-banner, Uncle Sam's coming to tuck you in."

Just then, the red X flickers and then disappears. A green circle replaces it and starts flashing.

"Whoa, phantom save." The president pulls back on the joystick. The person in the field looks up at the drone, takes a side step, and dives to the ground. The drone buzzes over the ground and then shoots up into the sky.

"Mission aborted" flashes on the screen, and is quickly replaced by "Drone under COMSAC control."

The president flicks his hand through the air as if he is trying to wipe the message from the screen. "I hate when they do that."

"Was that Afghanistan?" Scotty says.

The president grunts a little as he climbs out of the drone machine. "Something-stan." He walks back to his place at the boardroom table and takes a seat.

Brandon, Derek, and I return to our seats. Scotty stands next to the president, looking at him as if he's just found out the truth about Santa Claus. "How do they know who gets an X and who gets an O?"

"I don't know, son." The president runs his hand over the table like he's moving an imaginary piece of paper around. "Sometimes they get it wrong, okay? Not everything is as it seems in this world."

Scotty walks around the table with his head down, as if he is contemplating this confusing wisdom. He takes a seat next to me. I grab his leg just above the knee and give him a reassuring squeeze.

The president strums his fingers on the tabletop. "Where were we?" He looks at Brandon. "Are we done yet?"

"The impeachment," Brandon says. He looks at me and Derek. "We think that it would be best if you two stayed here until you're needed at the impeachment trial next week."

"Right here?" Derek looks around, thinking about this possibility. "No—I'd go crazy."

"This is the safest place for you." Brandon places a computer tablet from his briefcase onto the table. He taps his fingers onto the screen. The flat-screens hanging around us all come to life with movies, sporting events, and news stations from around the world. "We can get an Xbox and other game stations for you to use."

"Cool," Scotty says.

"Just stay away from my Talibanny-buster." The president squints one eye at Scotty.

"And whatever kind of food you want," Brandon continues, "anything you need to make yourselves comfortable.

Just name it."

"It'll be like a regular slumber party," the president says. "Hell, I'll probably come down here and hang out once in a while, it sounds like so much fun."

I think about when the president first recruited me, how scared I was in the White House, how I was willing to go along with his crazy plan just because I wanted to be a spy. "No," I say. "We are not staying. We're going to spend every free minute trying to find my wife."

The president looks at me as if he's sizing me up. His expression changes into one of respect.

"I assure you," Brandon says. "We are doing everything we can to find your wife."

"Like what?" Scotty says. "We're just sitting here. Dad's right. We have to go."

"I'll tell you who's right," the president says. "I'm right. I'm President Wright—get it?"

Derek laughs, but the president is not joking. "I order you to stay here until the impeachment trial," he concludes.

Derek and I, as employees of the executive branch, have sworn an oath to obey the orders of the president, the commander-in-chief of the United States.

The president massages his forehead. "God, I could use a Macwacky pill." He looks at Brandon, who shakes his head minutely.

"Maybe resigning isn't such a bad idea," I say. "You seemed warm to that possibility the last time we spoke."

The president slaps his hand on the table. "You'd just hand the country back over to Big Mac? After all we've done? You'd put our citizens under that oppression again? What's up with you, Thompson?"

If Vice President Carlson is truly a Big Mac lackey, I guess the president staying in office at all costs is our best choice. The president is under a lot of pressure, and he's also obviously still in withdrawal from Macwacky. I should give him some slack. "I'm just worried about my wife."

Brandon takes off his glasses. "Look, Mr. Thompson, no offence, but we have real professionals working on finding your wife. I know you did well on your last mission, but your methods were not exactly orthodox, and we think you benefited from certain random confluences."

Derek and I look at each other and shrug.

"You're saying we were just plain lucky?" I ask.

"I'm offended," Derek says.

"Don't believe it," the president says. "Those CIA spooks are just jealous. But you could benefit from some training." He talks to Brandon. "Until the impeachment trial, I want these two with Doctor Rod twenty-four seven." He looks back to Derek and me. "Spy training for the both of you. What a fantastic idea. Combine your methods with some real training and you really could be super-spies."

"You already said he was a super-spy," Scotty says.

"He could be a super super-spy," the president says. "Once you have proper training, you can join the team looking for your wife. We really could use some spies we can trust, Brandon."

"I don't have to follow your orders," Scotty says. "I'm a kid. You can't keep me here."

"That's right," I say. "Let's not involve a kid in this mess."

"President Wright kidnapped me. That's what I'll say," Scotty says.

"Ooh, man," Derek says. "The press will love that headline."

The president and Brandon look at each other. It's quiet as they consider what to do with Scotty.

"I was kept locked up in the basement of the White House," Scotty says.

I get an idea. "My mother-in-law and, er, father-in-law can watch him."

"Your father-in-law? You don't mean Archibald," the president says. "I don't want that goofball in the White House. We'll have someone drive the kid to your in-laws. Okay? Is that good?"

"No," I say. "Derek and I will deliver him personally. That's the only way I'll feel comfortable."

"And then you'll go through training?" the president says.

"And testify exactly the way we want you to at the impeachment trial?" Brandon says.

"Yes," I say.

"Sure," Derek says.

"Then it's settled." The president stands up, followed by Brandon. "Deliver your son to Archibald or Grandma or whoever, but make it close by and discreet. Both of you have to wear disguises—the kid, too."

"And we will be monitoring you the whole time," Brandon says.

The president leaves and walks into the elevator, followed by Brandon and Shawna.

I look to Scotty and Derek. Derek looks tired. He seems generally all right, but he's just not his usual upbeat, enthusiastic self. I suppose he's not thrilled to be here. He's also probably in more pain from his injury than he is letting on.

And now we're right back in the Big Mac mess. Will we be able to hold up and escape death again? Is Derek as leery as I am? Maybe we were just lucky last time. Derek has some military training, but I'm just winging it, thrown into the arena by a half-crazy president. I do need training, but what can I possibly learn in a week? Will Karen be able to survive that long?

"You were just joking, right, Dad?" Scotty asks. "I don't really have to stay with Grandpa and Grandma." Scotty is full of importance: ready to be a super-spy like his father, confident it will all end well, confident we will stick together to save his mother.

I don't say anything.

"Dad. Dad!"

Washington Monument

WE CONTACT ARCHIE on an encrypted telephone.

"Glad to have you home, hound dog," Archie says. "I've been worried about the Winnebago. Everything all right? How are the shocks? June and I have been thinking about taking another trip—extending our honeymoon, if you will—need them springs in good working order, if you know what I mean."

"We can talk about the Winnebago later. Right now—"

"What's wrong with the Winnebago? Everything was perfect when—"

"Shut up, Archie. Just listen to what I have to say." I tell Archie an edited version of the situation we find ourselves in. "The gist of the matter is, I need to meet you somewhere close to the White House, soon."

"The Washington Monument," Archie says. "I know a

security guard there. He can take us up after hours if we want. Scotty might like to see that."

It's eleven p.m. right now. "We'll meet you there at midnight."

In forty-five minutes, we walk out the side door of the White House with two dozen staff workers. Derek and I are dressed as White House servers, in classic tuxedos. I wear a fake mustache, an Orioles baseball hat, and a black Windbreaker. Derek wears a medium-sized, neatly trimmed Afro wig and gold wire-rimmed glasses.

Scotty walks several people ahead of me, hand in hand with a young white couple in their late twenties who seem happy to play the role of faux parents. They're both in dark suits and hold briefcases, the consummate DC power pair.

We walk along Executive Avenue, still within the White House grounds. Some workers walk to their cars, but most stay with us, as instructed. We turn right and continue to the 17th Street gate.

As we walk out of the gate, the group separates. Derek walks to the right. I wait for a moment, say goodbye to one of my "coworkers," and then walk left to follow Scotty and his chaperones.

I follow them down 17th Street until we reach Constitution Avenue. The night is still humid, but it's cooler now from a gentle breeze out of the west. Scotty and the young couple take a path that leads on a diagonal to the Washington Monument.

I wait for the crossing light at 17th Street and strain to see Scotty as he passes from the glow of a walkway lamp into a small stretch of darkness. He is only holding the woman's hand now.

I cross Constitution Avenue and continue on 17th Street,

casting quick glances to monitor Scotty as he approaches the monument. When I draw even with the monument, I take a left onto the path and walk directly toward it. It is late, but there are still groups of tourists milling around the base and looking up at the brightly lit white obelisk.

I walk up to the closed entrance doors and stand next to Scotty. The young lady lets go of his hand to text on her phone. After a moment the entrance door opens, and a guard sitting on a rolling swivel chair leans his head out.

"President Wright likes John Lennon," I say.

The guard stands up and moves aside. Scotty and I walk in.

"Two more?" the guard asks.

"Should be on their way," I say.

The guard shuts the door behind us. Another guard stands by an open elevator. Scotty and I walk in, the elevator doors close, and we head for the top of the monument.

"So, when are we going to shake them?" Scotty says.

I don't say anything.

"That's what this ruse about sending me to Grandma's is all about, isn't it?"

"Ruse—good word."

"Come on, Dad. I don't believe that Brandon guy. I don't think they're worried about Mom at all."

I've been thinking the same thing. Scotty's spot-on as usual. Karen's in danger, and the president is only worried about saving himself. And saving himself means saving the country, so I guess it makes sense that Karen is low on his priority list, but man—I've given enough over the last few weeks. Karen is my wife. She didn't ask for any of this. We're supposed to be on vacation, damn it. I'm loyal to my country, but there has to be a way I can work to save Karen and help the president.

"Dad!"

"Quiet, Scotty. We're on a mission."

The elevator doors open. We step into a small, dimly lit area. The walls are polished white marble. A solid rectangular window frames the view of the brightly lit capitol building that rests magnificently at the end of the national mall. There is a fresh lemon scent in the air, probably the remnants of the nightly cleaning.

"Dad. What's the plan?"

"Let's go this way." I lead us down a tiny hallway to the next viewing window. "Check it out. The Jefferson Memorial."

"I'm not going with Archie and Grandma. You can't do this to me."

I hear and feel the gentle rumble of the elevator ascending, and then the doors open.

"Roast beef with red peppers?" I hear Derek call.

"In a panini is best," I say.

Derek joins us in admiring the view.

"Pretty cool, huh?" I say.

"I've been up here before." Derek peers around the corner to the next window. "It's different in the dark, though, and with no one else around."

"It's kind of eerie," Scotty says.

Derek leads us to a window with a view of the White House. "Peaceful," Derek says. "I like it."

"Ahh!" A figure jumps out at us from around the corner.

Derek spins around with a roundhouse kick. His foot connects into a man's gut. The man falls backward onto the ground. Derek jumps on top of him and rears his fist back, about to strike.

"Stop," I say. "That's Archie."

Archie still has his bushy mustache and looks like a harmless bulldog. He puts his hands in front of his face to protect himself. "Easy there, Jackie Chan."

With two hands, Derek grabs Archie's shirt and pulls him to his feet. "What the hell are you doing?" Derek grinds his teeth and glares.

Archie speaks fast and sputters his words. "I was just joking. I thought it would be funny to sneak up on you spies."

Derek holds his shoulder and grimaces. "I don't see anybody laughing."

"Someday we'll have a good laugh about it." Archie looks around at us, smiling. "Ha ha, right?"

I shake my head. "Derek, this is Archie. Archie—Derek."

Archie grins with that dog-eared look of his and sticks out his hand.

Derek just looks at him.

"How did you get up here?" I say, trying to break the tension.

"I took the stairs. You know me. I like the exercise. I do it all the time."

Derek looks over at Archie's somewhat flabby physique. "This the guy who was hitting on your wife?"

"Hey, now," Archie says.

"No, no. It was Karen's mom. He just married my mother-in-law."

Archie makes a clicking sound with his tongue. "Yes, sir."

"Forget that," I say. "We need a—"

"A plan," Derek says.

Archie strokes his beefy black mustache. "That's some fancy wagtail you've got going on there above the lip, hound dog."

"It's fake, Archie. You don't think I'd grow something so ridiculous, now, do you?"

Archie looks perplexed. "Well, yes, sir, I suppose you gotta be a mighty stud to pull off a face hedge like mine."

"Plan?" Derek hisses.

"I'm staying with you, Dad," Scotty says. "I say we grab a cab, head for the subway, and ditch whoever is watching us. Then we track down Mom."

Derek still hasn't gotten over Archie's surprise attack. He continues to give him the evil eye. "I can appreciate that you don't want to go with your grandpa," Derek says, "but your dad and I operate better when it's just the two of us. You'll be helping out by staying with your grandparents."

Archie points out the window toward Constitution Avenue. "I brought the Winnebago. You, me, and Grandma can take a little camping trip—do a little catfish hunting down south in a couple secret watering holes I know about."

Sure enough, I see the Winnebago partially hidden by a tree, parked on Constitution Avenue like a normal RV, its recent adventures seemingly a secret. The same RV that Karen, Scotty, and I had been bonding in the last week. The RV that Big Mac had used to kidnap Karen, now probably bugged or worse.

"How'd you get the RV here?" I ask, trying to keep my voice calm.

Archie dangles a set of keys. "It's my Winnebago."

"But how did you find it? Where was it?"

"It was parked a block over from your place. I've been driving by to check up on the house and whatnot while you were gone. I came across it yesterday. Figured you must've tipped back one too many—guess I was right if you can't even remember where you parked it."

This has to be a trap. No way can I let Scotty go with Archie.

"A lot of eyes probably on that camper right now," Derek says.

"She's a little old, but she's still a beaut," Archie says.

"A lot of eyes on the monument, too, no doubt," I say.

"Yeah, there's still a number of tourists out there," Archie says.

Derek shakes his head at Archie. "You're a fool."

Archie's normal goofy smile disappears. "Your Bruce Lee kick surprised my surprise, but I'm ready now. Take that fool comment back, or I'll go Chuck Norris all over you."

"You led them right to us."

I care about both of these guys. The last thing I want to see is the two of them going at it, especially in front of Scotty. "Archie didn't know anything about Big Mac capturing the RV. It's not his fault he drove it here," I say.

A vibration in the floor indicates that the elevator has started moving.

"Someone is coming. It could be Big Mac." I look around. "We have to move."

The angry look on Archie's face disappears. His mustache twitches. "Big Mac?"

"Yes. Big Mac, or—I don't know. We just have to leave. I can feel the danger. Can't you?"

"I don't think Big Mac is in the elevator," Archie says.

"We can take the stairs." I grab Scotty's hand and run toward Archie. "The stairs. Let's go."

Derek, I think, is feeling my concern. "This way," he says. He opens the stairway door and leads us down.

Archie reluctantly follows. "The monument was guarded. Whoever is in the elevator has to be on our side."

Our voices and the clapping of our shoes hitting the cement echo throughout the stairway.

"We're escaping the president's men, too," Scotty says. "Right, Dad? We're going to find Mom."

I don't respond to Scotty. Archie's breathing becomes labored as he follows. Scotty is ahead of me, his feet barely tapping the steps as he hurries down with ease.

Scotty keeps looking back at me. "Dad? Dad?"

"Watch where you're going," I say.

We continue to descend, going around and around. After two flights Scotty looks back to me again. "Dad?"

"What?"

"Big Mac is out there watching. We should let them catch us. I bet they'd take us straight to Mom."

That's a great idea. Why didn't I think of that?

"That's not a bad plan," I say. "Now please, look ahead."

We reach the bottom. I open the door slightly. Only the guard standing by the elevator and the guard who is Archie's friend, sitting on his chair by the door, are in the small lobby.

I open the door all the way, and we walk toward the exit. Archie's friend stands up. "A group of Secret Service dudes just went up the elevator to make sure you were all safe."

"See? No Big Mac," Archie says. "You're way too nervous, Chris."

"Shut up," Derek says.

Archie's friend stands up. "Big Mac? I thought they were done for." He looks around. "That was a scary couple of weeks when they were in charge."

The light atop the elevator shows that the cab is moving

back down.

"Didn't any Secret Service agents stay down here?"

Archie's friend nods his head toward the door. "Outside. That couple who walked the kid in."

"Good," I say. "Here's what we're going to do."

"Run for the RV?" Scotty says.

Scotty has been an asset so far, I must admit, but he's only eleven years old: our little boy, the cement in Karen and my relationship, our reason for being.

"I'm sorry, buddy."

The eager look on Scotty's face evaporates as he realizes his fate. "I'm not going with Archie."

I try to put my hand on Scotty's back but he squirms away from me. "Not Archie."

I open the door and walk outside. The young couple who'd been walking with Scotty earlier are talking while they wait for us to return. The man is animated, his facial expressions contorting into different comical poses as he tells some story. She smiles at him and then laughs when he finishes. They make an attractive couple, and I realize that they are not just playing a role to guard Scotty; they are actually in love.

Derek, Scotty, and Archie shuffle out the door behind me. The young couple notice us and start toward us. The man puts his hand on Scotty's shoulder while the woman holds his hand.

"Dad?"

Archie gives me one of his overly dramatic confounded looks. "What's up, hound dog? I thought Scotty was coming with me."

Scotty stares at me, his eyes mixed with anger and sadness. But I have to do what is best for him. What sane parent would take their kid on a dangerous mission into Big Mac's evil clutches?

"Scotty will be safest in the White House. I realize that now. We all will." I nod to the young couple. "Change of plans. We're all going back to the White House."

"Procedures dictate we should wait for approval to change the plan," the young man says.

"Damn procedures," Derek says. "We don't wait. We move. We're going back, now."

"Derek's right," I say. "Time to move. You two take Scotty and return to the White House. Derek and I will wait for the rest of the team. We can follow and cover you."

"Yes, sir. If you order so," the young man says.

I'm surprised he has agreed so easily, but he is young, and Derek and I are somewhat legendary. We're probably intimidating to him.

"Dad. Don't you care what happens to Mom? Dad!"

The young woman smiles broadly and smothers Scotty with a hug. "She'll be fine, sweetie. Come on, now. We'll all be safe shortly."

She has calmed Scotty, and before he can protest further, the young man has grabbed his hand and they're leading him off.

"What am I supposed to tell June?" Archie says.

"Make something up." I hold out my hand. "Now give me the Winnebago keys."

"Do you think I'm drunk? I can drive."

"Derek and I need the RV, and it's going to be dangerous. Take a cab back to June and resume the honeymoon." I stick my hand out farther and look at him as if he's getting the better end of the deal. Archie considers, and I think the thought of resuming the honeymoon without any further delays has sealed things for him. He hands over the keys.

Derek and I leave Archie and walk toward Constitution Avenue and the Winnebago.

"You got a plan?" Derek says.

"Walk ahead of me casually, like we're returning to the White House. I'll jump in the RV and then come to pick you up."

"And then what?"

"We drive around until Big Mac captures us."

And just then, the lights to the Winnebago turn on, stopping both Derek and me in our tracks. The RV backs up slowly. Someone is in there. It's a trap. I look for the young couple and Scotty, hoping they are far enough away from whatever is about to go down. I don't see any sign of them.

The Winnebago moves slowly forward. "You armed?" I ask Derek.

"No. You?"

"No. Why the fuck don't we have any guns?"

"Wait up, dudes." I feel a hand on my shoulder. I turn around and see Archie, panting. "I got to thinking," he says. "One of the main ingredients of Juney and my honeymoon was to cruise around rockin' out the Winnebago, if you know what I mean." He gives me a thumbs-up. "You guys take a cab."

Derek points. "There—go get your Winne-fucking-bago, you fool."

The RV is on the lawn, careening over the footpath, and heading straight for us.

Little Joe

I'M GOING TO have a friend. A real friend. They told me today. Probably just for a few days, but still, I've never had a real friend. I told you that before, but soon I won't have to tell you again.

The president is stupid. The president takes drugs that make him crazy. That's what they told me. I've seen it on TV, too, but they seem to know more about it here.

I walked around the Washington Monument once. It's the tallest building in Washington, DC, and it's right across from the White House. Papa McGuffin says the president won't be the president very much longer. He says Vice President Carlson is going to be president, and he's one of our friends, so everyone is very excited here. They say something big is going to happen.

I wonder where my new friend is from? Will my friend be a

girl or a boy? I hope it's a boy. I heard girls get scared and don't like to do cool stuff. I like playing with the monkeys and messing with their minds. I bet my new friend will like the monkeys. We can put them in boxes and roll them down the stairs. That really freaks them out. I bet my new friend will like that.

Papa McGuffin said I might be president someday. He said it real serious, too, not like how they tell little boys and girls on TV that they could be president. He meant it.

I won't take any drugs when I'm president. My mind has to be clear. Papa McGuffin says I'll have to make the tough decisions, the decisions that will decide the lives and deaths of millions of people and ensure the greatness of Big Mac and America.

Papa McGuffin knows everything. He is like the most powerful general in the world. I wonder what my new friend will think of that?

Chekhov, Tolstoy, and Drineys

THE RV IS about to run the three of us over. At the last moment, we scatter and dive out of the way. The RV skids and spins to a stop. Archie and I lie next to each other, separated from Derek on the Winnebago's other side.

Archie is sitting on his ass, frozen scared and looking at the RV as six men in masks jump out the side door. I slowly stand up. "Run, Archie!" I shout, but Archie can't seem to function.

I'm knocked down by two of the men. They overwhelm Archie and me and drag us inside the RV. The men shut the door and the RV drives off.

I don't know what happened to Derek, but he is not on the RV. I so wish it were him and not Archie who's been captured with me.

My hands are cuffed behind me. I sit at the kitchen table across from Archie. The Winnebago's interior has not changed. My eyes are drawn to the refrigerator, where a magnet clips our family Christmas card from last year. Karen, Scotty, and I stand in front of our tree wearing obnoxious holiday sweaters. Scotty wears an image of Rudolph leading Santa's sleigh through a sea of bullets in an Xbox war game. I wear a replica Charlie Brown sweater, yellow with a black zigzagged line and a small patch featuring Charlie Brown's famously sad-looking Christmas tree. Karen sports a sweater with a round ornament adorned with sparkling plastic gems. I stare at the photo.

The RV shakes as it hurtles over the curb and back onto the street. The men, all in black masks, hold on or sit down where they can. And then a man covers Archie's head with a black hood. Everything goes black as someone does the same to me.

Archie is whimpering. "You've got the wrong guy. Tell them, hound dog. Tell them they've got the wrong guy."

I remain silent, as I know is best in these situations. Archie keeps whining, and then I hear the rip of tape. There is some commotion. Archie is now silent.

The RV moves on. I feel us make several sharp turns, and then we speed up and go straight for a while. I try to relax. This is exactly what I wanted. Big Mac, or whoever has kidnapped Karen, has now gotten me. It's undoubtedly Big Mac or some organization aligned with them. Who else would want to capture me? Surely they will let Karen go now that they have me. I had to be their original objective, right? Scotty should be safe in the White House by now, probably still fuming. At least

I won't have to worry about him.

We drive for about thirty minutes before coming to a stop. I am led out of the RV, a person holding on to each of my arms, a black hood still covering my head. The temperature is cool and it smells damp. I hear the echoing sounds of the RV doors opening and closing, and footsteps shuffle all around me. It feels as if we're in some kind of underground parking garage.

We walk, and I hear doors slide open in front of me with a soft whoosh. The echoes disappear and the sounds of the walking footsteps are now close and defined. We're walking down some sort of carpeted hallway, and all is quiet except for the soft breathing of the person escorting me on my left.

Someone stops me and then turns me to the right. I'm guided down a turning stairway. We descend what I think must be about three floors before I hear the clank of a door opening.

The black hood is pulled off my head. Bright lights blind me. I blink and squint as my eyes adjust. It looks like the interior of a hospital. I'm in a circular room where two hallways intersect. To my right is a nurses' station where two workers in light-blue hospital garb monitor vital signs on video screens. Archie is gone.

Standing before me, looking superior in a green army suit in full regalia, is the tall and muscular General George McGuffin. He has army-green battle eyes and a mostly gray crew cut shaved close to his white skin on the sides. A strong jawline outlines a still handsome face, even though he has a two-inch scar across his cheekbone, a battle souvenir courtesy of the Vietcong. I think the sinister mark has probably served General McGuffins' purposes well.

So this is the secret Big Mac headquarters. We must be in DC, or at least close by. Perhaps we are in the Pentagon, or some cave deep underground. I must pay attention and look for clues to our whereabouts.

The General nods to one of the three guards watching over me. I look around, but Archie is nowhere to be seen. The guard unlocks my handcuffs, and I rub my wrists in relief.

McGuffin sizes me up and doesn't look impressed. "Chris Thompson," he says in a commanding, condescending voice. "We underestimated your . . . your . . . lucky tactics, shall we say. You are one bumbling fool and a lucky son of a bitch."

"Nice to meet you too, General McGuffin. Apparently my luck has run out." I say it somewhat cavalierly, like I think James Bond would have done.

"Maybe not," the general says. "Maybe your luck has brought us together for a reason."

"What exactly do you want with me?" I ask. "What have you done with my wife?"

"Your wife is perfectly safe and being well taken care of, I assure you."

"I want to see her."

"Yes, of course, in due time." He seems to be thinking something over. "I want to show you something, Chris. May I call you Chris?"

"You just called me a son of a bitch." I look at the three guards. "I suppose you can call me whatever you want."

He laughs. "But we should be civil, even if we don't agree, though I do hope we will be seeing along the same lines someday. Perhaps soon, very soon."

The general is trying to turn me, I can see that right off. I've seen too much of Big Mac's evil: the torture, the mind control, the persecution of minorities. I never want to be a part of their nefarious plans, but I'll try to be conciliatory in hopes of freeing Karen.

I nod. "Thank you, General. Gentlemen should be civil, even in times of war."

I've touched a nerve. Regardless of his politics, General McGuffin has a reputation for being honorable. He nods back to me. "Indeed. Now please follow me." The general turns and walks down the near hall. He stops and waits for me in front of a heavy door that has an opaque window interlaced with wire mesh. The door buzzes, and the general opens it.

We step into a long room that smells like the inside of a barn. A cacophony of screams erupt around us. Wire cages containing pairs of hyperactive monkeys line the room.

"Silence," the general commands.

The monkeys become silent.

"Training an army of monkeys?" I say.

"No," the general says. "That is not the purpose for this project. Although these are very intelligent monkeys."

"I imagine that most monkeys will listen to you, General," I say.

The general shoots me a look that says he'd like to end my life right now.

A monkey reaches a hand out and grabs my back pocket, probing it with its fingers. Finding nothing, the monkey removes its hand, bares its teeth, and shakes its head wildly.

General McGuffin forces a smile to return to his face. "Look at the ones in each cage closely," he says. "Can you tell the difference?"

I walk the room and inspect the monkey pairs. "Twins?"

The general bends down in front of one cage. "Two plus two," he says.

One of the monkeys holds up four fingers. "Good, Tolstoy.

Now Chekhov." He motions the other monkey forward. "Two plus one?"

The monkey named Chekhov comes forward holding up three fingers.

"Very good, Chekhov." The general stands up, proud and satisfied. As chairman of the Joint Chiefs of Staff, he is a powerful man used to getting his wishes, and evidently these monkeys have not disappointed him. "The monkeys," he says. "They are identical in every way, but they are not twins."

"Clones?" I say.

"You are looking at the results of the everlasting life project." The general says this as if he is delivering the climactic line of a boardroom presentation. He seems disappointed when my deadpan demeanor does not change. "Think of the implications, Chris."

"The chosen ones in the shelter believed that they were part of some government eternal life program, but you eventually killed them. Do you expect me to be impressed with some cloning program that may have created rumors that fueled their false hopes?"

"I won't deny that we utilized some of the misconceived religious beliefs of the Emergence program. But it was all done for the betterment of Big Mac and for the future of the United States."

I try to hide my disgust—angering him will only make matters worse for me and Karen.

McGuffin walks up and down the line of monkey cages. The guards move out of his path. "We have perfected cloning. The monkeys' levels of intelligence, along with every other thing about them, are exactly the same." He stops in front of me and looks me in the eye. He puts his hands on my shoulders. "I want you to be a part of the everlasting life program."

"You want to clone me?" I ask, surprised.

McGuffin rears his head back and laughs. "Maybe. Just maybe. I like that we are starting to think along the same lines." The general gives a squeeze before releasing his hands from my shoulders. "Chris—we want you to be a Big Mac leader in the new world order."

"I'm not so sure we're thinking along the same lines," I say.

"You said you wanted to be cloned. We can do that if you really want."

"I didn't say that. I don't want to be cloned. I just want my wife back. I want my family to be safe."

"And they will. I promise you that you and your family will be well taken care of. But Chris. Do you understand?" The general's eyes go wide. His scar flushes red. "We can clone people."

I don't know what to say. I'm not sure why he is so excited.

"Think of what we can do." McGuffin touches the four gold stars on his epaulet, as if to make sure that they are still there. "The brightest minds, the greatest leaders, the most influential people the world has ever known—they could all be working for me." The general removes his fingers from his gold stars and puts his hand to one side. His eyes blink rapidly. "I mean, for Big Mac. And for the United States, of course."

I try to digest what the general is saying.

"Alexander the Great, Julius Caesar, Attila the Hun, Genghis Khan!" The general is actually shaking with excitement. "The greatest military mind of the last hundred years—Adolf Hitler!" McGuffin holds up his hands in front of me as if to stop any rebuke I may have. "We would have to keep him under control, of course. But to have Hitler working for us would be a dream come true."

"He could be your speechwriter," I say.

"Exactly. You're fitting in already, Chris."

"What about Mother Theresa, or Gandhi?"

"Sure, sure. A few notable religious figures to keep the population happy would be okay."

The general's phone buzzes. He looks irritated, but he answers it. He listens for a moment and then says, "McCarthy grew up on a farm. He raised chickens or something. Okay. You got it ready? Thanks, Skylar." He puts the phone back in his pocket.

Suddenly, I realize a scary possibility.

"Are you going to clone Joe McCarthy?" I ask this in a hushed tone, almost as if I am talking to myself, but McGuffin hears me loud and clear. He chuckles. "You think like us."

"You've already done it? You've cloned Senator Joe McCarthy?"

"He's our first human clone. Actually, he's our only human clone right now. We are very proud."

It's hard to believe, but I guess it makes sense. Bringing back their fabled iconic leader is exactly what these McCarthy-worshipping Big Mac nut jobs would want to do.

"How is a cloned Joe McCarthy going to fit into your plans?" I ask. "McCarthy was a witch hunter. He embodied the antithesis of the American spirit. Even his most ardent supporters renounced him in the end."

"Yes, in the end, McCarthy was wrongly maligned, but at his prime he was unstoppable. His charisma, his influence, his innate understanding on how to use power—these are skills you can't teach. Besides being the iconic symbol of the Big Mac party, McCarthy had the true skills to lead."

"But nobody really liked him."

"His followers loved him. We love him, and the true disciples of the party will worship and fight to the death for a reincarnation of their beloved leader."

"I don't doubt that," I say. "But I don't think the rest of America will feel the same way."

"The hell with the rest of America."

The general opens the door at the room's other end. We walk down another hallway and stop before a black glass door. McGuffin waves his hand, and the door slides open. "Come. I want to show you something else."

We step into a glass-enclosed viewing area. The door closes behind us. It is mostly dark but for dim safety lights that outline the floor and select spots along the walls and ceiling. I look out upon a large atrium. It must be four stories tall and five hundred yards long.

General McGuffin flips a switch on a control panel. A loud buzzing sound fills the room. It sounds like I have stuck my head inside a hornet's nest. I cover my ears with my hands. The general laughs. "You'll get used to it."

Is he going to torture me with hornets or wasps? Did Karen have to face the same terror?

McGuffin spins a dial on the control panel. "The rest of America will see the wisdom in accepting the rule of Joe McCarthy and Big Mac, or they'll face the consequences. The masses are ignorant. The people must be told what is good for them and the country—forced to do it, if necessary." He outstretches his hand. "Regard—the guardians of our future utopia."

The buzzing sound increases, becoming what can only be

described as a scream. A silver mass rises from the ground. The mass covers the whole length of the atrium and looks like a large blanket. The blanket undulates and waves like a stormy sea. The waves increase in size and frequency, and then the whole blanket separates into a million flying drone-like bullets, each of them looking exactly like the ones that chased Scotty and me in Yellowstone. General McGuffin pushes a button, and tiny red lights illuminate on all of the minidrones.

"I think you have seen a driney before," the general says.

"Nasty little buggers," I say.

The drineys scatter and dart in random directions. They look like they are lost, like they are searching for something in vain.

"When Big Mac regains control, we will release them, and the purification will begin."

The drineys look like a frightening hive of evil. "What do they do?"

"They will offer people a chance," the general says. "A chance to correct their un-American ways."

I lean close to the glass. A driney stops directly in front of me. Its red light flashes in my eye and then zooms away.

"Don't worry—yours is in another room."

"What do you mean 'yours'?"

"Each driney is assigned to one citizen. They will know instantly when that citizen is likely to commit an un-American act. The drineys will act as our nation's conscience."

"Tyranny," I whisper.

"Freedom," the general says. "If a target is constantly monitored, they're very unlikely to commit an un-American act. The nation will be rid of crime. Undesirables will be rehabilitated without need of the draconian incarceration methods we use today. Citizens will be free to experience a safe, wholesome American way of life in every corner of this beautiful country."

"Freedom," I say sarcastically.

General McGuffin slaps me on the back. "Now you see." He turns to the guards who have been standing in the shadows next to the wall. "Leave us for a moment."

The guards leave. McGuffin works the control panel and the drineys collapse to the floor all at once. To my relief, the buzzing ceases.

The general flips a switch and the whole room lights up. The drineys carpet the room, aligning themselves eerily in neat rows that all face the left wall. The general walks down to the end of the glass and then back, as if inspecting his army.

"So, are you ready to be a part of Big Mac?" he asks suddenly.

I'm not sure why he thinks that what he has just shown me would convince me to join Big Mac. Claiming he has cloned Joe McCarthy and demonstrating his Big Brother army of drones has, if anything, freaked me out. But I want to stay on the general's good side. The fact that he wants to turn me is my key to saving Karen.

"It's tempting. But surely, general, you can respect my loyalty."

"I do. Though there is no dishonor in correcting misplaced loyalty. Chris, it's understandable that you would have some concerns." McGuffin relaxes his shoulders. His facial expression turns into one of understanding, as if he is an empathetic father. "In time, I believe you will accept the wisdom behind Big Mac's philosophies. But until then, I wonder if you could just find it within yourself to trust me, if only a little bit. Understand that I have lived a longer life than you. I have seen and felt the darkness of war, but I also understand the goodness and greatness that is within every man." He pauses a moment. "Chris—we would like you to testify at the president's impeachment trial that the president was of sound mind during the last emergency. That he knew full well what he was doing when he allowed Vance Slater and Big Mac to take control."

"Impeaching the president would allow Vice President Carlson to become the new president," I say. "And he will undoubtedly pardon Vance Slater, and the country will fall back under Big Mac's totalitarian control."

"Exactly. And we want you to play a big role, too. Having a former enemy of Big Mac see the wisdom in our rule would do wonders for public opinion. People trust you, Chris. They like your everyman sense of right and wrong. Imagine, Chris—you could be head of the Customs Service, or be in charge of one of the borders. You could sit atop the wall and pick off Canadians with a high-powered rifle. Or how about this: you and your family could live in an old refurbished lighthouse, complete with staff. You could have an old howitzer and blast any foreign boats you see. Now that's real fun."

"I don't know," I say, somewhat mystified.

"Or you could head our division of superspies. I know you still have those boyhood fantasies of being James Bond."

"I do not."

"You, do, Chris, you do. You could be Big Mac's James Bond. We'd set up all of your missions so that you would never fail, of course."

"I don't need set-up missions," I say loudly. "I don't have James Bond fantasies. Go to hell, General—I'll never join you."

General McGuffin waves his arm toward the sleeping driney army. His eyes squint, and his scar becomes more pointed. "We can't keep you here. It would look too suspicious if you weren't able to testify, and it might possibly turn some congressional votes against us." He raises an eyebrow and makes a sly smile. "But we do have your wife."

I jump toward McGuffin and grab his meaty neck. My attack takes him by surprise, and he tumbles to the ground with me on top of him. I hear the sliding glass doors open as I squeeze his neck with all my might. The general's face turns red. His eyes bulge out at me.

Something hard hits me in the forearm, and then my other forearm. Hands grab my arms, my legs, my back, the hair on top of my head, and I am hoisted into the air.

The guards throw me into the hallway, handcuff my arms behind my back, and then lift me to my feet. The general marches out of the driney atrium looking furious. He walks close to me, but he doesn't acknowledge or even look at me. With a clenched fist, he flexes his arm and punches me in the gut. The wind sails out of me. Stomach acids rush up my throat. I want to bend over and collapse, but the guards hold me up, ready to receive another blow. McGuffin makes a low growling sound, and then he turns and walks away. He enters an elevator with two guards. The doors close, and he is gone.

I messed up. I let the general get to me and lost my cool. Perhaps he was testing me. I should have stayed calm, gone along with him for a while until I had a chance either to free Karen or to do some more harm to Big Mac. Damn my insecurities and love of James Bond. I don't know what to do now but wait for an opening, a mistake by a guard, anything.

Four guards are with me. They open a door. I brace myself for a beating, but the door leads to a stairwell, which they prod and pull me to climb. After three flights, we exit to a carpeted hallway that looks exactly the same as the one we left. At the hallway's end, there are two secure doors. One of the guards places his hand on a palm-print reader and then looks into a retina scanner. There is a click. The doors open and we enter.

I am in a darkly lit room. The walls are made of cinder blocks painted a desert-tank-colored beige. The room is two stories high. Across from me is a one story wall with two large windows. A balcony with a tubular metal railing extends backward from the top of the wall. The windows are blacked out. I feel uneasy. It looks like a place where you would interrogate prisoners or choose criminals out of a lineup. I search in vain for anything that might indicate our true location. I wish Derek were here.

There is movement up on the balcony: General McGuffin again. He walks toward the rail, patting his face with a steaming towel. He sees me and throws the towel to the ground. He puts his hands on the rail and looks down on me as if he is about to address a multitude of followers. An aide tries to adjust one of his award ribbons that is askew, but McGuffin brusquely brushes his hand away.

"I'm very disappointed it had to come to this, Chris."

"Me, too."

"I prefer to win converts to the cause with logic and reasoning, but as you are too stubborn to use either, you have forced me to use more intensive methods."

"You said yourself that it would look bad if I didn't testify.

And if logic and reason are on your side, why does it matter what I say? And who knows what questions they're going to ask me? I might not say anything that damages Big Mac's agenda."

The general smiles. "Yes. That is exactly what we want to ensure. In fact, we're certain your testimony is going to be downright helpful." He laughs and waves a hand into the air. "Light up number one."

A light goes on behind the window on the right side. Behind the window, I see what looks to be a simple hotel room suite with a queen-size bed, a small table, a sofa, and two chairs in a sitting area. Karen is sitting with her feet up on the bed, her back cushioned by pillows against the headrest. In front of the bed Archie walks back and forth, talking and pantomiming wildly. There is no sound, so I can't hear what he is saying.

"Karen." I run to the window and pound my hands against it. "Karen." The window absorbs my blows without sound or vibration. Archie continues talking as if nothing has changed. Karen looks bored out of her mind. She rubs her temple, and I can tell she must have one of her migraines.

I take a few steps back and look up at McGuffin. He looks confident, like he's enjoying this, like whatever evil he has in store for me will undoubtedly go his way.

"What's your game, McGuffin?"

"Game?" He looks up toward the ceiling, mockingly pretending as if he is considering my question. "There is no game—more like simple math." He puts his palms to his chest. "I subtract the two most precious things to you." He points his finger forcefully at me. "Which equals you testifying exactly how I tell you to at President Wright's impeachment trial."

"What demented math class did you learn that formula in?"

I force a laugh. "Assigning Archie as a 'precious' variable—that's funny."

McGuffin laughs a real laugh, a laugh that is unsettling to me. "I understand the equation, Thompson." He turns and stretches out his hand as if he's about to reveal the prize behind a curtain. "How do you like my X and my O? I believe you have already met Chip and Lexi."

Standing next to General McGuffin is the young couple who escorted Scotty from the White House to the Washington Monument.

McGuffin nods in satisfaction at what must be the horrified look on my face. He claps his hands. The blacked-out window to the left lights up to reveal Scotty sitting before a TV, playing a video game.

"Scotty," I whisper as my breath escapes me. I look up at Chip and Lexi. They are holding hands and looking down at me quite pleased with themselves. "How could you?"

"We support the evolution," Chip says.

"By kidnapping a young boy? Nice revolution."

"Ev-olution," Lexi says, plainly irritated by constantly having to make this correction.

"The time of glorifying the self is over." Chip holds Lexi's hand and raises it into the air. "We are in the midst of an evolution where small sacrifices must be made to optimize the superior attributes of mankind as a whole."

I'm not sure what Chip is saying, and I don't really care. The last thing I want to do is argue philosophy. "My family is my only concern, and they will not be sacrificed."

"Very glad to hear you say that," the general says. "We shall now complete the equation. In exchange for your testimony, we will spare your family. Do you agree, Chris Thompson?"

I'm in no position to bargain. Do I sacrifice my family in an attempt to save the country and millions of people? Is the individual more important than the whole? Is my family more important? This is no mere philosophical question; this is real. I see Karen and Scotty before me, helpless. I look at Scotty, playing innocently, and then Karen, still enduring whatever Archie is going on about. They are everything to me, no matter what evil is in control. I have to save them, and right now, it looks as if helping Big Mac is the only way.

"I agree," I say. "I'll say whatever you want if you let everyone leave safely with me."

McGuffin chuckles. "You would like that solution. But no, that would be too easy for you." He makes a motion behind him, and suddenly I can hear the electronic beeps and explosions from Scotty's video game.

"The thing about landing catfish is you don't need a fancy lure," Archie is explaining. "They'll go for a moldy piece of cheese. One time—"

"Scotty. Karen. Can you hear me?"

Scotty and Karen both look up, and I can see that they recognize me. A window on the wall separating their rooms becomes transparent. Karen runs to the window. "Scotty. What are you doing here?"

"Mom!"

Karen turns to me. "Chris. What is happening?"

"Silence!" McGuffin roars. "I will tell you what is happening."

Karen and Scotty both look up, wondering where the booming voice is coming from.

"I'm not such a fool as to let you testify without me keeping some insurance," McGuffin says. "But as a sign of Big

Mac's goodwill, I won't keep everyone prisoner. You must decide, Chris, which apartment will be set free. Do you want your son to go home with you, or your wife and best friend?"

"Best friend nothing," I say.

Archie presses his forehead against the glass. "You worried about the father-in-law thing, hound dog? We can still be best friends."

I walk close to Archie and Karen's window. "I don't care what you are, Archie. I don't want you alone with Karen for any amount of time."

"Aw, don't you worry about me." Archie stands in the back corner. "I'll stay here the whole time. I'll sleep on the floor." He walks to the opposite side of the bed from where Karen had been sitting and he touches the bed top just a few inches from the side. "Well, maybe I could sleep way over here." He lies down, barely on the bed, his one leg sprawled over the side. "I will be completely on my best behavior, hound dog." He inches a little more to the center and puts both legs on the bed. "Or maybe just this far." He inches farther to the center. "Or just a little bit more." He moves even farther so that he's completely on one side of the bed. "Or maybe here. Here would be good, don't you think, hound dog? Have a heart; a man's gotta sleep."

Karen is tapping on the window. "Chris. How can you even be considering? Choose Scotty."

I look from Karen to Archie and back to Karen again.

"I can handle Archie," she says. "There'll be no problems."

"No problems," Archie says.

"Dad." Scotty looks through his interior window. "Choose Mom. That was the whole mission, to rescue Mom."

"No, no, honey," Karen says. "You're just a child. You

have no business being caught in this mess."

"I can take care of myself, Mom."

"Mom's right," I say. "You're a kid, Scotty. You can't stay here. I'm sorry."

Karen looks at me with relief. "Make the choice, Chris, and take Scotty home."

"Scotty stays with me," a squeaky boy's voice says.

Suddenly, there's a husky black-haired boy an inch taller than Scotty standing next to him in the window. The boy puts his arm around Scotty's shoulders. "You can't take my new pal."

"Mom, Dad, this is Little Joe," Scotty says.

"Nice to meetcha," Little Joe says.

I take a step back and look up at McGuffin, who is smiling down smugly at me. "That's right. Little Joe McCarthy. The heart of the everlasting life project. Big Mac is at the forefront of genetic science. Little Joe here was miraculously born to us twelve years ago."

I stare at Little Joe. He is clearly in the midst of puberty, with a few pimples and arms and limbs that look too long and unwieldy for his body. Still, he has dark, bushy eyebrows, thin lips, and a curved smile, all traits of the infamous Senator Joe McCarthy.

"I'm a clone," Little Joe says proudly. "I'm going to rule the world someday."

"Dad." Scotty waves me over to his side to speak confidentially. "Dad. They're not going to hurt me. They want me to play with Little Joe. He doesn't have any friends."

"He's different than an average kid, Scotty."

"He does cheat and swear a lot, but he's no different from a lot of my friends. Don't worry, Dad. We get along."

"It's time for Little Joe to interact with real children," McGuffin says. "Think of it, Thompson—your son could have a powerful ally someday."

Scotty's right about one thing. They probably will take good care of him if he becomes Little Joe's friend.

Scotty taps on the window. "Dad. Do you really want Mom to spend a week in one room with Grandpa Archie?" Scotty twirls his finger next to his ear. "Because you know as well as I do, Dad, he's not all there."

"I don't think—"

Scotty pounds his hand against the window. "Don't be naive, Dad. Be a man. I like being here. I like being a spy. I can help us. I'll figure it out. Dad, please. Stick to the mission. Protect your wife."

"Decide now," McGuffin says.

I think it over. "Do I have your word the prisoners will be kept safe and returned immediately after I testify?"

McGuffin puts his hand over his ribbons. "As I pledge myself to the betterment of the United States of America, I pledge on my honor that your family will be kept safe and returned as promised."

He may be a little off his rocker, but McGuffin is a career military man, known for selfless heroic acts. I'm confident he will honor his pledge.

"Well?" McGuffin says.

It's the toughest decision I've ever had to make. Scotty or Karen, my heart and soul, my true loves.

"Decide," McGuffin says.

Ugh. I've never felt lower. Scotty is a kid; he's the obvious choice. But he's so good at this spy business. He's flown a plane, and he thinks clearly—better than me, even. Would I be the worst dad ever if I forsake my son just because he might do better than my wife in surviving imprisonment by Big Mac? I don't know.

"Now," McGuffin says.

Can I trust McGuffin's honor? In the end, I go with my gut.

"I'll stick to simple math," I say. "Logically, you having two hostages is better for you than having just one, so I choose Karen and Archie. Scotty can stay here until I testify."

"No!" Karen screams.

"Yes," Scotty says. He touches his temple and points at me. "Smart move, Dad."

Archie starts packing his things. "Tough choice, hound dog, but I'm not embarrassed to say that I'm happy to be getting out of here."

Karen takes off her shoe and throws it at Archie, hitting him square in the back of the head.

"Ow."

"You should be ashamed to be so happy at the expense of your own grandson." Karen turns to me. "And you. I . . . I . . . I . . ." She buries her face into her hands and starts crying.

Guards appear in Karen and Archie's room and escort them out. After a moment, the guards bring them to me. Karen is still crying.

Archie slaps my back and shakes my hand. "This spy stuff ain't for me. I appreciate you having my back, hound dog."

Karen grabs my ears and puts her face in front of mine. "Change your mind. It's not too late. Tell McGuffin you want Scotty."

"It is too late," McGuffin roars.

"Please, no," Karen says.

I wave to Scotty. "Hang tough, my man."

"I got this, Dad."

The guards are shuffling us out of the room.

Karen is crying. "I love you, Scotty."

Scotty waves. "I love you, Mom."

We exit the doors. Archie has nervous energy and seems excited to be set free. Karen is glum, disconsolate, livid. "You're not fit to be a father," she says.

"Karen," I begin.

"Fuck you, Chris."

I feel empty, like I have failed as a husband and father. A real spy would have taken action, found a way out, saved the day. Karen's right. What have I done? Big Mac's made up of a bunch of maniacs. What if they do crazy experiments on him or harm him in some other way? And then there's Little Joe. He's bigger than Scotty, and he's a clone—of Joseph McCarthy. He might bully Scotty, or worse. Scotty could die.

What's going to happen? Oh, god. I am a horrible father.

Polar Bear

ARCHIE, KAREN, AND I sit in the Winnebago with hoods on our heads. An icy voice speaks into my ear. "Remember. Testifying correctly at the impeachment trial is the only way to save your son. Big Mac will be watching."

I hear the door open and people leaving the RV. The door slams shut. It is quiet. We count together to a hundred, as instructed, Karen's voice barely a whisper. When we reach one hundred, we pull off our hoods. Thankfully, we are alone.

Archie jumps up and pushes open the side door. "We're at your house."

Karen and I follow Archie out, and we all stand next to the RV. It is awkwardly silent. Archie points at his car in the driveway.

"Right where I left it." He shifts around. "I'm really sorry about Scotty and all. He should be okay. That Little Joe seemed all right, and the food wasn't bad. You gotta admit, Karen, the food was pretty good."

Karen looks about to cry.

"Look whatcha done, hound dog. You should have left me and Karen. I wouldn't have touched her now, right, Karen? Have I ever made you uncomfortable? Okay, well, that one time, but I'm married now, and you can respect that I'm an honest husband. Okay. Well. I see y'all got a lot on your minds, and June will be missing me, so best I be going." Archie walks to his car. "We'll come back for the RV tomorrow." He gets in the car and is off.

I look upon our simple DC suburban ranch house. I haven't been home for nearly a month. The morning sun is just rising over the treetops in the nearby park. I'm so tired. I'd love to crawl into my own bed and fall asleep.

"I still can't believe it. How could you?" Karen is crying. "He's probably lonely and afraid."

"Little Joe is with him."

"A clone. We left our child with a clone."

"You have something against clones?"

"What if it's deranged?"

"Scotty will be well looked after. General McGuffin gave me his word." I try to put my hand on Karen's back, but she leans away.

"My baby. You gave my baby away."

"I had to choose. It made more sense. Scotty is probably going to love being a hostage."

She grabs at her hair. "Are you even listening to what you are saying? A hostage. Our son, our creation, my most precious—a hostage. What have you done?"

"He's precious to me, too."

"You didn't even tell him you loved him."

"What?"

"When we left. All you said was 'goodbye, buddy,' or something macho like that. When was the last time you told him you loved him?"

"I don't know, Karen. Come on. He knows I love him."

"A fine way you have of showing it, sacrificing him to prison."

Phyllis comes out of her house next door in her bathrobe heading for the morning paper at the street's edge. She hears us arguing and stops. "Oh, hi." She gives a wave.

Karen and I both wave.

"Let's go inside," I say.

"No. I don't want you inside. I don't want you here. You're dangerous. I thought you were a teddy bear, but you're really a polar bear." I try to get closer to her, but she pushes me away. "You eat your own cubs."

Okay. Maybe she's right. Scotty is the most important thing in our lives. Scotty is us, our love, our focus. What kind of man, father, husband am I? Logically, it's true: it was better to leave McGuffin with one hostage rather than two, and frankly, Scotty will probably do better in that environment than Karen would have. But that misses the point. How could I give up my own son to Big Mac?

"Honey, please," I say.

Her voice softens ever so slightly. "You can stay in the RV."

I think Karen has recognized that I regret my choice to leave Scotty behind, and I know that if I apologize and show remorse for my decision right now, we could end this fight and get on with the business of trying to find Scotty, but damn it,

I'm too proud, and I turn and walk into the RV.

"Fine." I slam the door. After a while, I'm pretty sure she's gone into the house. I lie down on the back bed, but the sun is now above the trees and bright light is streaming through the windows. The RV is quickly warming up. I won't be able to sleep here unless I turn on the power and run the air conditioning. And suddenly I don't feel like sleeping anymore.

I walk to the front. Our former captors have left the keys in the ignition. I turn the engine on and rev it. I look toward the house and see the curtains move in our bedroom. Karen must be peeking out.

I step on the gas and try to peel out, but instead the Winnebago lurches forward, and I have to slam on the brakes lest I knock over the Campbells' mailbox. Shit. I step on the gas again and move slowly off. My destination—the White House.

Roast Beef with Red Peppers

I FIGHT THROUGH morning rush hour traffic as I drive the RV into DC, down 17th Street toward the west gate. DC police cars and Secret Service vehicles are parked in front of the gate. Security guards stand in place. Police officers mill about, talking with each other and watching pedestrians file by. The midmorning sun is heating up, and it feels like it's going to be a hot day. I roll down my window and smell the diesel fumes from a tour bus a half block ahead of me.

Did the Secret Service see me captured at the Washington Monument? Derek must have seen for sure. Hopefully they were able to track the RV to find McGuffin's hideout. I have to let them know that Scotty is a prisoner and to take precautions so he doesn't get hurt in any rescue attempt. I need to talk to Derek and the president. I need to get inside the White House. I don't have time to call.

The only way for me to get into the White House fast is to get someone's attention. When I'm parallel with the gate I stop the RV, halting traffic. I lay on the horn and shout at the guards. "Hey, I need to bring this baby inside."

The response is faster than I'd have thought. Before I can say another word, my door opens, and I am pulled out and thrown to the ground. Security personnel swarm the RV with their guns drawn. They crawl on top and underneath with metal sensors and bomb-sniffing dogs.

"I'm Chris Thompson, here to see President Wright," I say with my face in the street while my hands are being cuffed behind my back.

A meaty hand grabs my collar and pulls me to a standing position. A tough, dark-skinned, obviously military man stares at me intensely. "And I'm, 'I don't give a fuck', here to make sure you never lay eyes on the president."

"Yo, Keith," a guard inside the gate with a phone to his ear calls to my captor. "They're looking for a Chris Thompson inside. That's not him, is it?"

"You got to be freaking kidding me."

"Show him to the camera."

Keith gently walks me in front of a swiveling camera perched atop a cement gatepost. After a moment, the motorized gate starts sliding open.

"Let him in," says the other guard. "Order came from the president himself."

Keith unlocks my cuffs. "Sorry, sir, but we have to be vigilant."

I shake his hand. "No worries—just testing. You did well."

The Secret Service arrives to escort me through the White House and into the same meeting room Scotty and I had been in last night. The room is empty, except for Derek lying flat on his back and staring up at the boardroom ceiling.

"Derek." I run to him. "Derek. You all right?"

Derek groans and rolls onto his side, his gut hanging over his belt and pressing his button-down shirt tight. "Hey, Chris. You made it back. What happened?"

"What are you doing on the table?"

"Just thinking."

"Anything wrong, man?"

"My back's been hurting. I think from favoring my arm, you know? It feels good to lie on the hard surface."

"Bullshit."

He sits up, dangles his legs over the table's edge, and gives me a cross look. "You don't think my back's hurting?"

"Oh, I think your back's hurting. I'm not doubting that. You just seem a little down and not your usual good-natured self—Cannonball."

The start of a smile begins on his face, but fades quickly. "I don't know."

"How's your girl? Her name is coming back to me. Ruh . . . Ruh . . . Rhon—"

"Don't say that name." Derek jumps off the table. "I don't ever want to hear that bitch's name again."

So that's what has been bothering him. Derek worked undercover at Emergence month on and month off, living with his girlfriend, Rhonda, during his off time. "I'm sorry, Derek. It's gotta be tough keeping a relationship going long distance like that."

"You don't know how tough. Especially when she's doing some other guy the moment I'm out of sight."

I don't know what to say. It's silent for a minute. "She wasn't for you," I finally say, stating the obvious.

Derek walks around the room pushing on the boardroom chairs, spinning them around and creating a general disorder. "This government job has done me no good. I'm sick of being their secret stooge." He plops down into the chair at the head of the table and puts up his feet.

I begin to tell him about what happened to me after we were captured at the RV. My story seems to shake him out of his despondency, and he becomes more riveted to my words the further along I get.

The elevator doors open, and a black man in a waiter's tuxedo enters the room and speaks to us with elegant deference. "The president requests your presence at lunch. If you please, follow me."

We walk after the maître d'. Derek appears next to me and puts his hand on my shoulder. "Shit, man. We gotta get your son, pronto." Then he smiles. "But we're about to dine in the White House, my good Chris Thompson."

I nod my head to Derek. "I can't think of finer company than you, honorable sir."

We exit the elevator on the ground floor and walk down a series of hallways. I look around for the state dining room, or perhaps a side dining room set up for a small party. But instead, we walk out the north door onto the long circular drive. Black Suburbans with dark tinted windows, along with a couple of military Humvees, surround Archie's old Winnebago. The maître d' opens the Winnebago's door and motions us inside with a regal flip of his hand. I take a tentative step in, look left and right.

"Come in. Come in." The president is standing at the kitchen counter wearing a red apron that says Da Boss. He waves us in excitedly. "I've been waiting to do this for a long time. Sit down. Sit down."

Derek and I sit close together at the table in the too-small booth seat. Shawna, with her launch code briefcase, sits uncomfortably on the bed in the back. Derek and I wave to her. She ignores us.

The president cuts submarine sandwiches in half with a serrated knife. He places a sandwich on a paper plate and slides it across the table to me. He then hands one to Derek. A grand smile spreads across the president's face. "Roast beef with red peppers sandwich. A little celebration to commemorate the last mission." The president spreads his arms wide like a conductor acknowledging his orchestra, but he still has a knife in his hand, and the flat edge smacks into Derek's face, spreading yellow mustard across his cheek. "Oh, sorry." The president tears off a paper towel from a roll hanging under a cupboard and dabs Derek's face, smearing the mustard even worse.

President Wright sits down across from us with his own sandwich. He takes a large bite, tearing through the bread and roast beef with his teeth and a quick turn of his head like a hungry tiger. "Being off the Macwacky sure has brought back my appetite."

Derek and I take a bite of our sandwiches. "These are pretty good," I say, "but I don't feel like celebrating. Big Mac is holding Scotty hostage."

The president wipes his lips with his fingers. "I know all about it."

"That young couple, Lexi and Chip—they're Big Mac

operatives. You should have vetted them better," I say.

"These things happen," the president says.

"Things happen? They kidnapped my son. Where was the backup? Why didn't anyone follow the RV? Why didn't anyone guard my son?"

"We did. Anyway, we thought we did. We wanted to." The president's eyes dart back and forth. He turns and looks out the window. "People defected. We didn't know who was who. The plan went bad."

"Nobody followed the RV? We still don't know where McGuffin is? This mission is slipshod, and we—Derek, me, Karen, and Scotty—deserve better. I want your best people on the job, like right now."

"Your testimony is what is most important, like right now."

"Bullshit."

"Thompson—" The president takes another gigantic bite of his sandwich. "There's a lot of Americans in danger out there beyond just you and your family. We're talking about the future of the United States. The future of nearly three hundred million people."

The president has been talking out of one side of his mouth, both of his cheeks swelling with food. I want to grab his head and squeeze his face. "You're starting to sound exactly like Big Mac. If difficult choices have to be made, I'm choosing my son."

"I'm the president, Thompson. You need to look at the big picture here. I have to think of all Americans."

"Right now Scotty is my only picture. You want me to testify for you? Then get my son back."

The president is a little taken aback that I'm speaking to him so forcefully. "We're working on it, Thompson."

"Not good enough." I point at and nudge Derek with my elbow. "Derek and I are going to do it. You said before that we could try and rescue Karen. Now we'll rescue Scotty."

"After you receive some training, I said. You need at least a month."

"Excuse me, Mr. President. You don't seem to be hearing what I am saying. I will not testify at your impeachment trial until my son is safe."

The president doesn't say anything. He just stares at me and chews and chews and chews.

"We don't need training," Derek says. "We just need a little intel on where they're holding the boy, and Chris and I will get it done."

The president is still chewing. He stops and swallows, and then he plops the last bit of sandwich into his mouth. "Here's what we'll do. I'll gather as much information as I can. You two start training with Doctor Rod." He looks around. "Goddammit, I could use some water."

"Check the fridge, Derek."

"Forget it." The president sticks out his tongue and coughs. "We're almost done. You testify next Wednesday. That's one week. Train, make a plan, and then before the trial, go get your son."

I want to save Scotty right now, but I did the last mission on nothing but Customs Service paper-stamping training. The chances of saving Scotty will be a lot better if I receive some real espionage instruction.

"Okay," I say. "I like a plan."

The president stands up and runs a hand over his throat. He forces a cough and then abruptly leaves.

I'm standing outside the White House, looking across the north lawn and talking to Karen on a secure cell phone the president has let me use.

"Gone for a week? What kind of training?"

She didn't exactly want me around earlier today, and now she's mad I'm going to be gone a week? "Training to rescue Scotty."

"You. Don't they have anybody better?"

"Derek's going to help me."

"Cannonball Derek? I don't understand. Why aren't they sending in Seal Team Six or some real pros?"

"Karen, listen, I don't have time. I'm working on saving Scotty, but you must know that the president is sending over two Secret Service agents to watch the house. You'll be safe."

"I'm not worried about my safety. I'm worried about Scotty."

The roar from a helicopter starting up deafens our call.

"Goodbye, Karen. I love you." Men are motioning Derek and me toward the helicopter. I hold the phone close to my ear, but I can't hear Karen say anything. The Secret Service agent takes it from me.

Derek and I run across the north lawn and climb into the waiting US Army Lakota helicopter. A lone white male pilot lifts the small copter into the air. We spin in a slow circle. The Washington Monument and the Capitol building, both brilliantly white in the clear sky, pan by the window. We point northeast and move forward, almost casually, like we are on a tour.

"A little different from our last helicopter ride, huh?" I say to Derek.

Derek smiles. "We sure kicked ass in that Black Hawk."

I think back to how Samuel, whom I'd thought to be a mild-mannered retiree, turned into a warrior and flew that Black Hawk through a gauntlet of fighter jets and Apache helicopters to help us attack Big Mac's Emergence headquarters and save his son, among others. And now I'm starting a mission to save my own son. Or rather, not yet starting—first, I have to receive training from some mysterious doctor. I sure hope I'm not wasting time while Scotty is in harm's way. I hope he's all right. He's tough, though, and scrappy.

After a ten-minute ride, a tinted black rectangular office building comes into view. It is at the center of an office complex and is surrounded by giant parking lots. I've always wondered what goes on in this mysterious place. This is the NSA, the National Security Agency.

The pilot lands us on a helipad on the top of the tall main building. We are on the president's daily packet run that transports secret documents back and forth between the White House and the NSA—documents and data too secret to be mailed or sent electronically.

Derek and I wear disguises again. We are in army fatigues. Derek carries the actual packet to be delivered.

We walk out of the helicopter to a small control-room structure built next to the helipad. Inside, a female guard and a young man in a suit wait for us. The man in the suit outstretches his hand. Derek transfers the packet to him.

The helicopter lifts off the pad and departs into the sky.

"You guys are new," the guard says.

"First time," I say.

The man in the suit leaves.

"We're to wait in the presidential room," I say.

Derek leans closer to the guard like he is about to reveal a secret. "And we're here to see—"

"Shush." The guard gives Derek and me a wide-eyed look like, how could you be so stupid? "The presidential room doesn't exist, and therefore you can't meet anybody there either."

"Sorry," Derek says.

She glares at us superiorly. "I hate newbies who don't know proper procedure. You have ID keys?"

Derek and I produce photo ID keys they made for us at the White House.

"This way." The guard exits the control room, and we follow her across the roof to a door and stairwell.

We stop one flight down in front of a door that says Maintenance. The guard removes a keychain hanging from her belt and unlocks the door. She opens the door and motions Derek and me inside. "Have a nice day." She closes the door behind us.

We are in a short, empty hallway that has another door at its end. "You think they're really going to train us?" I say.

"You smell a trap?"

"I'm not sure who to trust anymore."

The lights go out. I tense. It's completely dark except for small red and green LED lights on the keycard reader beside the door we're supposed to enter.

Derek has reflexively grabbed my shoulder. Nothing is happening.

"Maybe turning out the lights is just an energy-saving thing," I say.

"No choice but to go," Derek says.

"Let's do it."

"Let's go."

"Okay, here we go." I swipe my ID key and the door opens, filling the space instantly with intensely bright light.

I lead Derek into a giant, futuristic-looking room. We blink and rub our eyes. The room takes up the whole floor. There are no walls; windows frame every side. Large square and rectangular workstations are throughout the room, each containing different-looking contraptions and experiments: chemistry tubes, robots, guns, devices that look like bombs, and perhaps fifty other projects.

A cleaning lady is mopping the floor down a far aisle, but other than her, Derek, and I, the room is devoid of people. Derek and I meander about, looking at the different devices. He stops at a disassembled iPhone.

"Check this out," Derek says.

Next to the iPhone is a small spring-loaded dart. Derek picks both of them up and then holds the dart next to the open iPhone's back. "It fits right in here like this."

"Don't you touch anything."

The cleaning lady is walking toward us, pushing her mop in a rolling bucket. Derek sets the iPhone and dart down and holds up his hands. "Nothing is broken," he insists.

"Who are you? Who let you in here?"

I show her my ID key. Derek's hand searches his pocket until he finds his. He holds his ID out with a bigger-than-necessary smile.

"We are here to see Doctor Rod. Do you know where we can find him? You know, because we're here for some training." Derek looks around as if he's making sure nobody is listening. "We're kind of in the espionage business."

What is he doing? Is he trying to impress this cleaning woman? She's wearing a dark-gray pullover uniform smock with matching pants, and she's tiny, with wiry arms and legs, light-brown skin, and large black eyes. I'd guess she's in her midthirties. Her hair is tied back in a bun, but if she let it down and got rid of the glasses, she would be very attractive. I guess I can't fault Derek, but he should be a little more professional.

I give a little laugh and say, "My friend likes to joke a lot. We really just need to see—"

In an instant the cleaning lady thrusts the mop handle into Derek's groin. He gasps and doubles over as the mop handle swoops down to my ankles and knocks my feet out from under me. I fall toward Derek and land on top of his back.

Derek is moaning.

"Ugh," I say.

The handle is spinning and the mop head is arcing through the air, droplets of soapy water splaying around it. I try to move my head, but the mop lands flat on my face and spins, sliding spongy strings over my lips and up my nostrils in an instant swirly. Derek tries to roll over, and as he does, the mop lands square on his face as well.

The mop spins again and Derek and I each squirm to get out of the way, but we are only just tapped by the handle's end.

"Stand up," the lady says.

Derek and I do as we're told, somewhat dispirited.

The lady is angry at us for some reason. "In the espionage business—my buttocks," she says. "I've seen better reactions from my three-hundred-pound ex-husband, the lazy, fat, cheating son of a bitch."

"Cleaning lady, my ass," Derek says. "You've got more tricks than my ex-girlfriend, the money-sucking, two-timing devil of a woman."

With her finger, she touches a small splotch of mustard that's still on Derek's cheek, even after the degrading face wash. "Had lunch with President Wright, did ya?" A brief flicker of a smile passes over the woman's face but quickly disappears. "First lesson for you misogynists: never, ever accept appearances for what they seem." She pokes me in the stomach with the mop handle. "Chris Thompson." She pokes Derek. "Derek Allen."

"I don't like massages," Derek says. "I'm not a massage assist. Are you, Chris?"

"No. I don't like massages either." I force a smile. "You must be Doctor Rod."

"Obviously," she says. "I'm Doctor Michelle Rodriguez from the Puerto Rican island of Culebra. I have doctorates in quantum physics and artificial intelligence, but I'm also an expert in many other fields—ninjutsu, for example."

"You're a ninja," Derek says with respect.

She looks at Derek. "I'm happily single and will die that way. And that's all that you two need to know about me."

"So you're going to train us?" I say.

Doctor Rod doesn't say a word. She just looks Derek and me up and down slowly, like she is scanning us. "Pshh." She looks disappointed, almost sad. "Why does the president waste my time? There is so much important work to do."

"We saved the country from Big Mac," Derek says. "That was pretty important."

She looks at Derek doubtfully. "I thought Ninjenna and that computer guy Wizkid took care of that. I trained Ninjenna, you know."

"Wizkid. He was scared silly."

"He did save us," I say. "You know Wizkid?"

Doctor Rod gives me a look. Yes, I realize: as President Wright's secret agent trainer, of course Doctor Rod would know Wizkid, the genius computer science student from Arizona State who helped President Wright create the fictitious invasion from Mexico and Canada, a farce which then comically ensnared me into the espionage world that I cannot seem to escape from.

"And of course you trained, Ninjenna," I say. "That makes perfect sense."

Derek flexes his chest proudly. "She did, you know, play a big part. But you should ask President Wright. Chris and I were the mission leaders."

Doctor Rod waves her hand. "I've got the report, but I didn't get past your names. What's the point? Big Mac is trying to take over again. I can't spend my time on you two."

Derek explains that we are scheduled to testify at President Wright's impeachment next Wednesday.

"So have the president get you a lawyer. You don't need me."

"Big Mac is blackmailing Chris. He may not be able to testify favorably for President Wright."

Doctor Rod looks at me as if I am weak, both physically and mentally, exactly the opposite of her. "Bite the bullet and do your duty. Defeating Big Mac should be the prime objective, regardless of your personal problems."

"Big Mac has captured my eleven-year-old son. And I can't testify for the president until I know he's safe from them— which means I have to get him back. Which means you have to train us."

The tension in Doctor Rod's face vanishes. Her shoulders

sag, and her small body seems to deflate a little. "Your son?"

"Yes, Scotty. They have him with a twelve-year-old clone. They've cloned Senator Joe McCarthy."

Doctor Rod returns to full alert. "A clone. A human clone? Are you sure?"

"Pretty sure. General McGuffin showed me. He was awfully confident. The resemblance between Little Joe and the 1950s communist-hunting McCarthy was pretty eerie."

"Are they using the somatic cell nuclear transfer method?"

"I don't know."

"Where are they? Where are they holding your son and this Little Joe?"

"I don't know. That's one of the main problems."

"Think, Chris Thompson." Doctor Rod ushers me over to a lab chair and I take a seat. "Tell me everything that happened with McGuffin."

Little Joe

MY NEW FRIEND'S name is Scotty. I like him. Scotty is really cool, but his dad is our enemy. His dad is Chris Thompson.

Everyone here hates Chris Thompson. He's like a terrorist or something, although he didn't look like a terrorist to me. He looked scared and like he didn't really know what to do. I don't think we have to worry if Chris Thompson is our enemy. But maybe he's just acting. Maybe he really is a threat and doesn't want us to think so. I've been trained not to trust people like Chris Thompson, people who don't believe in the righteousness of Big Mac and who want to corrupt you with their weakness. Chris Thompson makes Papa McGuffin and everyone here nervous, even though we seem to have control over him. Chris Thompson must be dangerous. I must not forget that.

I was scared at first because I thought Scotty would be like his dad, but he isn't. He's really cool, like I said, and we are friends.

Scotty and I play Xbox. He's better than me and has tons more games at home, he says. I don't mind—it's just so fun to have someone to play with.

I told Scotty I was a clone, and he didn't believe me at first, but then I convinced him. I showed him science pictures about how they do the cloning. I showed him photos of myself when I was alive before, when I was a kid living in Wisconsin in the 1910s. I looked just like I do now. I've never had to tell anyone that before. Most people here know. That's why I'm special, they say. But some of them don't like me, I can tell. They look at me like they do the monkeys, like I'm an experiment and not a real person. On TV, clones are always bad, or something is wrong with them and they eat people or act like zombies. I was worried to tell Scotty, but after he believed me, he thought it was the greatest thing ever. Scotty wants to be a clone too, which I thought was pretty funny. Scotty has lots of friends, but he doesn't have any brothers or sisters, so he thought having a clone of himself was the best idea ever.

I'm going to be president. I told him that.

Scotty thinks his dad is great, which is kind of strange. I didn't say anything about his dad being a terrorist and our enemy because I don't want Scotty to get mad. His dad just left him here, too. It's great for me, but what a jerk. I felt bad for Scotty, but he urged his dad to do it. I think he was just being brave for his mom; I don't think he really wanted to stay here. When his parents left, I saw his lips quivering and I thought he was going to cry. I could tell because I feel the same way sometimes, like when I'm in a debate with one of the instructors and I mistakenly take a position Big Mac doesn't believe in, or when I say I want to go on vacation in another country, or when I get caught watching Japanese anime on the Internet. I can't help it—I like anime so much better than American cartoons. But it's wrong not to like anything American the most, and if I make a mistake, they yell at me so much that I don't know what to say, and I feel like crying. I never do cry, though, not anymore. But sometimes my lips quiver just like Scotty's were quivering.

Chris Thompson seemed kind of wishy-washy, but he didn't seem like a dad who would yell a lot. That would be nice. I guess having a dad must be okay, even if you have a bad dad like Scotty.

I would have been really bummed if Scotty's dad chose him instead of his mom. I kind of do wish they would clone Scotty, because you know, I'd be pretty sad if he ever had to leave.

Amazonian Curare

I TELL DOCTOR Rod about how I came out of the Washington Monument and handed Scotty over to Chip and Lexi. She stops me several times and asks detailed questions, getting frustrated when I can't remember everything. I'm at the part where I'm in the monkey-clone room with McGuffin.

"You said McGuffin talked to someone on the phone. Who was it?"

"Uh, let's see. The monkeys were Chekhov and Tolstoy."

"That doesn't do me any good. Who did he talk to? Think."

I try to think. "He talked about what Joe McCarthy liked to do as a child. He said the person's name. It wasn't that common. Earthy, or Moon."

"Celestial bodies," Derek says. "Was it Celeste? or Mars?"

"Something to do with the sky," I say.

Doctor Rod snaps her fingers. "Skylar."

"That's it."

"Skylar is a psychologist I worked with long ago. I know exactly where they are."

"Where?" Derek and I ask at the same time.

Doctor Rod looks deadpan at us. "Not until you finish your training."

"What? Tell me where my son is right now."

Doctor Rod gives me a look of the kind a pit bull would give to an annoying cat. "I can't have you making plans or sneaking off trying to save your son when you're not ready. You need total concentration if you want to succeed."

"But . . . but—my son. At least tell the president where he is. He can send in a team to rescue Scotty right now."

Doctor Rod nods. "I will tell the president, but your training continues until we hear differently." Doctor Rod puts a phone to her ear and walks away to the far corner of the room, looking out the windows. She's talking on the phone, but we cannot hear her.

Okay. I have hope. Scotty may be rescued soon. Karen was right—real professionals like Delta Force could do a better job than me. Or could they? Would another team care enough about Scotty to make sure that he is safe, that he survives?

Doctor Rod returns, as serious as ever.

Derek has been looking over at a cot stored underneath one lab table. "Doctor Rod. Do you live here?"

Doctor Rod breathes in heavily through her nose. "I spend a lot of time here, but I go home. Sometimes. The packet helicopter takes me. I have a life too, you know." She clears her throat. "I just spoke with the president. We'll try and learn more details about the layout of Big Mac's location. For now, though, we train. If you are testifying on Wednesday, we'll need to attack on Tuesday, so there's no time to spare."

"Tuesday. My son is in danger. Why doesn't the president send in a team ASAP?"

"The president isn't sending anyone else. He wants you two to go."

"What!"

Doctor Rod looks over Derek and me with discouraged apprehension, like she just can't believe that we're the president's choice. "He says he can't spare the resources to rescue civilians, nor can he trust anyone else as much as you two to take on Big Mac. Basically, if you want to ensure your son's safety, you need to do it yourself."

I have to agree with the president on this one. I feel somewhat proud he has such confidence in us. "Okay. The president believes in us. So—heck with training. We go now."

"I don't agree with the president's rosy view of you two." Doctor Rod still looks at us disparagingly. "Your son will be in real danger if you couple of softies bumble up the rescue with a shit-ass plan. Tuesday will give me the most possible time to teach you anything."

I've always wanted to be a true spy. Here is my chance to get some real espionage training from an expert. And Doctor Rod's right, too. We can't mess this up.

"Okay. We train twenty-four seven. Derek and I will stay right here with you. If you think we are ready for the mission early, then we go early. Deal?"

"Deal," Doctor Rod says. "Let's get started. Tell me what else happened after McGuffin talked with Skylar."

"Wait a minute. What about me?" Derek says.

"What, you're not in?" I say.

"Well, yeah, I suppose. But why don't I get to say deal?"

"Say deal, then."

"I just might."

"Then say it. Say deal."

"Deal," Derek says.

I tell Doctor Rod the rest of the story in as much detail as I can remember. When I finish, she paces between two lab tables, holding her chin.

"You have confirmed my biggest worry. Big Mac has drineys."

"You know about the drineys?"

"I worked to develop them. It was a top secret joint project between the Pentagon and the CIA to gather intelligence in Afghanistan without having to use human assets. There were two physicists on the team, scary guys, both from the CIA. They were all for weaponizing the drineys and using them for offensive purposes, to take out enemy combatants with virtually no danger to the operator."

"And did it work?"

"I'm not sure. I was moved off the project and over here to the executive branch's clandestine operations during the early stages. But last month when Big Mac took over, those two physicists totally went over to the other side. They sent me emails trying to recruit me back onto the team, but I ignored them."

"Weren't you worried?"

"No. Nobody knows where I am. But I was worried about what Big Mac and these two guys would do with the drineys. And from what you're telling me, it sounds as if they have finished the planned development of hive and tracking technology. The question is whether they have offensive capabilities."

"McGuffin didn't say, but he implied that the drineys would be a key part of Big Mac's enforcement policies."

"It's unfortunate, but it's not surprising that Big Mac would use the drineys. It's a perfect way for them to control a lot of people with few resources. But the good news is that if the drineys are in the same location as your son, we can take them out at the same time as we rescue him. Big Mac will have nothing."

Derek is striking karate poses and throwing punches. "I had some hand-to-hand combat training in the marines, but maybe I need a little brushing up."

"Earlier you got mopped up. Now you can get brushed up," I say.

"Ha, ha." Derek bares his teeth and makes a move on me like he is about to chop me in half. "Damn comedian."

"Stop it," Doctor Rod says. "At your age and physical conditions, you two both need weapons. Each of you: browse the room and pick out the weapon that you think you'd be most comfortable with. In the meantime, I'm going to work on this driney problem."

I meander about the room looking at all the different weapons. Some look normal enough, like guns and knives and hand grenades and whatnot, but there are others—a Rubik's cube, a pair of hockey skates, a life jacket, and many more whose purpose I can't imagine.

Derek heads straight for the iPhone he saw before. He starts flipping the phone around and pressing different buttons. I can't see exactly what he does, but somehow he figures out how to snap it all together.

"You going to text someone to death?" I say.

He shrugs. "Just might." He tosses the phone into the air, passing it from one hand to the other. I hear a slight beep and then feel a sharp pain in my nose. A thin metallic dart has pierced my left nostril.

"Oh, suck a shit, Derek." My eyes water as mucus floods into my nose and blood drips down from the puncture wound. I quickly become a bloody, snotty mess.

Doctor Rod walks quickly toward me.

"This thing isn't going to kill anybody," Derek says.

"Tips are laced with enough Amazonian curare to paralyze a victim's respiratory muscles within seconds. Death will soon follow."

"Oh, no." My vision blurs and everything goes blank.

When I open my eyes, Doctor Rod is applying some ointment to my nose. "Am I alive?"

Derek is standing behind Doctor Rod laughing. "There was no poison in that dart. You needn't have passed out, CT."

Doctor Rod is about to put a Band-Aid on me. "If you ever wanted a nose ring, now's the time to do it."

I sit up. "No. I'm good."

"Time for you to pick out a weapon," Doctor Rod says.

"What? That dart-shooting phone is going to be Derek's weapon?"

He spins the phone around in his hands, pretending to shoot it in different ways. I flinch and cover my eyes, and Derek laughs and continues his antics. He lifts one leg and pretends to shoot me from under it.

"Don't worry," Doctor Rod says. "It's not loaded. He won't get live darts until he proves his proficiency."

I stand up and walk between the tables, searching for a suitable weapon. After a while, I find a shoulder-mounted Stingray missile launcher. I strap the weapon on and spin slowly toward Derek. He is practicing quick-drawing the iPhone from his crotch zipper.

I shout, "Is this baby loaded?" I run toward Derek, aiming my shoulder missile right at him. "Argh!" I yell, like a marauding pirate.

"No, no, no," Doctor Rod says.

Derek dives under a table, just as Doctor Rod does a backflip. She jumps from one table to the next and then through the air toward me. I stop in my tracks, and she lands on her feet before me, ready to fight. I lower the missile.

"I'm just joking. I just wanted to scare him."

Derek's head appears from under the table. "Truce?"

"Truce," I say.

"You are grown men," Doctor Rod says. "Why do you act like boys? How did you ever save America from Big Mac?"

"We think different," Derek says. He walks over to inspect my weapon.

"You don't think at all." Doctor Rod removes the missile launcher from my shoulder. "If you do think, then you should be ashamed. You, Chris Thompson, have a child in danger, and you make jokes. And you, Derek Allen, are fat and out of shape, but you act with such bravado. Why don't you take your obligations to your country seriously?"

Doctor Rod couldn't be more right. Scotty's a hostage, and I'm acting like a moronic fool. If Karen knew that I was joking around instead of concentrating all my power on saving Scotty, she'd question the very foundations of our marriage, and who could blame her? "I'm sorry, Doctor. Please forgive me. I'm ready to work."

She walks with the missile launcher and replaces it on the table where I found it. "You can't work with this rocket. Our mission is clandestine. Why do I have to tell you these simple concepts? Find a weapon like Derek's. Find something you can conceal."

Derek raises his eyebrows at me and looks at me with a class-pet superior smirk.

I roll my eyes at him and continue my search for a weapon. I walk between the tables and over to the far window, looking at more spy gadgets. I don't know what half of this stuff does. I should ask Doctor Rod, but she and Derek are talking, and I'm sure that whatever I say would somehow irritate her.

I come upon a muscular male mannequin. He's wearing a formfitting, long-sleeve upper-body pullover made with a thick, plastic-looking fabric. I run my hands over the solid gray material. There's an invisibly thin but very strong tubing running through the fabric, and four thicker tubes run down the top, bottom, and sides of the left arm.

"Not a bad choice." Doctor Rod stands behind me. "Are you left handed?"

"No."

"Good. It's better to have your weak arm bionified."

She spins the mannequin around and unties straps, and then she unzips a thick zipper that runs completely down the middle of the back.

Derek has now joined us. "Bionified?"

"A term I made up for battle wear enhanced with bionics."

She removes the suit and holds it out to me. "Take off your shirt. Hurry up. No time to be shy."

I reluctantly take my shirt off. I hold my arms out, and Doctor Rod slides the suit over my arms and torso. She struggles to zip up the back.

"Help me here."

I feel my rib cage constricting as Derek pulls back tight on the fabric and Doctor Rod zips it up.

"There," Doctor Rod says. "That will do."

Derek is laughing. "Oh, man. That is not pretty."

I look myself over. My chest and arms are taut and muscular. I feel strong. The problem is at the point where the bottom meets my waist. All the skin and flab that has been displaced by this new faux physique is undulating out the bottom of the suit like a melting glacier of brie cheese.

"It will have to do. I can't help it that you're so fat. It's the only bionified shirt I have."

"How does it work?"

"The left arm is bionified. I recommend you do normal tasks with your right arm only." Doctor Rod points to the other end of the floor. "See that open space between the desks? There's a wrestling mat there. You two go practice on each other."

"Practice what?" Derek says.

"I don't want to be shot again," I say.

"Don't be pansies. You practice fighting. Do what's natural. Become one with your weapons." Doctor Rod gives me a disparaging look. "Just for you, I'll give Derek the soft tipped practice darts."

119

In the practice area, we are stripped down to our boxers and black socks. Doctor Rod has gone to plan our strategy, leaving us alone. I have the bionified shirt on. Derek has on a white tank top T-shirt. He starts doing forward rolls and shoots at me.

"This is really no fair." Doctor Rod has forbidden me from touching Derek when I have the bionified shirt on, as apparently it is too dangerous.

I throw some punches, dodge and block, prance around, and generally look like an ass. The shirt feels natural. I really don't notice anything different. I do some pushups. I'm up to twenty and starting to sweat. My right arm is aching, but my left feels like it could go on forever. I lift my right arm and do one-armed pushups with my left. Easy. My breathing slows. I'm comfortable. I increase my speed and pump pushups out at what must be a record pace.

Derek walks back and forth, pretending to talk on the phone. Every time he turns, he shoots a dart at me. He's getting good. "In the leg," he says, and a dart hits me in the leg. "In the head." A soft dart hits me in the ear. "In the back. In the head again." This is really starting to get irritating.

"In the nose." A dart smacks me in the nose exactly where my Band-Aid covers my wound. Ow, that one hurt. I stop doing pushups and plop down onto my stomach. I turn my head away from Derek, who is still shooting at me. On a nearby desk, a paper towel roll rests on its end. I stand up, walk over, and bring my left palm down hard, smashing it into what looks like a lopsided Frisbee. I pick it up, and like a seasoned southpaw, I fire a whooshing discus throw into Derek's gut.

"Ugh," he says, falling to his knees and gasping in vain for air.

I run my hands over my bionified shirt. "I think I'm getting the hang of it."

After a minute, Derek recovers. He stands up slowly, holding his gut. "He touched me. Chris broke the rules. He touched me."

"I did not."

Derek laughs. "Son of a bitch."

I laugh too. "What the hell are we doing?"

"We're going to save your son."

"Yeah, I know. I just wish we'd get on it with, you know? I don't think Doctor Rod-in-her-butt knows how we operate."

Derek hems and haws a little. "She's all right. Give her time."

"What? Really? You got a thing for her?"

"No. That's not what I'm saying. I've just got this feeling that she's been through some pain. I think all that bitchy bluster is just a mask."

As I'm thinking this over, I hear a faint buzzing sound. Derek swats at something. Drineys. I see three, four . . . there must be a dozen—no, more, perhaps twenty—circling in a swarm and diving around us. Derek is spinning, pointing his iPhone at them, but it is futile. How did they get in here? One brushes my neck. Panic shivers rush through my body, and I swipe uselessly at it.

Derek is freaking out, swatting wildly. "Get them off me."

I don't know what to do. Can we get outside? Or maybe I could throw water on them, or a blanket or something, or smack them with a flat board? I grab a towel and crouch low, preparing to attack them with a bionic-powered spinning towel, when I hear something behind me. Someone is quietly—and somewhat maliciously—laughing.

"Rod in the butt, huh? How'd you like a driney in the ear?"

Nuseum

THE TWENTY DRINEYS swarming Derek and me suddenly rise toward the ceiling. They form a circle and hold their position in midair.

Doctor Rod walks calmly toward us, a joystick device in her hand. She glares at me.

"I'm sorry," I say to her. "Did you say they can fly in my ear?"

"These? Lucky for you, no." She steps over to a lab table and puts the joystick down. "That was one possible goal of the original project, though: making the drineys able to fly right into your ear and scramble your brain. But I really don't know whether they figured out how to do that."

Derek is brushing himself off, as if the drineys were gnats and they were possibly still on him. "I don't like those things. They're creepy. You say Big Mac has millions of these, Chris?"

"McGuffin said that they'd have one for every citizen."

Derek, leery, watches the hovering drineys. "Man. Take them down. Put them away, please."

Doctor Rod looks at him, and then she reaches into her pocket and pulls out a small, red metal container. She opens the lid, and I think she is about to offer us a mint, but it is full of miniature white spheres that look like fish eggs. She sets the container on the table, and with tweezers, she picks up a tiny sphere and deposits it in an empty pillbox. The drineys continue to hold their position, buzzing softly.

"Are we doing an experiment? Is this part of our training?" Derek says.

Doctor Rod puts a lid on the pillbox and hands it to me. "Shake it." She picks up the joystick, and the drineys start to fly around again. "Shake it."

The drineys fly at Derek and swarm around his head. He tries to swat at them, but they are too fast. He closes his eyes and puts his hands over his ears.

"Shake it," Doctor Rod says to me. "Shake it to save your friend."

"The pill container?"

"Shake it!" Derek screams. "Shake it!"

I shake the pillbox.

"Faster," Doctor Rod says. She moves the joystick around and smiles at Derek's discomfort as the drineys bump against his head and face.

"Faster!" Derek yells. He still has his hands on his ears, and he is twisting his body and head, flaying at the drineys with his elbows. "Faster, Chris, faster."

I switch the pillbox to my left hand and shake it fast enough to hear a rapid rattling sound.

"Open the box," Doctor Rod says.

I open the pillbox, and for a brief second miniature sparks, like glitter, flash in every corner of the room. Just as fast, they disappear.

The drineys go dead and fall to the ground. Derek opens his eyes and looks around. He uncovers his ears, relieved. A faint sulfur smell, like rotten eggs, lingers in the room.

Doctor Rod is pleased. "The power of magnetics. Crystallized neodymium particles, which I've combined into a salt powder with another element I will not name. I like to call it nuseum."

"Like a new museum," Derek says.

"New you see 'em. New you don't," I say.

Doctor Rod stares at us. "Something like that. The nuseum's magnetic properties confuse the drineys' laser guidance and in effect disable them."

"I don't know," I say. "Shaking one pill is going to stop millions of drineys? And what if they're spread out?"

Doctor Rod takes the pillbox from me. "As soon as I suspected Big Mac was working with drineys, I went to work on developing a solution that could counteract the drineys on a large scale, if need be."

"And it need be," Derek says.

"That's all fine, but what's the plan to rescue my son? That's the solution we should be working on first."

"Bigger minds work on bigger problems," she says.

"She got you there, man," Derek says.

I'm starting to feel alone here. "Scotty's supposed to be our primary mission, at least if the president wants me to testify. That's the deal. Now what's the plan to rescue my son?"

"That's trivial," Doctor Rod says.

"Excuse me. Trivial?"

"I think she means that the amount of planning we'd need to do in order to save Scotty will be simpler than taking on all of Big Mac and the drineys, if necessary," Derek says.

Doctor Rod is staring intently at Derek. "Doesn't she see that keeping the president in power is our number one option for controlling Big Mac?" I ask.

Derek rubs his chin contemplatively. "I think she's worried that Big Mac might be a problem regardless of what happens at the president's impeachment trial."

I look back and forth between them. "Is this a mind meld? Is she speaking through you?"

Derek and Doctor Rod both laugh.

"You need to lighten up, Chris," Doctor Rod says. "Derek has merely deduced my thoughts through logical reasoning." She looks at Derek. "Very impressive."

These two are starting to worry me. "If it's so trivial and easy to make a plan, then let's do it. Right now. How are we going to save Scotty?"

"Keep experimenting with your weapons," Doctor Rod says. "When you are comfortable, I will train you to be experts with them, and then we can talk about attack plans." She walks away.

Derek reloads his iPhone. "You want to run around while I try to shoot you?"

"I need to call Karen," I say.

"You can't call her. We're undercover."

"I want her to know that we plan to rescue Scotty."

"And if Big Mac finds out we're here, our plan will be blown."

"I just want to talk to her."

Derek paces back and forth. "She basically kicked you out and told you to find your son. That's what you're doing. God. Why do you always have to call her? We're on a mission. What kind of spy are you? Suck it up, man."

Derek's right. We can't compromise the mission. But still, I hate knowing Karen is out of her mind with worry about Scotty.

We practice with our weapons for the rest of that day until we are too tired to stay awake. Derek and I each select a table and make our own living areas, like we are kids constructing forts on a sleepover. The president sends us clothes and supplies, and we settle in to train every waking moment until next Tuesday—the day we attack Big Mac.

In the morning we begin our training with Doctor Rod. She is tough, efficient, and, as she said, an expert.

By the end of the day, Derek has become an Apple iPhone genius. He masters all the apps—the camera, social media, books, etc.—and at the same time, he can fire darts out of either hand: before him, behind him, while talking on the phone, or while searching the internet.

I spend most of my time learning to control my arm's power, gauging the exact amount of force needed to, say, smash a table just enough so that the debris stays contained, or to lift Derek to the ceiling without hurling him into it, or to disable a man with a quick karate chop while making it look as if I'm doing nothing more than brushing a piece of lint off his neck.

Each day we train and improve. Although we have many new ways to kill, each of us perfects one go-to maneuver that we practice over and over so that we can perform it with our eyes closed, or injured, or mentally impaired from a hallucinogen.

Derek's expert move is to accidentally drop his iPhone from any position—talking, texting, or pulling it out of his pocket—but then actually setting it off so that it fires accurately at up to two targets as it falls.

My move is to fake fall, or trip, but then to catch the ground with my left hand, flip, and spring myself up in the air with the bionified arm and down onto any assailant with a hard strike. I've been practicing into a box of sponge cushions. I've never been able to do even a cartwheel, so becoming a sudden high-flying gymnast is exhilarating. The only thing keeping me from springing higher into the air is the ceiling.

I never do get to speak to Karen. I hope she is managing and not worrying too much. Who am I kidding? She's probably out of her mind. If I could only assure her that everything will be all right. Doctor Rod has informed me that the Secret Service will be picking her up on the night before the mission to keep her safe from any retaliation from Big Mac. On Tuesday night, if all goes well, we will be together as a family, protected in the White House, as I prepare to testify and begin the process that will hopefully defeat Big Mac for good.

On Monday, one day before we're scheduled to make our

move, a note for me arrives in the packet mail. It's from the president.

> *Thompson. Got wind of your plan from the Doc. I like it, but I've changed my mind. You can't be on the rescue team. We can't afford to have you captured by Big Mac. Let Doctor Rod and Derek handle it. That's an order.*
>
> *President Oscar I. Wright.*

I don't show the letter to Doctor Rod or Derek.

I ask myself: do I ignore a direct order from the president of the United States, whom I've sworn an oath to obey as my commander and chief? I know what Karen would say. Scotty is an ordinary citizen—a kid, no less—and he deserves to be saved before anything else happens. Karen and Scotty mean more to me than anything. So I guess the answer is yes. To save my son, to save my marriage and family—yes. I will commit a treasonous act. I will disobey a direct order from the president.

Impeachment

LATE ON MONDAY, I hear a helicopter land on the roof. After a moment, it occurs to me that this is strange: the daily packet from the White House has already arrived. But suddenly, Doctor Rod and Derek are walking toward me with two men in dark suits who are obviously from the Secret Service.

"We have to go," Derek says. "They're here to escort us back to the White House."

"Why?"

One of the men is white. The other is Latino. They're both bald and look like they do nothing but lift weights and eat protein during their spare time.

The Latino man casually opens his suit jacket, revealing his Uzi submachine gun. "No discussion," he says. "We go now."

The Secret Service agents usher us into the helicopter. It's small, and Derek and I are practically sitting on top of each other.

I'm seething. This must be some ploy by the president to ensure that I don't go on the mission tomorrow.

"Relax, dude," Derek says. "They promised they had orders to bring us back here on tomorrow's packet. The mission is still a go."

Derek doesn't know about the note. The mission may be a go for him, but I'm worried that the president won't let me out of his sight until the impeachment. "I don't like this. Something's not right."

The NSA buildings pan underneath us as we head straight toward the White House.

"Maybe you'll get to see your wife. She's supposed to be coming to the White House today, right?" Derek rocks back and forth in his seat like he's disco dancing. He elbows me in the arm. "Maybe you and your missus will be, mm, mm, you know, getting down on it—in the White House—mm, mm."

I don't want to laugh, but I can't help it, and that makes it all the funnier. "The White House—yeah, that'd be better than the Mile High Club."

"West Wing Wango Tango."

I'm still laughing. "You're a Nugent fan?"

"You mean like that stuff inside of candy bars?"

"I didn't think so."

Derek is still rocking back and forth, humming a different song.

"Easy back there," the pilot says. "I have to land this thing."

Derek stops rocking, and the helicopter sets down uneventfully on the White House's north lawn.

We are escorted at a brisk pace into the White House and then down into the underground situation room, where there is a flurry of activity. Every chair is filled with lawyerly types working on laptops and rifling through stacks of paper. The flat-screens are showing different news stations: local, national, and international networks. Aides walk around, assisting those at the table. A loud chatter fills the air, and I can feel the excitement. I wonder what's going on.

Brandon sits at the table's end. He looks up briefly when Derek and I walk in, and then he does a double take and stares at us, alarmed. "Call the magic makers. These two need clothes."

Derek and I are in our workout gear, and we look like a couple of weekend warriors better suited for drinking than for exercise. Normally I would have felt embarrassed to be so out of place, but I'm wearing a long-sleeve jersey over my bionified suit, and even though I may look like a dork, I feel totally confident.

Brandon stands up and walks over to a side conference room. "They're here, Mr. President." Brandon waves us over.

"Just one more level," the president calls.

Derek and I walk over and stand next to Brandon. The president is playing on his Talibanny machine. "Hooyah!" he yells, throwing his arms into the air. He climbs out of the machine and walks toward us, his hands still in the air. "High five." Derek and I each raise a hand and slap the president a high five. "They can run, and they can hide, but with the Talibanny-buster and"—the president points to himself—"numero uno at the stick, they are going to die."

Male and female hands are touching me and Derek. It's the magic makers—the White House tailor team that had instantly outfitted me with an Armani suit during my original mission. They are measuring us and pulling our clothes off as we speak with the president.

"Change of plans," the president informs us. "You two are going to testify today."

"No—we have to rescue Scotty first." I feel a hand on my bionified suit zipper. I swat the hand away. "This stays."

The president runs his hands over my suit. "Nice. I heard about this. I'll have to get me one." He looks at Derek, who is standing in nothing but his boxers, his large round belly hard not to notice. "What's up, Cannonball? Doctor Rod didn't let you have a muscle suit?" The president looks at the ground and smiles, like he is remembering something. "She's really not so tough, you know. Treat her with compassion—she deserves it."

Derek holds up the deadly iPhone he has been clutching in his hand. "I got this."

The president rocks his head back and forth. "Who you gonna call?"

"Stop it," I say. The room goes silent and everyone looks at me. "Mr. President, please, sir." I lower my voice, but my anger still shows as I start to put on a pair of black suit pants that an old tailor has been holding out for me. "You must have planned this to ensure that I wouldn't get hurt trying to save my son. But I'm not going to testify for you."

"Thompson, please. First of all, the Speaker of the House, whom I have absolutely no influence over, made the schedule change. And second of all, I really had no doubt that you would obey my order and keep yourself safe for the trial. But I guess I should have doubted it."

He's got me there. A white dress shirt is put on me. I start buttoning it from the bottom, but when I get midway up, one of the buttons is hard to put through. My hand is shaking. "I . . . I haven't disobeyed you yet."

The president pushes my hand aside and slides the button through. He continues to button my shirt. "Thompson, you have to relax," he says. "The country is counting on you. The free people of the United States of America want to remain free, and all you have to do is tell the truth."

"And then Big Mac will—"

He pats my face. "And then you and Derek will be flown immediately back to the NSA, where you can infiltrate the building and save your son with Doctor Rod and whatever personnel or other resources you need."

"The NSA?"

"Yes. The mission will go today. Ten minutes after you testify, we'll hit 'em hard."

"The NSA. Scotty, McGuffin, the drineys—they're all at the NSA?"

The president shrugs. "Same building as you, underground levels. Didn't Doctor Rod tell you?" He gives a little chuckle. "Whoops, maybe I wasn't supposed to tell you."

"That's bullshit," I tell the president. "Thanks a hell of a lot. My son is in danger and my own side won't reveal that he's in the same building as me. I could have saved him."

"Time to go," Brandon says.

"Yes, Thompson. Of course you would have tried to save him," the president says. "You would have jeopardized the whole mission."

"The mission to save Scotty or the mission to testify and save your ass?"

"It's all one and the same. To save your son. To save our country." The president is shouting. "There is only one mission." He clasps his hands over my face and looks intently into my eyes. "We can do this, Thompson. You're on our team. The right team. Testify—and then all of us, you included, hit those Big Mac fucks hard and save your son. Are you with me, Thompson?"

The president is starting to bring me around. Crazy as he is sometimes, I do feel loyal to him. But I still want to ask him whether it will take McGuffin, or anyone else with Big Mac, more or less than ten minutes after the testimony finishes to decide whether or not to hurt Scotty. Would they really do it—hurt a child? I think of all the young men and women in the Emergence program, men and women who were totally loyal to Big Mac and who believed they would have an everlasting utopia through the government. No—they wouldn't have any moral qualms about harming Scotty. But McGuffin is in charge, and I believe he's honorable. I can't imagine he'd make the decision to hurt Scotty so easily.

With that, it's decided. The plan is shaky, but I will be able to take part in Scotty's rescue. Derek and I will pull it off somehow. I'll stay with the team.

I reluctantly mumble something which could possibly be construed as a "yes."

The president slaps me on the shoulder. "Thank you, Thompson." He turns and walks back to the Talibanny-buster.

We are now impeccably dressed in fine wool suits. Brandon leads Derek and me toward the elevator. As soon as we arrive, the elevator doors open, and standing there with a Secret Service escort, staring wide-eyed at me, is Karen. And suddenly I'm not so sure about what I've decided.

"Chris. What is happening? Have you found Scotty?"

Karen looks really frazzled. It feels like forever since I have seen her, and I've missed her. "Yes. We've found him." I open my arms and she falls into them. We hug tightly, our past argument forgiven on both sides without words.

"You have him?"

"No. We're going to go and get him this afternoon."

"Not until they testify," Brandon says. "Now if you'll excuse us."

Karen pulls away from our hug and grabs my lapels. "Chris, you can't testify for the president. They'll kill him. You heard that general. They'll kill him without a thought."

"Don't worry. We'll get to him first," Derek says.

"Karen, I'd like you to meet Derek."

Karen looks Derek in the face, caught between being upset and wanting to be friendly. "Cannonball Derek?"

Derek reaches out and gives Karen a big bear hug. She is a little stiff at first, but then hugs Derek tight. "Thank you for watching out for Chris."

"We have to go," Brandon says, leading us into the elevator. Karen releases from Derek and follows us in.

"Please do what is right. Do what is right for Scotty, right for our family, right for you and me, Chris."

I touch the side of her cheek. "I'm going to tell the truth. I have an obligation. I'm going to testify for the president."

Karen shakes her head, words failing her.

"Derek and I have this," I say. "Please honey, don't worry. I can save Scotty. And the president—and our country."

With that, Brandon gently separates us and pushes Karen out of the elevator. The doors close, and we ascend.

"I don't care about our country!" I hear her scream.

The dome of the Capitol building looms large before us. Derek and I begin the long climb up the steps, following Brandon and the Senate security guards. At the top, reporters and photographers surround us.

"Chris Thompson."

"Have you been in contact with the president? Will you maintain his innocence?"

"Is Macwacky a real drug? Did you take it with the president?"

We push through the reporters and make our way under the marble columns and into the main reception atrium. We are ushered over to a corded-off area, where we pass through security. As I walk through the metal detector, a female guard nods to me. "Chris Thompson, super-spy."

I nod back to her. "Super-witness." I smile and she laughs. Super-spy. God, that felt good.

Derek and I enter the Senate chambers, where there is a bustle of activity. Senators stand talking with each other or sit at their wooden desks while pages scurry around. The second floor gallery is filled with spectators and reporters. TV cameras are positioned in key locations.

Derek and I walk on the blue carpeting down an aisle toward two wooden tables set before the main podium. Cameras turn toward us and follow our path. Senators return to their seats. Noisy chatter comes from the spectators in the gallery above us. Papers shuffle and laptops open. We reach the table and sit down, Brandon positioning himself between Derek and me. He will act as counsel for us both.

Presiding over the proceedings in place of Chief Justice Lancaster is an old white woman Supreme Court judge. She has yellowish hair worn in a 1950s style. I can't remember her name—Gerber or something like that. The judge pounds her gavel and someone shouts a call to order. The room quiets. Derek and I are sworn in. Everything is happening so fast. I look around at all the faces that are staring at us. They don't want justice. They want a spectacle.

A tall, thin white senator with perfect pearl-gray hair paces before Derek and asks him some perfunctory questions. I look to my right and get a shock. There, in a seat against the wall, is President Wright's former chief of staff, Senator Joseph McCarthy's former aide, and the grand master of the Big Mac Party: Vance Slater. I knew there was a possibility he would be here, but I expected him to be in handcuffs, or at least guarded. But Slater sits there in a fine suit, unencumbered, smug, relaxed, even. Is he waiting to testify? He catches my gaze and stares back at me with deadpan, malignant eyes. In his pocket, I can see the outline of a cell phone. Something tells me he wants me to see it.

I hadn't counted on Slater being free. General McGuffin has too much honor to kill a child easily, I know, but Slater would kill Scotty within seconds. So the question is: who's really in charge? With a chill, I realize that I'm no longer sure.

Derek is talking. "I had no contact with the president during the Big Mac takeover."

"And so your opinion that the president was acting against his will was only hearsay from Chris Thompson?"

"Um."

"Was Chris Thompson your only source of information regarding President Wright? Yes or no?"

Derek closes his eyes and thinks. "Yes," he finally says.

"No further questions." The senator walks to a lectern and consults his computer.

It's my turn.

"Mr. Chris Thompson." The senator points and walks forcefully toward me. "Is it true that you were one of the masterminds of the fake invasion from Mexico and Canada?"

"No."

"Let me rephrase the question." The senator paces before me. "Is it true that you, the president, and a computer genius known as the Wizkid were the only people who had any knowledge of this fake invasion?"

"Well—"

"Yes or no?"

"Yes."

"Thank you." He stops before me and relaxes his shoulders, as if we are now friends. "Is it true that you were sent as the president's liaison to the secret Emergence center to direct the torture of innocent foreign nationals?"

I didn't like the way this was going. "No, absolutely not."

The senator sighs a confident sigh, as if he is disappointed that he will have to go through the routine, but certain he will prove his point. He asks, "Were you not the presidential liaison to Emergence?"

"I was."

"And at Emergence, did you not see a Canadian prisoner there accused of infiltrating the border to undermine the government of the United States?"

I think of Walter, and how he had to die for no reason. "He didn't do anything."

"So you agree the Canadian was innocent?"

"I do. He was innocent." I suddenly realize I am agreeing to all his questions, on my way to proving his initial point.

"And as the presidential liaison to Emergence, you oversaw the torture and murder of this innocent Canadian?"

"No."

"You did not see the Canadian tortured?"

How was I going to explain that I did see Walter tortured, but that I was naked and hiding in a crate, or that I tried to save him by running out in my flip flops? They would laugh me down. It would sound unbelievable.

"I refuse to answer the question under my rights granted to me by the Fifth Amendment," I say.

A murmur spreads through the room.

The senator's eyebrows raise. I look around. Slater glares at me.

"So you are worried you might incriminate yourself?"

"I plead the Fifth."

"By pleading the Fifth and refusing to answer the question, you are affirming my supposition." The senator pulls on his lapels and rotates around the room as he speaks. "I want everyone to know that Chris Thompson has refused to answer my questions regarding whether or not he was in charge of the president's torture program at the Emergence center."

I stand up. "That's a lie."

A gavel pounds. "You are out of order. Sit down, Mr. Thompson."

I sit down. The senator's tactics are right out of old Joe McCarthy's playbook. I'm pretty certain there are laws to protect me against these types of statements and questions, but no one seems to be on my side.

"Let us move on." The senator smiles, suddenly my friend

again. "The president claims he was under influence of some concocted hallucinogen called Macwacky. Did you ever see the president take any drugs?"

I saw the president being led away by Big Mac operatives to take them, and I saw a package intended for the president, and I saw him clearly out of his mind on something. But no, I had not seen him take any drugs. "Not personally," I say.

And now, I knew, here it was. "Did you ever see the president acting strangely, as if he was under the influence of a hallucinogen?"

This was the key question that Big Mac wanted me to answer with a lie in order to save Scotty's life. I don't look, but I can feel Slater's stare.

I ask myself: what is more important, the individual or the state? The individual or society? My love for my son or my duty as a citizen? I imagine Karen in front of the television, both hands to her face, biting into her knuckles. Derek touches my shoulder and looks at me with a kindness that says he will be there for me whatever I say.

And I realize: I'm no Abraham. The heck with this circus. I'm saving my son.

"No. I never saw the president acting strangely," I say, and I feel relieved and guilty at once.

"Objection," Brandon shouts.

"Overruled."

The senator is now my best friend. "So you believe the president acted of sound mind and body to create a fake invasion and a national emergency?"

Brandon is hissing in my ear. "Say no and retract your previous statement, Thompson. This is your last chance."

"Mr. Thompson? I repeat—do you believe the president

acted of sound mind and body to create a fake invasion and a national emergency?"

"I do." It's easy now that I've taken the first plunge into the liars' sea.

Brandon gathers his papers and folders and slams them on the table. "You and your family are on your own now," he whispers as he stands up and walks out of the room.

"And you believe that on his own volition, without any coercion from Vance Slater, President Oscar I. Wright bypassed the judicial and legislative branches and issued illegal and oppressive executive orders in order to give himself dictatorial powers and create a totalitarian regime over the United States?"

This was, of course, total bullshit. "Yes," I say. "That is what I believe."

A roar goes up throughout the room. A gavel pounds. I have just sold out the president of the United States.

The questioning is over. It's chaos. The wardens herd Derek and me out of the room into a swarm of reporters who thrust their microphones, cell phones, and cameras at us.

"Follow me." Derek lowers his shoulder and charges. I put my hand on him like a good halfback and follow him out of the building. We run down the stairs, dodge more reporters, and sprint toward Constitution Avenue and a line of taxis.

I hear a familiar voice. "Chris." It's Karen, running on a diagonal to cut us off. I stop, and she runs into my arms. She squeezes me tight and showers my face and neck with kisses. "You did the right thing."

Still holding on to Karen, I take a small step back to speak to her. "Derek and I are going to get Scotty."

"I want to come," she insists.

I shake my head. "We could be in danger. The president still has some power, and he's probably infuriated with me. And who knows what Big Mac has in mind for all of us? You go with Archie and June and hide somewhere until this all blows over. Archie has a favorite fishing hole in West Virginia. Stonecoal Lake. Let's meet up there, and we'll figure out what to do next." I kiss her again. "I love you."

"I love you, too."

Derek has hailed a cab. I slide in next to him. "NSA building as fast as you can," I say.

But the door on Derek's side opens. Two hands reach in and push on his shoulder. It's Karen. "Move over, Cannonball," she says.

"What are you doing?" I say.

She squeezes in next to Derek and slams the door shut. She looks at me. "You're not shoving me off with Archie and Mom. I'm going to get my son."

"Are we going?" the cabbie asks.

There is no time to argue, and by the look on Karen's face I have no chance of winning anyway. "Yes, go."

Un-American Activities

WE HAVE INFILTRATED the NSA. It was easy. They let us in the front door like special guests. Now Derek, Karen, and I stand before General McGuffin in the hotel-like prison rooms. Scotty and Little Joe are playing a video game on the TV. Armed guards stand around the room. Karen has run up to the window and is trying to get Scotty's attention, but he cannot see or hear her.

"There's been a change of plans," McGuffin says to me.

"You gave me your word," I hiss.

McGuffin is looking at the ground, embarrassed. He starts to talk—"I"—but then stops. He raises his head and looks directly into my eyes. "My hands are tied."

Just then, a figure walks above us on the balcony and leans over the rail. Vance Slater. "Thompson, I'm glad you could join us." He speaks in that gravelly voice that grates on my nerves.

"I held up my end of the bargain. Now give me my son."

"But look how well they are getting on," Slater says. "The interaction is good for Little Joe. A future leader of the world needs to have friends."

"I'm guessing you never had any," Derek says.

Slater does not like the comment.

Karen walks backward toward us, looking up at Slater. Her voice is slightly panicked. "What's he saying? What is going on?"

"I've decided that your son—in fact, all of you—are going to be staying with us for a while longer," Slater announces.

"You can't do this," Karen says.

"President Wright has been impeached." Slater takes a step to the right and puts his hands on the rails and leans over. "Vice President Carlson is being sworn in as we speak."

"Impeached for trying to stop exactly what you are doing," Derek says.

"Ironic," I say.

"Yes, how ironic," Slater says. "You two buffoons thought you could stop us, but in the end, you were merely pawns in our plan." Slater's face puffs up and turns red. "We win. Big Mac is back. Big Mac is in power." He shakes a fist. "I'm in power." He paces back and forth. "You are mine, now. Take them away."

He turns and disappears into the dark.

"You gave your word," I say to McGuffin.

"I did," McGuffin says. He looks different now that Slater is obviously in charge. He's lost his charisma and his honor, and he stands deflated.

I look around at the guards. I run my right hand over my left arm and wonder if I could smash it through the window and snatch Scotty.

But before I can act on this, there's a commotion inside the prison room. Scotty and Little Joe are running around playing with a monkey.

"They really like Tolstoy." McGuffin turns to walk away. "Come with me."

"I'm not going anywhere," Karen says.

McGuffin keeps walking. "Do you want to see your son?"

Karen quickly steps forward, and we follow McGuffin through an armored door behind the prison rooms. Two guards follow us. One of the guards takes out keys and unlocks a door that should lead into Scotty's room.

"We won't need you in here," McGuffin says to the guards. They're not going anywhere. He opens the door slightly and peers in. "Quickly, so Tolstoy doesn't escape."

McGuffin, Derek, Karen, and I enter the room, and within a second, Scotty and Karen are in an embrace. Scotty gives me a knowing eye, touches his temple twice, and points at me. I wonder what he's up to.

Little Joe, stupefied, watches Scotty and Karen hug like he is witnessing an unimaginable event. For him, perhaps that is sadly true.

Tolstoy runs around, screeching and jumping on everything.

"Time for Tolstoy to go back in his cage," McGuffin says. He nods at Scotty. Quick as a monkey, Scotty chases and gathers Tolstoy up and walks with him into the bedroom.

We're about to follow, but McGuffin stops us. "Wait a moment," he says. He appears to be counting to himself, and then he nods and walks into the bedroom as well. We follow him in.

Inside, a rolling cart sits next to bunk beds. There is a cage on the cart with a beige canvas draped over it. Neither Scotty nor Tolstoy can be seen.

"Scotty's not in the cage with that monkey, is he?" Karen asks, upset.

McGuffin walks over to a closet door. "It's a little trick to get Tolstoy in his cage. Scotty hides in the closet and Tolstoy hides in his cage."

Little Joe brushes past McGuffin, runs to the closet, and opens it slightly. He has a big grin on his face and is very excited.

The general encourages us to look into the closet. Inside, there is a small laundry hamper. Little Joe opens it and reveals Tolstoy resting quietly inside. Tolstoy smiles and puts his index finger over his lips.

What is happening? I look to McGuffin.

"I gave you my word," the general says, looking straight at me.

I look at Derek. His eyes light up in recognition.

Karen walks over to the cart. She lifts the canvas slightly and is about to speak.

"Please don't disturb Tolstoy." The general walks quickly over to the cart. He takes the canvas from Karen and lets it fall, but before it does, I see Scotty's red tennis shoe. Karen sees it too.

"We will return Tolstoy to the lab," he says loudly, "and then I will show you to your quarters." The general motions us into the other room. He follows us, pushing the canvas-covered cage with Scotty inside and shutting the bedroom door behind him. "Quickly now." He leads us out the main door and nods to the guards.

"Are the rooms for our guests prepared, Sergeant?" he asks.

The sergeant glances at the other guard and looks a little uneasy. "The guests are to be transferred to SUBCOM 23, General."

"Yes, I had forgotten." The general suddenly looks like a man with a mission. He starts barking orders. "Sergeant, retrieve my briefcase." He looks to the other guard. "You, man. I need the Mercury file. Captain O'Brien has it." McGuffin looks at his watch. "Meet us at the underground transit center in fifteen minutes."

The sergeant shifts uncomfortably. "We have orders, sir. Not to leave our guests."

"You have new orders now, Sergeant," the general bellows.

"Yes, sir."

The sergeant leads the other guard out via the door we originally came through. McGuffin pushes the cage in the other direction.

"Where are we going?" I say.

Karen is pulling on my arm. "He's helping us," she says forcibly in a hushed tone. "Scotty is in the cage. Haven't you figured that out?"

"Shush," McGuffin says.

The hallway we are walking down ends in a T. Slater's speaking over the PA. "I want them under video surveillance in the Waikiki twenty-four seven."

McGuffin puts his keycard through a slot and opens a side door. He pushes the cart and leads us into a dark room with hundreds of desktop computers. Video screens cover the walls. A woman in civilian business clothes approaches us.

"Can I help you, General?"

"A quick tour for some important guests," McGuffin says.

"Of course." The woman is composed and looks eager to explain. "In this room we monitor social media for terrorist activities."

"Un-American activities?" Derek says.

The woman gives a slight nod. "One and the same. Don't you agree?"

Derek nods back with a sly smile. "Of course."

"Can I check Facebook?" Karen says.

"Tommy can help you." The woman motions to a nearby man, who swivels around in his chair and displays his computer screen to Karen.

"Can you see who's been looking at my photos?" she asks.

The man gives Karen a confident smirk. "Oh, I can show you more than that."

Karen leans over his shoulder, and they bring up her Facebook page.

The woman in charge launches into a polished tour speech she has doubtless given many times before. McGuffin is anxious. We all are. We need to leave. But the woman keeps rambling on.

"Big Mac will be able to use home security systems, game consoles, televisions, cell phones, anything with a camera, to ensure that all Americans are safe inside their homes."

"Oh my—Jesus." Derek is looking toward the back corner of the room.

The woman smiles. "You've discovered our newest program." She waves her hand toward the back screens. They're showing people having sex—normal looking people in normal looking places.

"Our ASS program."

"ASS program?" Derek says.

"ASS program. American Sex for Space."

"They get paid cash for having sex?" I say.

The woman laughs. "No, we do. These people have no idea we can see them. People pay big money for this. These Americans having sex will fund Big Mac's space program. American sex will hump us through the cosmos." She laughs with pride.

"Thank you—we have to go." McGuffin pushes the cage toward a door opposite where we came in.

"Let's go, Karen," I say.

She laughs and holds up a finger. "Just a minute. We're inside the Goldmans' house. I've always wanted to see their kitchen."

"Karen," I hiss. She looks up, and I nod toward the cage. "We have to go."

Karen wises up, and we follow Derek and McGuffin out the door. We are walking quickly down a brightly lit hallway.

"Where are we going? What's the plan?" I say.

We stop in front of an elevator. McGuffin pushes the Up button repeatedly. "Straight to the roof to an escape helicopter. Doctor Rod is waiting."

"You know about Doctor Rod?" Derek says.

"I know—and knew—all about your little training program and rescue plan." McGuffin laughs. "It is in the same building." He presses the Up button again.

"Why are you helping us?" Karen says.

"I gave my word."

"They'll know it was you," Derek says.

He hesitates. "I believe in Big Mac's goals for America. But Slater . . . he has no honor. He is not a man I can follow anymore." McGuffin is introspective, sad even. "I'm escaping with you."

"Freeze!"

Lexi and Chip, the demonic couple I entrusted with Scotty's care, stand at the hallway's end. They're both drawing guns.

The elevator door opens. Immediately, the general rolls the cart containing Scotty inside. I push Karen in after him. Derek and I jump in. A shot rings out, and General McGuffin falls, a bullet hole in his forehead. The doors close.

Derek has already pushed the top-floor button, and we are ascending.

From beneath the canvas comes the sound of crying.

"It's okay, baby." Karen is trying to calm Scotty, but she looks pretty shaken up herself. She reaches down. "You can come out now."

The elevator stops.

"No." I grab Karen's arm. "He's safer hidden. Stay quiet, buddy. We're almost there."

I hear the sound of a sniff.

The doors open and I peer into an empty hallway. "Let's go."

Pushing the cart ahead of us, we run toward the maintenance door that leads to Doctor Rod's laboratory. The door opens, and there stands Doctor Rod. Next to her is the female guard who first greeted us when we arrived in a helicopter last week. The guard has a gun to Doctor Rod's head.

"Turn around and go back down in the elevator," the guard says.

We stand frozen.

"I said, turn around and—"

She slumps to the ground, a tiny dart in her neck.

Derek has his iPhone in hand. He blows on its top. "There's a new sharpshooter in town," he says. "You couldn't handle the guard?"

Doctor Rod gives a look that would scare tougher men than Derek and me. "I was just testing you boys." She reaches out a hand to Karen, and all sweet-like, she says, "I'm Doctor Rod. Are you Karen? I've heard so many nice things about you."

Karen is trying to compose herself. "Nice, too."

Bringing Doctor Rod with us, we turn and run up the stairs to the roof. I carry Scotty's canvas-covered cage with my super arm as if I am holding nothing at all.

On the helipad sits a helicopter. Not just any helicopter, but a VH-3D Marine One presidential helicopter. The hatchway is down, and President Wright is inside, waving. His two pilots, Captain Pearson and Lieutenant Singer, are with him.

We slide the cage into the helicopter and then quickly climb in ourselves. The rotors begin to turn. The president has a margarita in his hand and couldn't be happier.

"Welcome to Marine One. Well, it's not really Marine One, because I'm not the president any longer. But still, hot damn."

"Finally." Karen starts to remove the canvas from the cage to free Scotty. Derek, Doctor Rod, and I collapse happily into the seats.

"Last ride for me," the president muses. "Gave me a sendoff like Nixon."

And then Karen screams.

I turn around. Sitting in the cage with a smile on his face is Little Joe McCarthy.

Little Joe

IM ON A helicopter. The President of the United States's helicopter. He's not the president anymore. He's crazy, they say, and I can see that for myself now.

Getting here has been the most exciting experience of my life so far. Scotty and I were playing jumping tag with Tolstoy. He's a monkey and can really jump. The game is just like tag, but you have to jump the whole time.

Then Papa McGuffin came in and said that Scotty had to leave. He said that Big Mac was taking over, which was good, but that they were breaking a promise, which he didn't like. He said that even good governments make bad choices sometimes. So to help save Papa McGuffin's honor, we have to help Scotty escape. I was really mad at Big Mac for making Scotty leave and for hurting General McGuffin's honor.

He showed us President Wright being impeached on the

TV. I was excited, but Scotty was really worried. He said things were moving too fast and all in Big Mac's favor.

Scotty laughs at me when I yell at the newscasters on TV and call them pinkos and commies, like a real Big Mac person should. I said the Reds are still out there, waiting to ruin America. Scotty says that this is weird and that nobody talks like that anymore. I don't like when he laughs at me. I don't want to be weird.

Then I had a great idea. I said that I should escape instead of him. I could be his dad's hostage, and he could be Big Mac's hostage. How fun is that? I could find out what people are really like. See if anybody else thinks I'm weird. Scotty liked the idea of switching, too. He said that if we switched, his dad would be more safe, because Big Mac wouldn't want to accidentally hurt me by hurting him. Plus, if we are both hostages, they will switch us back for sure later, Scotty said.

I don't like it when Scotty talks bad about Big Mac. But I want to be friends, so I don't say anything.

Scotty's dad and mom showed up. They seem nice. Real nice. His mom gave him a really big hug. It made me feel strange inside. It made me kind of want to cry. It made me kind of not like Scotty. Just a little bit.

But still, this is the most fun I have ever had. We switched places real quick when we were in the room alone, and I escaped in Tolstoy's cage. It was a fun ride. I spun around, and it felt like we were going real fast. Papa and other people were doing a lot of talking, but it was hard to hear what they were saying. I heard gunshots, and someone hitting the floor. That was easy to hear. I hope it was a bad guy, one of the president's terrorist spies, who died. I thought I was going to die, too, but then I didn't.

And now I'm on an old Marine One—with the enemy. They all keep looking at me. I think they're scared. Scotty's mom is crying, pointing at me and calling me a clone. Maybe she's not so nice. This other lady, Doctor Rod, is screaming at the pilots to take off. I wish they would. I really want to fly and escape this place for a while. I want to go on an adventure.

Scotty's mom and dad are arguing. The helicopter is shaking like it's ready to jump into the air. The former president is yelling to pull up the hatch. He yells, "Whoop-de-doo," and circles his fingers in the air, and the one pilot gives him a thumbs-up. That seemed pretty weird to me.

Scotty's mom is furious. She leaps off the helicopter. The hatch goes up and we lift off. Scotty's dad puts his face against the window and we climb higher. I see Scotty's mom run back inside the building. What's she gonna do? What're the rest of them gonna do?

Whatever they do, they know Big Mac will come for them now. I'm Big Mac's destiny.

Puerto Rican Standoff

I SHOULD HAVE stayed with Karen. No. That makes no sense. She'll be caught immediately, and I would have been too. We have to regroup and make another plan, be happy we escaped at all. It's not my fault Scotty wasn't in the cage. I thought he was with us. We all did. I've done the right thing. So why do I feel so bad?

Thousands of silver bullets are flying out of a lower window of the NSA building, forming an ominous, rapidly growing swarm. "They've released the drineys."

We all look out. There are countless drineys now, flying out of the swarm in all directions.

"Where are they going?" I ask, but no one answers.

"Hey. What the hell? Is anybody going to let me out of here?" Little Joe rattles the cage.

Derek and Doctor Rod look at me as if it's my decision. I look out the window. I can't see either Karen or the NSA anymore. Chip and Lexi, or some other troops in Slater's Big Mac army, have probably captured Karen by now. I hope they put her with Scotty. I hope they don't harm them. I know Slater wouldn't hesitate to kill them in a second, but we have Little Joe, their precious icon and future ruler. That gives us an advantage for now.

"Goddammit, have some decency," Little Joe says.

"You have no decency, sir." The president gulps some more margarita. "Or something like that, remember? Keep that witch hunter in the cage."

"He's not really Joe McCarthy," I say. "He's just a kid."

"I really am Joe McCarthy. One hundred percent," Little Joe says.

The president is refilling his margarita glass from the frozen margarita machine he's had custom installed into Marine One. "He's a clone. He's as real as real can get to Senator Joe McCarthy."

"Little Joe's valuable," Derek says. "He's your key to guaranteeing Karen and Scotty's safety. We can't let him escape."

"Escape to where? We're in a helicopter, morons," Little Joe says.

I reach down and open the cage door. "I certainly wouldn't want Karen and Scotty to be kept in a cage." I give Little Joe a hand and help him out.

He sits in the seat next to me. "Thank you. You're a good fella, a straight-up guy."

Before I can say anything, there's a pinging sound against my window. More pinging sounds all around the helicopter.

There are several drineys flying next to us, bouncing against the helicopter, trying to reach us inside.

"What are we going to do?" A driney taps against the president's window, and he cringes, spilling his margarita all over his suit. "Get it away from me."

Doctor Rod casually reaches into her lab coat and pulls out a plastic bottle of pills. She opens the lid and drops one pill into her hand.

Derek points at the pill. "Salt powder and neodymer something."

Doctor Rod looks at Derek, impressed he has remembered. "Nuseum," she says.

"Driney busters," I say.

Doctor Rod looks around. "I need some type of container."

Little Joe fishes into his pocket and produces a plastic Easter egg. He opens it, removes some gelatin-slime-like material into his hand, and then gives the empty egg to Doctor Rod. Doctor Rod puts the pill into the egg.

President Wright is slapping his hand on the window next to the insistent driney. "Go away, go away."

Doctor Rod, calm, hands the president the plastic egg. "Shake it, and your dreams will come true."

The president looks at the egg curiously. "Shake it?"

"Shake it," Doctor Rod says matter-of-factly.

The president shakes the egg. He shakes it harder and starts singing, as I have seen him do before when he is under pressure.

"Faster," Doctor Rod says.

The president's face is red. He has both hands covering the egg, and he is vigorously pumping it up and down and side to side.

The air quickly flickers with sparkles, and I smell the sulfur smell again. The drineys outside pinging against the windows at once fall and disappear.

"Drop us below the radar," I say to Captain Pearson.

"Woo-hoo," the president says. He's looking around wildly. "Did you see that? Did you see the lights? We're going to heaven."

Captain Pearson turns to look at the president. He's now fumbling with the margarita machine.

"Woo-hoo means yes," Doctor Rod says.

Captain Pearson nods. She's seen the president's antics before. The helicopter dives for lower altitude.

"Where should we go?" Derek says.

"Canada," the president says. "A perfect place for draft dodgers, traitors, and impeached presidents." The president raises his glass in a toast to himself.

"Communist pussies," Little Joe says.

"Kingston, Canada," the president says. "I have to go to Kingston."

"Yes, Canada," Doctor Rod says. "Do not turn north until we are under radar."

"What about Scotty and Karen?" I say.

"Big Mac has released the drineys," Doctor Rod says. "I only have so many nuseum tablets. We need a safe haven."

"Scotty's a lot safer where he is than with you losers," Little Joe says. "You think you can escape by flying low? Big Mac has a lot more than radar to squash you with."

"What did you do with Scotty?" I put a threatening finger in front of Little Joe's face. "How'd you get in the cage?"

He looks bewildered. "Scotty's my friend." His shoulders relax, and his face softens. "I would never hurt Scotty. We switched when you left the bedroom and the general wasn't looking. It was Scotty's idea."

"Scotty's?" I say. "That makes no sense."

"Okay. It was my idea, but Scotty agreed. Scotty figured you'd all have a better chance of staying alive if you had me as a hostage." Little Joe smiles smugly. "I am pretty important to Big Mac."

"That makes a lot of sense," Derek said.

"It makes no sense," I say. Actually, though, it kind of does. Damn Scotty; he was just too smart. "But don't you like Big Mac?"

Everyone looked at Little Joe, hopeful that maybe after all Big Mac's efforts, their clone wouldn't buy into their crazy ideology.

"Ah, go fuck yourselves. I love Big Mac." Little Joe laughs a slightly maniacal laugh. It's hard to tell if he's pretending or not. "Scotty and I are just playing a game. We can disagree about Big Mac and still have fun."

What would Karen say if she knew that her son had conspired with Little Joe to keep himself hostage? She'd assume that Scotty had gotten this crazy idea from listening to me and all my old James Bond spy fantasies, and I'd be to blame.

The helicopter was now only a couple of hundred feet off the ground and heading straight north.

"Will we have enough fuel to make Canada?" I ask.

Lieutenant Singer taps on a gauge. "We can make it."

President Wright has fallen asleep. Doctor Rod takes the empty glass from his hand and places it in a cupboard in the back.

We ride on in silence. Night descends. The cockpit instrument lights and the drone of the rotors create a peaceful, relaxing sensation within me. I feel calm, comforted, and secure in this ship as we race north. If Scotty and Karen are together in the NSA prison/hotel room, they should be all right. Little Joe is the key. He's Big Mac's prize asset. Slater has to make a deal for a prisoner exchange and for our future security, doesn't he? I hope so.

Will Karen ever forgive me for leaving her with Scotty to endure Big Mac on their own? Will she ever forgive me for wanting to be a spy?

After three hours, the lights of Syracuse appear off to our right. Karen and I have married friends there from our college days, Bob and Jill. We see them every year or so. I wonder if we will ever have friends again, go out as couples, be invited over for game nights. Will we ever have a normal life? Why did I ever want to be a spy?

"We will be flying over Lake Ontario and entering Canadian airspace shortly," Captain Pearson says.

Doctor Rod and Derek have been whispering to each other. She turns and looks out the port-side window. "Can we see Niagara Falls? I do love Niagara Falls."

"Too far to the west," Lieutenant Singer says.

There's a deafening roar, and in the same instant, we see the afterburners from several fighter jets zoom past us.

The president wakes up and plasters his face against the

window. "Get us to Canada. To the Kingston airport."

"Antimissile systems activated," Captain Pearson says.

"They won't shoot at us," the president cries.

A missile goes zooming by the front of the helicopter.

"Just a warning, I'm sure," Derek says.

"The FUC Wall." I point out at the monolithic Forever United against Canada border wall. Giant spotlights light up the black Teflon-like structure that outlines the American shores of Lake Ontario. It reaches five hundred feet into the air and stretches east and west for as far as we can see. It looks exactly the same as the section of the wall Derek and I were conscripted to work at near Sunburst, Montana. Lasers shooting up from the wall create a neon checkered pattern all the way into space.

"Just detection lasers," the president says. "They won't harm us."

We've almost reached it when another missile goes whizzing by. President Wright is right. They're just warning us. I'm sure Slater wouldn't mind shooting down the president, but no way is he going to harm Little Joe.

We fly through the lasers and over the wall. I look down onto the walkway running along the top of the wall and to the American guards manning their posts against any potential harm from the Canadians.

Derek raises a fist into the air. "We made it."

Fighter jets surround us, dangerously close. They're trying to force the helicopter to turn, but Captain Pearson keeps Marine One steady.

"The official border is halfway across the lake," she says.

Captain Pearson slows down and dives the helicopter. The move catches our escorts off guard, and they fly ahead of us on their original course. After a moment, they turn around and start to intercept us, but in the end they pass us by and continue back over the wall. They're no longer following us. We're safe for now.

"We're across the border," Lieutenant Singer says.

"We should fly as far north as we can," I say.

"We could hide out at a fishing lodge somewhere," Derek says.

"No. Kingston." The president points out the window. "Right there."

I can barely make out the runway on the small airport. Why does the president want to go here? "We're too close to the border. It might not be safe."

"Kingston," the president says.

Captain Pearson salutes. "Yes, sir. Kingston."

The lights of Kingston airport welcome us. We land on a helicopter pad next to some small hangars. The hatchway goes down, and the president is the first one to scramble out.

"The boy stays in the helicopter," he shouts.

The rotor blades slowly come to a stop as Derek, Doctor Rod, and I follow the president out. We can hear waves lapping against the shore of Lake Ontario nearby.

The president calls us in around him. "We have to kill him, you know."

"Who?"

"Little Joe?" Derek says.

"Yes, the clone. We have to kill him. We can't have McCarthy terrorizing our country again."

Little Joe sticks his head out the doorway and looks around. I can't tell if he has heard the president or not.

"Come here, son," the president says.

"Stay right where you are." I take a step toward the president. "I can't believe you'd even think to do what you just said. He's a child."

"He's a clone, and he's a threat to the United States."

Little Joe looks back and forth between the president and me. Clearly he does not like the content of our conversation. He takes a step and then jumps over the hatchway stairs and hits the ground running.

The president reaches into his suit, pulls out a giant Smith & Wesson Model 29, and aims it at Little Joe. "Freeze."

Little Joe has no intention of stopping. He's running toward the hangar, which oddly has its door open, even though it is dark and looks deserted.

The president's gun follows Little Joe, and his face goes taut. He's going to shoot. In an instant I flick my left hand out, grab the president's wrist, and lift his hand and gun to the sky. He fires just as Little Joe disappears into the hangar.

"We have to find him," Doctor Rod says.

I squeeze the president's wrist, and the Smith & Wesson drops to the ground. Derek picks up the gun and points it at the president. "I thought we were on the same side," he says.

"So did I. What side are you all on?" asks the president.

"The side that doesn't kill children," I say.

"The pinko side that can wipe my American ass someday." Little Joe is walking out of the hangar toward us, but clearly against his will. Holding him by the collar, pushing him along, is Fixer.

Fixer has a gun in his free hand pointing at Derek. "Drop it."

The president laughs. "Fixer. What a pleasant surprise."

"Yes, what a pleasant surprise." Lieutenant Singer stands at the front of Marine One with a gun in her hand pointed at Fixer.

"What are you doing?" Captain Pearson says. Her own gun is pointed at Derek. "We're here to protect the president."

"We've safely delivered the president to his destination. Now he's not the president anymore." Lieutenant Singer has a crazy look in her eye as she addresses Fixer. "You said you loved me."

"Love?" Captain Pearson says. "I thought you only had one date?"

"She was a two-date mission, actually," Fixer says, a triumphant grin on his face.

Lieutenant Singer adjusts her aim and explains to Captain Pearson. "The little motherfucker. I'm not wasting this chance. If shots are going to fire, Fixer is going to die."

"A Mexican standoff," the president says. "Like an old western movie. These are so exciting."

"Well, technically no," Derek says. "You see, we have four guns, but no one is aiming at Captain Pearson or Lieutenant Singer, so really they have—"

"A Canadian standoff," the president cries, pleased with himself. "That's what we'll call it."

I sense a slight movement next to me, and then Doctor Rod is somehow in midair.

"Break the clone's neck," the president shouts to Fixer, but in an instant Doctor Rod lands on Fixer, cuts his legs out from underneath him, and snatches the gun out of his hand. She points the gun toward our pilots.

"A Puerto Rican standoff," she says in a thick accent.

"Fire up the helicopter," I say. "The president will be safe." I look to Fixer. "I assume you were taking him?"

Fixer nods. "F117 stealth ready to go in the hangar."

"Either we take Little Joe, or Big Mac gets him," I say to the president. "They know where we've landed. If we stay here they'll be coming for him, and us, soon."

President Wright waves his hand to the pilots. "Fine. Take them."

Captain Pearson and Lieutenant Singer run into the helicopter. Derek throws Little Joe over his shoulder and climbs in after them. The rotors begin to turn. I jump in. Doctor Rod follows. She flips Fixer's gun back to him. Marine One floats up and away from the president and Fixer on the ground. It's just Derek, Doctor Rod, and I, and of course our hostage, Little Joe.

"What are you going to do with me?" asks Little Joe. "The president. He . . . he . . . he really was going to kill me."

"We're not going to kill you," I say.

Derek gives Little Joe a mean eye. "Long as you do what you're told."

"But what are we going to do?" I say.

"I have a plan." Doctor Rod points toward the pilots. "Tell them to take us to—"

Derek grabs her hand. "No."

Doctor Rod gives him a fierce look.

"They can't know where we're going," I say. "Otherwise, we can't let them go back."

Doctor Rod nods. "Of course. I wasn't thinking."

"Landing in five minutes," Captain Pearson announces.

"That's too soon," I say. "We're in danger so close to the border."

Captain Pearson taps on a gauge. "No choice. Out of fuel."

Skunk

WE HAVE LANDED on a concrete pad off the taxiway on the remote south side of Ottawa International Airport. By skimming in low over the farm fields with all the radar jamming and other stealth equipment running, we have not attracted attention.

It is two in the morning, and the airport is quiet. Captain Pearson and Lieutenant Singer have agreed to sit tight with the helicopter until somebody notices them. Hopefully the rest of us will have several hours to escape before Big Mac catches up with Marine One.

Doctor Rod, Derek, Little Joe, and I have walked through the grass past a sleepy building with a sign that reads Canada Border Services Agency. We crossed a country road, and we are now walking on a golf course fairway.

"Is the place we are going to close by?" I ask Doctor Rod.

"No."

"Is it in Canada?" Derek asks.

"Yes."

"Will I be able to play outside?" Little Joe asks.

"Yes."

"Animal, vegetable, or mineral?" I say. "Good God. Can you please tell us where we are going?"

"No."

Meandering around a golf course can do us no good. I like to have a plan. "Are we just going to walk around all night?"

"No." Through the moonlight, Doctor Rod points between a group of short pine trees to a maintenance building on the other side of a putting green. "We need a vehicle. Golf courses have vehicles."

An overhead light illuminates the front sliding doors, but otherwise there is no security. I try to open the doors, but they are locked from the inside. To the side is a regular door. I ready my strong arm to break through.

"Stop," Doctor Rod hisses. "Try to leave no evidence that there was a break-in."

"Here." Derek has prodded open a window, and he is pushing Little Joe through.

In a minute, the front sliding doors have parted. Little Joe has a big grin on his face. "See? I can help."

In the dim light we can see lawn mowers, tractors, and other equipment.

"There." Doctor Rod points to the side wall and a line of golf carts. "We take the one at the far end. Hopefully it will take them a while to figure out that one is missing."

"Shh. I hear something," Derek says.

We all stop moving and listen intently, but there is no

sound.

"We have to move quickly." I rummage around on a workbench and find an electric drill. On the last car I drill holes around the ignition until there is enough room for me to slip my fingers inside the fiberglass. I rip out the ignition lock and wires. I bite off the ends to the two ignition wires and twist them together. I step on the accelerator, and the electric car slowly moves.

"I want to drive," Little Joe says.

There's a soft metallic bang outside.

Derek motions to me, and we edge toward the open main doors. We walk around the side of the maintenance building where the noise has come from. Derek has his iPhone out. I have my fists clenched as we walk side by side. There's a clanging behind some garbage cans, and then out walks a skunk.

Derek and I step slowly backward, but the damn skunk is ready to fight. He turns at us and sprays: a direct hit. Derek and I look at each other like two soldiers about to die. Derek gives me a frightened smile, and then a horrendous smell envelops us like the black death. His face shrivels in disgust.

Doctor Rod drives out of the building on the golf cart with Little Joe sitting next to her. She jerks to a stop when the smell reaches her. "Oh no."

Derek and I walk toward the cart, grimacing, contemplating our noxious predicament.

"You commie bastards stink." Little Joe puts his hands over his nose.

"On back." Doctor Rod points to the rear. "Maybe the smell will trail behind us."

Derek and I stand like two giant golf bags on the back of

the golf cart. Doctor Rod drives over the course and stops at the edge of the road.

"I want to drive," Little Joe says.

Doctor Rod looks at the stars to gather her bearings.

"Where to?" I say.

"Let me drive," Little Joe says.

"South," Doctor Rod says. "We go south."

"We should stay in Canada," I say.

Doctor Rod pulls onto the deserted road and heads south. "We will stay in Canada." She pinches her nose. "We can't drive fast enough. You two smell so awful."

"Let me drive. I'll drive faster," Little Joe says.

"Where are we going?" I say.

"I demand to drive," Little Joe says.

"I demand to know where we're going," I say.

"To the St. Lawrence, and hopefully passage on a discreet boat."

"And how far is that?"

Doctor Rod looks up at the stars again. "I don't know. Thirty, forty, fifty miles?"

"The max range for an electric golf cart is about thirty miles," Derek says.

I give Derek a look: how would you know that?

"I was a bartender at the Round Robin in DC, remember? I learned a lot of useless crap from a lot of useless rich fuckers."

Little Joe is bouncing up and down and rocking the cart. He looks furious. "Let me drive, I said."

Doctor Rod pulls over. "Fine."

"Fine? What?" I say. "You're going to give in to that temper tantrum?"

Doctor Rod shrugs. "Little Joe needs to experience real

life."

"Real life? We're escaping for our lives on a golf cart in Canada. You call this real life?"

"Lay off," Derek says. "It's just a golf cart."

The cart lurches, and we are off. Little Joe heads straight for the center line and tries to hold it, but keeps veering to the left.

I see headlights far down the road. "Car. Pull off the road."

Little Joe keeps going straight. The lights close in on us rapidly. Yellow fog lights outline a semitruck's trailer. "Truck. Pull off."

Little Joe seems frozen, uncertain, unwilling, or just too scared to do anything. Doctor Rod reaches over and tries to grab the wheel. Little Joe tries to avoid her and turns the cart hard left off the road into the ditch. Derek flies off the back. The truck goes whizzing by.

We push the cart back on the road, and Doctor Rod resumes driving.

Little Joe sulks in the seat next to her. "I could have done it. We would have been all right. I have a destiny, you know?"

We've been driving for about two hours without talking when the cart's battery dies.

"Ditch the cart in the woods and walk," Derek says.

"No," Doctor Rod says. "No loose ends."

Doctor Rod, Derek, and I push the cart while Little Joe gleefully steers.

"You guys stink so bad," Doctor Rod complains. "I've trained some of the world's best spies. How did I end up here?"

"Derek and I get the job done," I say.

"That's right, CT, that's right." Derek laughs. "Our methods may be a little unorthodox, but Chris Thompson and I will always set things straight."

"I don't care what you say," Little Joe says. "You guys stink."

"I agree with Little Joe," Doctor Rod says.

We push for a laborious two or so miles before we come to a crossroad, Boat House Road, which runs parallel to the St. Lawrence River. On the other side of the river, the mighty FUC Wall looms.

We turn down Boat House Road. The road runs along a small river harbor lined with houseboats. There are also docks with fishing boats and pleasure powerboats.

It is still dark, but the sky is turning just a shade lighter in the east. There are about twenty houseboats made of wood and aluminum. They all seem rickety and run-down. Two of them have lights on the inside. Doctor Rod points to the more dilapidated of the two.

"Fisherman." She walks toward the house. "You two smell. Stay here." She waves at Little Joe. "Come on, Little Joe. Try and look cute." Little Joe smiles superiorly at us and hustles after Doctor Rod.

Derek and I sit on the golf cart and watch as an older man in a T-shirt and boxers opens the door. He listens to Doctor Rod, runs his hand through his wild, wispy gray hair, and invites them in.

"How we going to get rid of this stink?" Derek says.

I nod toward the harbor. "Dip in the pond?"

We are dripping with skunk. Derek looks longingly at the water. We both start walking.

"Maybe we should wait," Derek says.

"I can't wait anymore," I say.

We reach the water's edge, strip down, and dive into the harbor. The water is freezing and smells a little like gasoline, but it is all wonderful to me. I scrub my hair, arms, and body with nothing but my hands, trying to remove the awful skunk smell.

"We need soap," Derek says.

I swim to the harbor's edge and stand on the murky bottom, the water just over my waist. I reach down and scoop up some mud and scrub myself with it. I dive under, wash myself off, and start to repeat the process. Derek joins me. "I think it's working," I say.

I come out of the water to my knees to better scrub my legs.

"It is working," Derek says. He walks up next to me. "Can you get my back?"

I scrub mud on Derek's back. We are knee deep in the water, naked, covered with black mud.

"Eh. What the hell you Yankee hosers doin'?"

The same old man that had let Doctor Rod and Little Joe into his house boat is now standing on his back wooden patio, aiming a rifle at us.

Derek dives under the water. I dive after Derek, but on a different angle so as to create two targets. Once underwater, I swim for the center of the harbor as far as my breath will take me.

I pop my head out of the water. The man points his gun at me. Derek pops out of the water thirty yards to my left. The man swings the gun toward Derek.

"Stop. They're with us." Doctor Rod is walking onto the porch.

A red beam of light shines on the old man. A familiar whooping sound comes from the FUC Wall. I turn and see that a red laser light is being aimed from the wall's top. Men are scurrying around to their alert positions.

I yell to Derek. "Alert yellow. Enemy combatants spotted."

"Possible WMDs," Derek says.

The old man puts the gun down and raises his hands in the air. "All right. All right."

The beam of light turns off, and the whooping alarm from the wall stops.

"I hate that wall," the old man says.

Doctor Rod has the old man's attention now. She seems to be apologizing or explaining Derek and me to him.

"Another attack on America foiled," Derek says.

Derek and I sit wrapped in blankets in the open-air stern of a decently sized fishing trawler. We are cruising up the St. Lawrence, heading toward the sun, which has just risen above the horizon. The golf cart is secured on the deck close to us, covered in a plastic green tarp. We pass by the green meadows, maples, and pines of Canada on our left. The never-ending expanse of the FUC Wall is ever on our right. We are wearing the old man's clothes: baggy jeans and flannel shirts. We still stink of skunk, but not nearly as badly as before.

Doctor Rod walks back to us and hands us Styrofoam cups filled with coffee. I'm about to ask her where we are going, but she senses my predictable impatience and says, "I'll tell you when we get there."

I nod my head toward the front of the boat, where through the windows, we can make out the small bridge and the old man operating the helm. "How'd you convince him?"

"How do you convince anybody?" Derek says. "Cash. You must have a secret stash of cash for espionage activities. Am I correct?"

"No." Doctor Rod says. "iNuggets."

I'm not sure I heard her correctly. "iNuggets?"

"Who has iNuggets?" Little Joe has just come out the cabin door. "You don't know what iNuggets are?"

"Should we?" Derek asks.

"What century do you guys live in?" Little Joe has a greedy gleam in his eye. "iNuggets. Internet gold. I wanted to get some, but General McGuffin would never give me a computer powerful enough to mine for them."

"Apparently the captain has them."

"Captain Carpy?" Little Joe looks toward the captain, who'd told us we could call him Captain or Carpy, since that was his fishing specialty—carping.

"Enough to make him a rich man," Doctor Rod says.

"Oh, I get it." Little Joe has it all figured out. "You gave a bunch of iNuggets to Captain Carpy so he'd take us to wherever he's taking us." He leans in front of Doctor Rod's face. "How many iNuggets you got?"

"As many as I want."

"Give me some."

"You don't even have a computer. I transferred them to the

Captain on his house computer."

"I'll get a computer. I'll get online. Then you'll give me some, right?"

"No."

Little Joe's face puffs up and turns all red. "I'll make you give them to me."

"Easy, Joe," I say.

"I'm Little Joe," he insists. "I won't be Big Joe until I rule the world."

"Is that what you want?"

Little Joe looks up to the FUC Wall. "Maybe. That's my destiny, isn't it?"

"No. That's not your destiny," Derek says. "That's what you've been taught by some evil people."

He doesn't seem to want to think about this. "Give me some iNuggets," he finally screams.

"No," Doctor Rod says.

Little Joe storms off and enters the cabin by opening and then slamming the door.

Derek shakes his head. "Future dictators. What pains."

I look at Doctor Rod. "I'm guessing, since you have an unlimited supply of iNuggets, that you're the person who created them."

Doctor Rod shakes her head. "The identity of the creator of iNuggets is one of today's greatest secrets. A brilliant mind, they say—now one of the richest people in the world."

"Wow," Derek says.

"Yes, wow," I say with respect. "And we know you."

Doctor Rod laughs. "I'm flattered, but I didn't create iNuggets. I wish I knew who did."

I hear a clanging noise. We look up and see Little Joe

climbing the mast.

"Hey. Get down from there," I say.

"I hate you guys. I want to go home." Little Joe keeps climbing. He has something in his hand. It's a handheld VHF radio. He pauses and brings the radio to his mouth. "Hello, hello. This is Little Joe McCarthy, and I've been kidnapped."

He's going to rat us out. Scotty, Karen—it will all be for naught. And suddenly the stress of the past weeks has caught up with me, and I'm furious at him, at everything.

I put my foot on the port gunwale and propel myself to the top of the cabin.

"Hello. Hello. I'm on a fishing boat in Canada."

I run to the mast and climb up the metal rungs as fast as I can.

"Hello, hello? Can anybody hear me? This is Little Joe—"

I reach up with my bionified arm and grab Little Joe by the throat. The radio falls to the ground.

I climb down still holding Little Joe by the neck. His face is red and he is squirming. I reach the deck and throw him down, my hand still squeezing his neck. Time slows. Little Joe's face is turning deep purple. His eyes twitch with terror.

Little Joe

THE BIG MAC people all talk about the wall. I'm glad to finally
see it. It's the biggest thing I have ever seen, no joke. It's to
keep Un-American people out of America. And it's to keep
American people inside America. The idea is that America stays
like America. Keeping America like America is part of my
destiny.

But now that I'm here, I'm so bored. The wall goes forever,
and I don't want to see it anymore. I want some iNuggets, but
Doctor Rod says no. I want to drive the boat, but Captain
Carpy says no. I tell them both to go to hell, and they laugh. I
tell Captain Carpy he should do what I say if he knows what's
good for him, and he says it's good for him if I'd just shut up
and not drive the boat. That pisses me off good.

Scotty's mom didn't get on the helicopter. His mom must
love him a lot. Nobody here loves me at all. They even talked

about killing me. They must be afraid of my destiny. They truly are enemies of America.

So fuck these people. They're all traitors. I'll show them.

I take a small handheld radio behind Captain Carpy when nobody is looking. I go outside, hiding the radio in my pants, and I climb up the ladder toward the lookout or crow's nest. All I want is to sit up there and turn the radio on and dial channels and quietly talk into it, calling for Big Mac. I want to be rescued. I want to be a hero. I want to go home.

That's all I want, and Chris Thompson tries to strangle me for it.

And I really believe I'm about to die, when finally, his grip releases. I can breathe. I gasp deeply, looking furiously at everyone.

"What am I doing?" Chris Thompson says. "What have I done?" He looks bewildered and then reaches out to touch my face. "I'm sorry," he says.

I slap at his arms. "Stay away from me."

Finally, Doctor Rod puts her arms around me, and I calm down. We sit on a bench and I lay my head in her lap. She softly strokes my hair and cheek and it feels so good. I want to cry, but don't. Instead I close my eyes and wonder what it would be like to have a real mom.

Maple Syrup

DEREK SLAPS ME hard in the face. "Get a hold of yourself. Stop crying."

"Am I a killer?"

"Chris, look at me. You're under a lot of stress. Your emotions got ahold of you. Killers are unemotional." Derek pulls my head to his shoulder and gives me a hug. "You'll be all right, CT."

"He was calling Big Mac. I had to stop him." Little Joe, in Doctor Rod's embrace, looks at me with wide, scared eyes, but otherwise seems okay. I lost it. I didn't have to hurt him. I only needed to get the radio. "I'm sorry, Little Joe. I don't know what got into me."

Little Joe closes his eyes and doesn't say a word.

The boat continues on up the St. Lawrence. The midmorning sun is slowly taking the chill out of the air. Doctor Rod has stopped comforting Little Joe, but he still sits close by her in his own chair. We ride on in silence for an hour.

Derek stands up and looks over the boat's port side into the murky river water. He clears his throat. "I thought you wanted to see some things—experience the real world."

"I do," Little Joe says.

"Then why you'd pull that stunt with the radio?"

"I didn't want to go back. I just wanted to get you in trouble." Little Joe looks at me like he still wants to get me in trouble.

"But why?" Derek says.

"Because you wouldn't give me any iNuggets," Little Joe says with a spark of defiance that betrays his recent timidity. "And you won't let me drive the boat."

"That's Captain Carpy's decision," I say.

"Make him. I want to drive the boat."

"You just can't make people do things," Doctor Rod says.

Little Joe looks at her with genuine surprise.

Doctor Rod leans closer to him. "If you make people do things, it won't work out the way you want, or it will feel wrong somehow. People have to really want to do something for it to be done the best."

"How can I make him want to let me drive the boat?"

Doctor Rod laughs. "Again, you can't make Captain Carpy do anything. Why don't you go talk to him like a friend? Show some interest in what he's doing."

"Inside, now." Captain Carpy's voice comes through the

deck speaker.

I look out. Farther up the river, there's a US Coast Guard cutter moving in our direction. "Quickly. Coast Guard," I say.

We move inside and sit on the low, vinyl-covered benches that line the port and starboard cabin walls. The windows are tinted, but even so, Derek and I still hunker low and peer out at the cutter. Men are positioned all around it, but it's hard to tell if they are operating normally or specifically looking for us.

The cutter is nearly upon us, and we all duck and wait with strained silence. The rumble of the Coast Guard boat's engines vibrates our windows. Are they going to board?

And then, out the rear window, we see the cutter pass our stern, continuing on, not concerned with us.

Derek stands up and wipes his brow. "Whew." The wake from the cutter rocks us, and Derek falls into the port couch.

Little Joe claps and laughs with glee. Derek sits up, smiles, and then laughs, too. The laughter is contagious, and soon Derek, Doctor Rod, Little Joe, and I are all laughing. Little Joe loves it; he can't stop. It's a brief respite from our predicament. In just a short time, we have been through a lot together, and I think, if just for a little bit, we have had a bonding moment.

The trawler's motor vibrates the steel hull, and we continue our sail up the river. By noon, we are far enough north into Canada that the river is no longer the border. We watch without sadness as the giant FUC Wall takes a direct landward turn toward the east and gradually fades away.

The river becomes busier with barges and small motorboats. Sailboats dart through the traffic and make the mood on the water seem more cheerful as we curve around busy Montreal.

Little Joe stands by Captain Carpy for hours and jabbers on incessantly. At one point they are holding the wheel together, and then Little Joe takes the helm solo. He concentrates hard and does a good job of holding her steady, but then he looks around for us, smiling. "I'm driving the boat." The boat swerves, and we laugh as Captain Carpy grabs the wheel.

We continue on through the rest of the day into evening, Little Joe taking turns at the wheel, enamored with the whole process.

Derek and I sit in the stern and relive our first mission against Big Mac and Emergence headquarters, laughing about our time at the sorority party at ASU. Doctor Rod occasionally forces a smile at us, like she is trying to be polite and keep herself from commenting on our tactics and espionage goofs. Most of the time she looks out at the scenery, thinking. She seems to enjoy cruising on the boat.

Finally, the evening fades, and the cool Canadian night descends on us. The captain motors on, oblivious to distraction or a need for sleep. The rest of us find spots in the cabin and drift off.

In the morning we approach Quebec City. The blue and white flag of Quebec and its four fleurs-de-lis have now replaced the red-and-white maple leaf flags we had been seeing on the passing houses and buildings.

A fortress wall surrounds old Quebec, and the grand Chateau Frontenac sits imposingly at the highest point on the bluff.

Captain Carpy motors on. He is one with his boat, never resting, steady-as-she-goes.

"Are we there yet?" I ask.

"Yeah, really. Are we there yet?" Derek asks.

Doctor Rod sits on the back deck with us, sipping at a coffee. She does not respond, but just looks out, taking in the city as we slowly pass.

Little Joe opens the cabin door and sticks his head out. "We're almost there."

A sly smile spreads across Doctor Rod's face.

Little Joe closes the door and returns to the ship's bridge.

"You told Little Joe where we are going and not us?" I say.

"Little Joe has a knack for getting what he wants."

"You say that as if it's a good thing. Do you not remember how dangerous McCarthy's affable personality turned out to be?"

Derek scoots closer to Doctor Rod. He puts his hand on her shoulder, and I can't help but notice that she doesn't seem to mind. "Ease up, Chris. You don't have to explain the dangers of McCarthyism to Doctor Rod."

Quebec City fades in the distance, and the green Canadian forest returns as we motor on.

"Ease up?" A large landmass directly ahead of us divides the river into two. "There's a giant wall enclosing the border of the United States. There are drineys loose across the country by now. Big Mac has Karen and Scotty and is doing who knows what to them. You want me to ease up?"

"Yeah, ease up," Derek says. "Don't insult us, man. We're professionals. We know the score, and I'm telling you that in order for us all to succeed, you need to ease up."

I take a deep breath and exhale slowly. After a moment,

Derek reaches out his fist to me and I lightly fist bump him back. He slaps me on the shoulder. No words are necessary.

Captain Carpy guides the boat to the left of what Doctor Rod explains is a large island. We pass under a long suspension bridge that connects the island to the mainland.

Doctor Rod jumps up. "Montmorency Falls." A foamy waterfall, stark white against the blue sky, is a half mile up a small tributary to our port side. Doctor Rod has a dreamy look in her eyes. "I just love waterfalls."

"Is that where we're going?" I ask. "Mont . . . Mont . . . waterfalls? Why are we going there?"

"Not these falls," Doctor Rod says. "But don't worry, Chris. You'll get to visit a waterfall soon enough."

I think back to Yellowstone, where Scotty and I swam underneath those waterfalls, hiding from Big Mac. I wish I could be back on vacation again with Karen and Scotty, relaxed, without a worry in the world. "I don't care about waterfalls. I just want to know where we're going, why, and when we're gonna get there."

Doctor Rod points to the island. "Our destination. The Ile d'Orleans. We have arrived."

We continue along between the island and the mainland for several miles until we reach the point where the two branches of the river meet up again, and the island ends. We come around the point and motor for a short while until we pull up to an old, rickety dock. There's nothing around but forest. If this is the plan, I am not impressed.

Captain Carpy puts down the plank, and I walk out onto the dock. Doctor Rod and Derek follow me. "So now what?" I say.

There's a loud clang. "Look out!" Derek shouts.

Little Joe is in the golf cart, barreling down the plank straight for us.

Derek has already reacted. He jumps off the dock, pushing Doctor Rod and me along with him. We fall at once, splashing into the cold St. Lawrence water.

Captain Carpy pulls the boat away. He stares at us without a hint of emotion on his face. "I never saw you. I hope never to see you again." He hits the throttles and rumbles off.

I lead Doctor Rod and Derek out of the water and onto the shore, shivering. Little Joe stands next to the golf cart, laughing maniacally. "I thought for a second you all were going to drown," he laughs.

Little Joe badgers us relentlessly to let him drive us in the golf cart. We are too tired to argue with him, and he gets his way. He drives us across a shoreline road and then onto a deserted gravel road toward the center of the island. Derek and I stand in the golf bag spots and lean over to hear Doctor Rod talking.

"The Ile de Orleans is about twenty miles long and eight miles wide," she explains. "It is broken into six municipalities, each anchored by a beautiful church."

"Have we come here to pray?" I say.

"We can keep trying churches until we find one that works," Derek says.

"We've come here to hide," Doctor Rod says.

This surprises me. The bridge we had gone under on the other side of the island had been full of cars, and the small towns and churches we'd seen while going around the island in the boat looked crowded with tourists.

Little Joe swerves the cart, aiming for a rabbit darting across the road.

"We will not be sightseeing," Doctor Rod says. "Where we will be going, the island is deserted. You can do all the praying you want, but it won't be in a church."

With that, the road ends. Little Joe fishtails the car and it stops.

We stand before a formidable wrought iron gate. A tall chain-link fence with a barbed wire top extends to the left and right as far as I can see. The main gate post is made of stone, and on top of it stands a black iron decorative maple leaf. Beyond it, all I can see are trees.

"Help me out, will you, Derek?" Doctor Rod says.

Even with his sore shoulder, Derek effortlessly lifts Doctor Rod up to the maple leaf. She touches something on the leaf's side, and it spins around. She looks intently into it with a big smile on her face as the gates open.

We hop back on the golf cart, and Little Joe continues our drive. The gates shut behind us. We are in the middle of a maple leaf forest. Many of the trees are tapped with metallic buckets.

"A maple syrup farm," Doctor Rod says.

"I love maple syrup," Little Joe says.

After a mile, in the midst of the maple leaf forest, we come to a single-story wooden building. It's a long, rectangular shack. Vertical planks of cedar, unpainted and weatherworn, have been nailed together haphazardly into walls and an overhanging roof. Steam rises from the backside of the building, and we walk around to investigate. An old man, skinny and coarse like a strong tree limb, stirs a vat of boiling sap with a long wooden ladle.

Doctor Rod walks toward him. "James."

He looks up and opens his hands wide. "Careful. I'm sticky."

"As always." Doctor Rod embraces James wholeheartedly, not caring whether he is sticky or not. James smiles and holds his hands away to protect her from the sap.

A door slams behind us. A skinny older woman, a perfect complement to James, walks toward Doctor Rod.

"Ella." Doctor Rod and Ella hug. "Been a long time," Doctor Rod says.

After introductions are made, James and Ella open an old, rickety door and welcome us into their shack. We are in a small room with a couch and wood-burning stove. It seems comfortable enough, but I can't imagine anyone out here surviving the winter, or even a thunderstorm.

James, Ella, and Doctor Rod are talking at once, catching up like true friends.

"Anything or anybody new we should know about?" Ella says coyly.

Doctor Rod scoffs. "Why do you always have to ask me that?"

"Because someday I hope you will say yes."

"We just want you to be happy," James says.

"Work makes me happy," Doctor Rod says. "How's the work here? Keeping busy?"

"Ahead of schedule," James says.

"That's good to hear," Doctor Rod says.

I wonder why Doctor Rod is interested in their syrup schedule. Perhaps she's just being polite and making small talk. Ella catches me watching them. "We'll be ready to deliver this year's first batch of syrup next week," she says loudly.

I lean over to Derek and say in a whispering hiss, "This is the plan? We're going to make maple syrup with a couple of old Canucks?"

"We Canucks make a lot more than maple syrup here," James says, overhearing.

"I'm sorry. I didn't mean anything by—"

"We're on the same side, Chris Thompson. I don't need any apology. Save it for when you do something really stupid. For example, when you call your wife collect from a strip club."

Clearly, James knows about my last mission.

"Or when you kiss sorority girls on YouTube," Derek says.

"She kissed me. I was a victim of circumstance in both of those cases."

Derek laughs. "You're a victim of a lot of circumstances."

The victim of my own doing, I guess. Why did I ever want to be a spy? After ten years, my application to the CIA has come back to haunt me. What a joke. But I don't think any of it is funny anymore.

"Are we going to do something about Big Mac, Scotty, and Karen?" I ask. "Or are we just going to sit around all day and make maple syrup?"

"Let's make pancakes," Little Joe says.

Ella smiles at little Joe. "I can make you pancakes, sweetie."

"Pancakes?" I can't believe it. "Pancakes! Pancakes!"

Doctor Rod nods to James. "Show him."

Ella puts her arms around Little Joe. "Let's say you and I get started on those pancakes."

Little Joe seems surprised, but then warms to the affection. "Okay."

Ella leads Little Joe outside. "The first step is checking

some buckets for sap. Will you help me?"

Little Joe seems mesmerized by her. "Okay."

Behind the couch, there are some family photos hanging on a paneled wall. As soon as Little Joe is gone, James pulls the couch away from the wall. He removes one of the photos, turns a latch, and pushes on the panels, opening a hidden door.

Okay. So more than making syrup is going on here. What could Doctor Rod be up to? Is this some sort of safe house? We've come a long way to get here, and I'd better see something useful to help save Scotty or Karen. If this place is just a shack to hide from Big Mac in, I plan on leaving soon.

We follow James through the door. The wall behind the panels is two feet of thick concrete. The room—or building, possibly—could withstand a hurricane, and for sure a Canadian winter.

James closes the door behind us. We're standing in a small, brightly lit room. Two flat-panel TV screens are on one wall. The other walls are covered with scientific charts and data. James moves the mouse at the computer and taps some keys. An image of Times Square comes up on one of the monitors. "This is a hidden webcam CSIS has let us tap into." He presses another button. "Take a look at this footage we captured yesterday."

Times Square is bustling with traffic and people as usual, but for one big difference. A driney hovers ominously behind each person.

"Watch closely," James says.

Derek, Doctor Rod, and I lean in closer to the screen. We watch as a man wanders out into the middle of traffic, shouting at the cars. He is inebriated, or possibly mentally deranged. His driney circles around his head, stops in front of his eyes, and flutters back and forth, as if it is warning him. The man swats at the driney. The driney circles around to his side, backs up a few feet, and then in an instant, dives into his ear.

"Whoa," Derek says. "Did that just—?"

"Yes," James says. "The driney flew inside his head through his ear."

James moves the mouse and replays the video in slow motion. We watch at slow speed as the driney again circles around and dives into the man's ear. James returns the video to full speed. The man stumbles and falls to the ground, apparently dead.

"They come for him," James says. "They zip him up into a body bag and throw him into the back of a garbage truck."

On the other television screen I see Vance Slater talking, but we can't hear him. "Special Election in Five Days" reads a banner on the screen.

"The United States is having a special election," James explains. "A vote on whether or not to cede all power to the Big Mac party."

"The people won't vote for that," Derek says.

"I bet somehow they will," Doctor Rod says.

"Oh, they will. They've learned very quickly," James says.

"Learned what?" Derek asks.

"The power of the driney," I say.

James nods. "That's about it. Anybody says anything against the Big Mac party, and—"

Derek slaps his hands. "It's a driney in the ear."

"Nobody in their right mind will even think about voting against Big Mac," Doctor Rod says.

I risked my life and my family to defeat Big Mac at Emergence only to have them come back stronger. The drineys have given them power. The double-edged sword of technology—freedom versus control—has cut through to the wrong side. I wonder if Karen and Scotty each have a driney assigned to them, ready to kill them at the slightest mistake they make.

"We have to get rid of the drineys." Furious, I grab a glass paperweight from the desk. I shake it fiercely, forgetting about my strength, and I crush it with my hand. Glass shatters and flies in all directions.

Watching the glass splintering reminds me of nuseum activating.

"The nuseum," I say. "We have to get a shitload of nuseum, shake it like hell, and get rid of the drineys."

As soon as I say it, my heart sinks. The idea is futile. How could we possibly activate enough nuseum to take down every driney in the country?

Doctor Rod gets a sly smile on her face. "Good plan, Chris. That's exactly what we are going to do."

Sugar Shack

"ARE YOU JOKING?" I say. "Even if we had enough nuseum, I just don't see how we can disable every driney in the country."

Doctor Rod again gets that smug smile on her face, like she is going to show me up again. She's starting to irritate me. "Shall we show him the next room, James?"

What could they possibly come up with in this sugar shack in the middle of nowhere? "Yes, please, show me. What's behind door number two?"

James opens up the next door, and we follow him in.

Derek snickers. "This is kind of fun. Reminds me of going room to room in one of those roadside mystery houses. I sure would like to get some maple syrup, though. You like maple syrup, CT?"

"Shut up—don't be a sap."

We walk down a metal stairway into a brightly lit two-story room, partially submerged in the ground. The room is large. Very large. There is a semitruck and trailer before us, and there are vats, tanks, and chemical processing equipment. It's a modern scientific manufacturing center.

"I think I know where I can get some maple syrup." Derek hurries over to the semitruck. On the flatbed trailer is a giant oak barrel with a logo that says "James and Ella's Isle de Orleans Homemade Maple Syrup." There are drawings of maple syrup jugs and maple trees. Derek pats his hand against the barrel. "Aunt Jemima time, baby."

We walk down and stand in front of the oak barrel. Derek walks back and forth, looking up at it with hungry eyes. He laughs. "Sap. I get it."

The barrel is tied down with straps. The truck looks ready to roll. "This, this giant barrel is our—"

"Our plan? It sure is," Doctor Rod says.

I look around at all the scientific equipment in the room. "You've been making nuseum, haven't you? The barrel is filled with nuseum."

Derek's face drops, as if the ice cream truck has just ignored him and driven away. "No maple syrup?"

Doctor Rod walks over to a machine that looks like an MRI scanner. "We shoot the nuseum into this mini-accelerator until it becomes slightly unstable. I won't bore you with the scientific details." She walks over to some large cylindrical tanks. "We then process the unstable nuseum into a somewhat solid form, which, Derek and Chris, you have already seen work in the pill form."

"Really? No maple syrup?" Derek says.

"My work for the president was top secret. I had access to

funds to use as I saw fit. I knew of the potential driney problem a long time ago. This maple syrup farm hidden in Canada is my solution to that problem."

I walk completely around the semi and the barrel. "This is the answer to the problem? How are we going to shake it? How are we going to save Scotty and Karen?" The smell of oak from the barrel permeates the room, but I can also smell a faint bit of maple syrup. I turn around and see a tank with a spigot and shelves of plastic half-gallon bottles that have the James and Ella Isle de Orleans maple syrup company logo.

"We shake it. Just like you said," Doctor Rod says with an excited gleam in her eyes.

"I bet you can just drive this truck over a bumpy road. Will that do the trick?" Derek asks.

"No," Doctor Rod says. "We're going to let Mother Nature do the work for us. And when I say Mother Nature, I mean waterfalls." Doctor Rod looks at me, waiting for my reaction.

I grab a plastic jug, walk around the truck to join the others, and shove the maple syrup into Derek's gut. "Waterfalls," I say.

"Pancakes," a voice says. It's Little Joe. He and Ella are standing at the top of the stairs with a platter stacked with pancakes.

"Get him out of here," I yell. "This is top secret."

Little Joe looks around and then glares at me suspiciously. "Top secret syrup?"

Derek laughs. "Yes." He walks toward Little Joe holding up his jug. "Let's go eat some pancakes."

We sit outside on a long, rickety picnic bench. Derek and

Little Joe happily eat pancakes as fast as they can. Derek has them stacked five high, syrup completely covering them like frosting on a cake. Little Joe eats them one at a time, a fork in one hand and pouring syrup on them with the other. He sets the syrup down only to grab another pancake, and then he resumes his indulgence.

There is an engine noise. James comes around the building. He's riding on a red Honda four-wheeler. He wears an open-face helmet on his head and clutches another in his arm. James pulls up next to us. "What do you say, Little Joe. Want to go for a ride?"

"Would I?" Little Joe shoves half the pancake left on his plate into his mouth and jumps up.

"Oh no, I don't think so." Ella reaches out and touches little Joe's shoulder and tries to hold on to him, but he is too quick for her and runs toward James. "Those machines are too dangerous."

James hands Little Joe the helmet. "Psh. He'll be fine." He turns the four-wheeler around. "Follow me, Little Joe. We have another one of these babies in the shed."

James and Little Joe disappear behind the main building.

"Little Joe's not the best of drivers," Derek says.

"He could kill himself on one of those things," Ella says.

We hear another motor start, and soon James and Little Joe come racing by us and head down a path into the forest.

Doctor Rod walks around the table picking up empty plates. "Maybe that wouldn't be such a bad thing, you know, if Little Joe had a little accident."

"You can't be serious, Michelle," Ella says.

"Who is Michelle?" I say.

"Michelle Rodriguez," Derek says. "Doctor Rod."

196

"Oh, yeah?"

Doctor Rod ignores us. She looks deadly serious. "Little Joe is too dangerous. I'm starting to think the president was right when he wanted to shoot him. We could eliminate one of Big Mac's future hopes right here."

"But he's just a child," Ella says. "He's simply adorable."

"We have to do what is best for the country," Doctor Rod says.

"I'm a scientist, not a murderer."

"And I'm a scientist too." Doctor Rod picks up Ella's plate. "But we work for the United States of America."

Ella stands up, clutching a knife and fork in each hand like weapons. "If the United States of America is going to condone killing an innocent boy, then we are no better than Big Mac, and I want no part of it."

I think of all the innocent boys and young women that Big Mac killed with the secret Emergence program. And to defeat that evil, I had to kill a not-so-innocent young man. The image of X-ray charging and the bullet from my gun splattering into his forehead still haunts me. I had no choice. Would I do it again? Yes, and to think that I may have to kill again makes me angry. I slam my fist into the picnic table, smashing it in two.

"Chris. Whoa, dude." Derek rolls off the tilted bench. He clutches at my leg. "What's going on?"

I look at Doctor Rod. "Nobody is going to hurt little Joe."

The wind picks up and low gray clouds skim over the island from the west. Derek and I resume our training. I dash around the trees and swing up into their branches while Derek shoots at me with rubber darts from his iPhone.

Ella and Little Joe play bocce ball, back and forth between the shack and the kettle of boiling sap. Little Joe bowls his ball and knocks Ella's out of the way. He cheers, and she laughs.

Three rubber iPhone darts hit me in the side of the head. Derek pumps his fist. "Eliminated. You're slowing down, CT."

I point at the bocce ball game. "I was distracted."

Doctor Rod comes out of the shack. She and James have been making final adjustments to the nuseum barrel. James joins the bocce ball game, coaching Ella on her form.

The semitruck emerges from the far end of the shack. The gears grind, and it slowly moves up the inclined drive. Doctor Rod is driving, and she pulls it around to the front gravel road, stopping before Derek and me. She hops out. "Time to go, superheroes."

I pick up the rubber darts from the ground and hand them back to Derek. "I wish we had some real superheroes to fight against Big Mac."

"We're super spies with super weapons. We got this, CT."

Doctor Rod walks toward Derek and me. She points her thumb back to the truck. "Only two bucket seats in the cab. You two have to ride in the back."

"Back where?" I say.

"There's room for you two in the barrel. Let's go. We have a long drive, and I want to drop this thing over the falls before daylight."

"The falls are just over the bridge," I say. "Why don't we wait for dark? We can make a quick clandestine drop and be back within an hour or two."

Doctor Rod scoffs at me. "Montmorency Falls don't have enough power to destabilize the nuseum."

"What falls do?" I ask, and then I realize the answer. Doctor Rod smiles. "Yes. Niagara Falls."

Emigrants

"NIAGARA FALLS." I try to calculate how far away that is. "That's like a, a—"

"A ten hour drive," Doctor Rod says. "So let's go. Just like we planned. James and I will sit up front. You two super spies ride in the barrel."

Derek and I look at each other. On our last mission, we had been lassoed together by a wire and were forced to sleep together on the bottom bed of a bunk. He looks at the barrel with a wary eye. "How much maple syrup is in there? That could get a little sticky."

"None," Doctor Rod hisses. "The nuseum is around the outside, where it will receive more force. There will be plenty of room for you two."

"What about Little Joe?" I say. "We can't leave him here

with Ella."

Doctor Rod looks over to where James, Ella, and Little Joe continue to enjoy their game. "Sure we can. They're getting along great. This place is secret, safe, and I think they'll be happy," Doctor Rod says.

I stretch my arms over my head, and Derek backs up a few steps. "What's the plan for the Thompson family to be safe and happy?"

Doctor Rod's face softens. She puts her hand on my shoulder. "Relax. We won't forget your family. But first we drop the barrel over Niagara. A rescue operation will be much easier with the drineys disabled. It may not even be necessary if Big Mac loses the election."

I have to admit her logic is right. I just get flustered when I think about Scotty and Karen in danger because of me. "Okay. Let's go."

We are on the road. Doctor Rod and James are in the cab, taking turns driving. Derek and I are in the barrel. It's actually not too bad at first. We're in a hollowed-out stainless steel cylinder, protected from the nuseum packed between us and the outer oak planks. It smells like tinfoil. There's enough room for us to lie down end to end, but it's also comfortable to sit along the curve, stretched into a half moon.

After two hours, we're not so comfortable anymore. We can't stand up, nor can we see outside. A small battery-powered lantern provides us light, but there is nothing to see but stainless steel and each other. Body odor fills our cylinder.

"Ever wonder what it would be like to be inside a pop

can?" Derek says.

"No."

"Well, now you know."

"I didn't want to know."

"Well, now you do."

"What's happening?"

The vibration from the road has stopped, and there's silence. The hatch opens and fresh air seeps in.

"Thank God," Derek says.

Doctor Rod pokes her head in.

"Are we there?" I ask.

"No," she says. Derek and I groan. "Shut up," she whispers, and she motions us out. "We're outside of Toronto. Couple more hours to go. Quick break and we're on our way."

Derek and I climb out and stretch our legs. It's two in the morning, dark and cool. We are resting in a Walmart parking lot. A few RVs are parked on the other side of the Walmart gas station from us, but all is quiet.

We take turns guarding the truck and using the gas station restroom.

"All set?" James says.

Just then, there's a screech of tires in the distance. A small Toyota pickup truck swerves into the parking lot and races toward us. Men fill the back cab. One stands, holding an American flag. He screams what only can be described as a rebel yell.

"Let's move," Doctor Rod shouts, but it is too late. The truck skids to stop next to us. The men are young, scraggly in blue jeans and T-shirts.

"Y'all hiring?" one of them says, pointing at the logo of the maple syrup company.

"No. We're leaving," Doctor Rod says.

"We just left." The flag bearer waves the flag. "And now we're free."

"No more drineys," another shouts.

"We're good workers," the flag bearer says. "We need to find jobs before the others get here. So do you know of anything?"

"No. I'm sorry," I say. "But what do you mean, before the others get here?"

"The wall is open."

A ragged man in overalls stands up. "We is emigrants."

"For the next two days, emigrating is legal. Big Mac haters and anyone else is free to leave the United States," the flag bearer says.

"There's a mad rush of freedom lovers like us a comin' through," one says.

"They closed the wall to people wanting to leave?" I say.

"We've been discriminated against," the overalls man says. "Wanting to leave has been illegal for days. They call us illegal emigrants."

"And wallbacks," the flag bearer says.

"Because they walked under the wall," Derek explains to me. "Get it?"

"I got it."

Doctor Rod looks worried. "But now that you're here, you won't be able to vote against Big Mac in the election."

"Lady," the flag bearer says. "The drineys have control. Nobody is voting against Big Mac."

A parking light flickers and then goes out, casting a darkness over our conversation. We wish the emigrants well and they tear off in their Toyota.

"Time to go," Doctor Rod says.

"Niagara Falls," Derek says.

"Step by step. Inch by inch. Slowly I turn." I laugh at my joke that only I seem to understand.

Little Joe

I'M IN A secret terrorist camp for sure, but I'm having a blast.
I'm going to stick around a little bit longer, I think.

They make maple syrup here, and pancakes. Ms. Ella
showed me how to cook. I made pancakes for everyone, and
they liked them. But that's not the best thing. They have a four-
wheeler. I can drive it and go as fast as I want and wherever I
want. As long as I stay inside the fence of the camp, that is.

They are all terrorists and Chris Thompson is planning
something against Big Mac, exactly like Scotty said. They have a
scientific laboratory hidden under a cabin. They're making a
bomb for sure, I think. I'm going to figure out what it is. Then
I'll be a hero to Big Mac and the United States. Scotty might
not be so happy if I turn in his dad, but he can still be my
friend. I bet if he stays with me he will learn to think like me

and be on Big Mac's team. Scotty's smart, not like his dad and his friends. He'll see the truth sooner or later.

Ms. Ella plays games with me, like bocce ball and other things. She's super nice. I wish she could be my mom.

Centripetal Force

"NICE MORNING FOR a barrel ride," Doctor Rod says.

We are standing on the Canadian shore of the Niagara River, about a mile from the falls. It is early morning, and dark. The ever-present wall, lit up from the glow of the laser-grid reaching into the sky, looms over us from the United States border. We don't use any lights, and even with the gleam from the wall, it is difficult to see.

"Some of them crazy barrel riders actually make it," Derek says.

I step back from the water. The current is fast and makes me nervous. "Let's roll this baby in and scram."

James laughs, as if he knows more than I do. He is behind us atop a small bank standing next to the truck. A cool mist floats over the water and dampens our skin. A distant rumble, constant and ominous, sounds from the falls.

We loosen the straps and use them for leverage to gently lower the barrel to the ground. One strap holds it back from rolling down the bank and into the water. I reach down and grab the fastener, ready to pull. "Shall we?"

Doctor Rod clamps my wrist with her hand. "Wait. There's something we have to do. A key element to ensure that the nuseum activates."

"Do we set in on fire?" Derek asks, with the enthusiasm of a kid waiting for a fireworks display.

Doctor Rod touches the faux maple syrup barrel's side. "The barrel needs added centripetal force when it crashes. Otherwise, there won't be enough energy to activate the nuseum."

"How about dynamite?" Derek says, rubbing his hands together. Derek must have a thing for fiery explosions I didn't know about. He's a former marine and has proved himself adept with all sorts of firearms. Perhaps he is skilled with bombs and grenades and such too.

"How about we just nuke it?" I say.

"That would work," Doctor Rod says.

"Like there are just nukes lying around," Derek says.

"We were just trying to diffuse Buster Alpha a few weeks ago," I say. "Our having a nuke seems about as likely as our carting around a load of dynamite."

"Are you nuts?" Derek says. "Do you know how easy it is to obtain dynamite versus a—"

"Boys." Doctor Rod says. "Shut up. This is a stupid conversation. We're not going to explode anything. We're going to have to spin the barrel to obtain the centripetal force."

I reach down for the latch again. "Okay. Let's spin this

baby into the water."

"No," Doctor Rod says.

James laughs, a superior laugh, like he's known all along what is coming.

Doctor Rod opens the top hatch. "We're going to spin it from the inside."

Derek gets a petrified look on his face. "But, but—"

"Yes," Doctor Rod says. "You, Chris, and I are going over the falls."

"Not me," I say.

James points inside the barrel, almost gleefully. "You get on your hands and knees and spin it like running hamsters."

"Why don't you spin it like a hamster then, if you're so excited about it?" I say.

Doctor Rod looks at Derek and me. "We're the spies here. We have the training. It's up to us to carry out this mission."

I don't particularly like waterfalls, and I certainly have no inclination to go over Niagara Falls in a barrel. "I have no training in spinning barrels or jumping waterfalls. I'm not doing it."

"Be a man," Doctor Rod says. "You work for the executive branch. You took an oath to protect your country."

"The country I took an oath to no longer exists."

"Yeah, be a man," Derek says.

What? I look to Derek. I thought he'd be on my side, but I can see that he has gathered his courage and is looking to impress Doctor Rod. I'm now outnumbered. "My commitment is to Karen and Scotty. Taking a barrel over Niagara Falls is a death wish. I can't die on them."

"Your country is more important than your family," Doctor Rod says.

"Is it? Really? How many kids do you have?"

Doctor Rod takes a threatening step toward me, but Derek puts an arm around her.

"It's partly your fault Slater has Scotty and Karen, Chris. Come on, man. We can do this."

"And you have the bionified arm," James says. "You're the most important one."

Damn it. Of all the crazy ideas, going over the falls has to be the worst. I think back to all the daydreaming I used to do about James Bond and wanting to be some super-spy. What a stupid idiot I was. A steady job, a nice family, a simple life— that's the American dream. That's what I want. Was I some kind of egomaniac to want any more; to think that I deserved any more? And why do I even care about Big Mac anyway? America will probably be a safer place with them in power. I obey all the laws. I'm a good citizen. The drineys will never bother me. Only the real criminals will have to worry.

"Come on, Chris." Derek is looking at me, as if he can't believe I would be having doubts.

And then I remember: Derek is black. How would he fare under Big Mac? I think about Big Mac clamping down on Mexican-sounding businesses when we were in Arizona, trying to make the neighborhoods more "American." I think about Walter being tortured, and the innocent young men and women being killed at Emergence. Sure, I'd probably be fine under Big Mac, but at what cost to my conscience? Fear of going over the falls in a barrel is causing me to have doubts. If I die, I die. If I live, at least I have tried to do what I thought right. Whatever happens, I will feel free.

"Okay." I tuck my shirt into my jeans. "Let's do it."

Doctor Rod nods and smiles at me politely.

Derek, on the other hand, is looking scared again. I think he was counting on me to keep protesting, or perhaps he is just realizing that we're actually going to do this.

"It will be pitch-dark in there," Derek says.

Doctor Rod reaches in her pocket and cracks a small glow stick. She tosses it inside the barrel.

"Do we all have to go?" Derek says. "Chris could spin it just as fast by himself."

"We're a team. We all go." Doctor Rod holds Derek by the elbow. "You first."

Derek shoots me a look like, what the fuck? He ducks his head and climbs into the barrel.

"You're in the middle with your arm." Doctor Rod ushers me in. I think she had Derek and me go in first just to make sure that we would.

I climb in and sit next to Derek. I shrug my shoulders at him like, oh well, here we go again.

Doctor Rod climbs in. "Once we hit the water, we will have ten minutes before we reach the falls."

James looks inside. "Ready?"

"Release us in one minute," Doctor Rod says.

"Will do. Good luck and Godspeed." James closes the lid.

Doctor Rod looks at her watch and presses a button on it. "Prepare yourselves."

My body is completely tense. I don't know what to do to prepare myself.

There's a soft katunk, and then we roll. Around and around we tumble. Derek yells. There's a thud and then a floating feeling. We rock, but our weight stabilizes the barrel, and we no longer spin.

"Nine minutes and we start spinning," Doctor Rod says.

"I don't feel so good," Derek says.

The dim glow stick makes us all look green. This is the most disorienting boat ride I have ever been on. "Uh, yeah. Me too."

"Shut up, you pansies, and concentrate," Doctor Rod says. "Think about how fast you're going to spin this barrel."

We continue toward the falls, floating haphazardly in an uncomfortable motion. I think back to how I got sick on that DC-10 when Fixer flew us into zero G, and then again on the Osprey. I have to concentrate, like Doctor Rod says.

I press my face against the cool metal. I think about Scotty and Karen and tell them I love them, trusting my message to whatever mystical power can transport it through the cosmos.

"One minute." Doctor Rod positions herself on her hands and knees. "Ready?"

Derek and I position ourselves. "Ready," I say.

"Boohah," Derek says.

"Spin," Doctor Rod says.

We start crawling like hamsters, and the barrel slowly moves around us.

"Faster," Doctor Rod says.

We crawl faster. Derek is huffing. Some water has seeped in and the metal is slippery. A roar from outside is getting loud enough to hear. The barrel still floats, but now it reverberates with the sound from the falls.

"Faster. Now. As fast as you can go, Chris."

I put all my strength into the bionified arm, pawing the barrel as fast as I can to make it spin. My bionified arm is revolving our tin can prison so rapidly that my other arm cannot keep up, and I look like a one-armed hamster. The spinning metal pulls on my jeans until they slide down my legs, exposing my boxer-brief underwear. My legs no longer move. My knees press against my jeans as the barrel interior spins under them. I continue to claw away with one arm.

Derek screams and then vomits. "Fuck."

"I can't keep up," Doctor Rod says. "Don't stop."

As the barrel spins faster, Doctor Rod and Derek falter and collapse. Pressed against the interior, they revolve around and around like they're on a nightmare version of the floor-dropping rotor ride at a carnival.

I keep my arm going, spinning faster and faster. The roar from the approaching falls becomes louder and louder. Derek's vomit covers everything in slippery slime; its foul odor fills the container. Everything goes black. The glow light has either gone out or it's covered by Derek and Doctor Rod's spinning bodies. But still, I spin.

And then the rocking stops. Gravity disappears, and we float inside the barrel. Panic shoots up my nerves from my stomach and into my throat. We are falling.

Trust

WE ARE IN the pitch-black, sound-deafening roar of a free fall. My mind is blank. I should say a prayer or think about my life, or about Karen and Scotty, but nothing.

Without any thought I say, "Mom."

Boom. My shoulder and back absorb a terrific force. We flip, turn, and tumble. The thundering sound from the falls continues unabated. There's a loud creaking that sounds like bending metal. Is that the nuseum activating, exploding out into the air? Or is it just the barrel collapsing, about to smash us to bits? Derek, Doctor Rod, and I collide against each other in a melee of arms, legs, heads, and bodies. Water is rushing in from the hatch. I think we are going to die.

And then the tumult ends. We are floating again. We have survived the falls, but we're far from being out of danger.

Water continues to flow in.

If we die, I can only hope that this crazy plan has worked, that the nuseum has activated, that Scotty and Karen will be set free.

"Open the hatch," I say.

"I can't move," Doctor Rod says.

I feel around. Doctor Rod and Derek are now below my legs. I reach up and touch the hatch. I unlatch and push, but I can't open it. Water pours in more. Do I try and hold the hatch shut to stop the water, or do I open the hatch and let the water in until the pressure equalizes and we can escape? As long as we're still floating, which is only an assumption, stopping the water from coming in seems the best option. I use my bionified arm to pull on the hatch in an attempt to tighten it. The water coming in slows to a trickle.

"Everyone okay?" I say.

"I'm okay," Doctor Rod says in a weak voice.

Derek says nothing.

I give a wake-up whistle. "Derek. What's going on, man?"

"He has a heartbeat," Doctor Rod says. "But he's out cold."

Thud. We lurch, and it feels like we've stopped. I release my hold on the hatch, and water no longer flows in. I try to open it, but it is still stuck. The metal around it is misshapen, and the damage must be holding it closed.

I put my palm on the hatch and push hard with my bionified arm. The hatch flies open. Cool air rushes in, followed by water. I stick my head out. We are wedged against a rock on an angle, but the hatch is partially submerged. We are close to the American side of the falls. The FUC Wall fills my vision. Spotlights from the wall randomly crisscross the water, but they never stop on us.

The barrel shifts and more water flows in. "We have to go," I say.

"Derek's still out."

"He'll drown soon if he stays here."

"You go." I help Doctor Rod climb out the hole. She swims and holds on to the barrel. I crawl back inside. I grab Derek under the arm.

"Come on, Cannonball. You can explode at any time, right? Where's your spark?"

Derek doesn't react.

"Okay, Big Boy, you'll be all right."

I lift him onto my shoulder. I wedge my feet against the side and slowly climb. I push Derek's head out of the hole. I position my shoulder and arm under his body as Doctor Rod helps guide him from the outside. It's a struggle, but we get him out.

Doctor Rod is holding on, struggling to keep Derek from floating away. "Hold him," she commands me. "He's too heavy for me."

I reach out and grab hold of Derek by his shirt back. His face momentarily ducks into the water, but Doctor Rod and I swing him around. I hold him by the arm. Doctor Rod cups his head out of the water so he can breathe.

I climb out. Doctor Rod and I hold on to Derek and the hatch, our bodies dangling in the water. The outer wood planks and the nuseum are now gone. All that remains is the metal container.

"We have to swim for it," Doctor Rod says.

"Which side, American or Canadian?"

"Don't be stupid. If we want to be free, we have to stay in

Canada."

Derek is heavy, and Doctor Rod and I struggle to get him into a good position. We each hold him under an arm. I use my bionified arm to swim, and soon I have such a powerful paddle going that I am able to drag both Derek and Doctor Rod along with me.

We swim for the Canadian side, away from the United States and the FUC Wall, and we have perhaps a couple hundred yards ahead of us. I didn't see any sparkles in the air, but I know that they disappear quickly. More disconcerting, though, is that I haven't smelled any sulfur. Perhaps I am too close to the water, or perhaps I've been too busy to notice. The current is swift, and as we make our way across we drift downstream. The bank approaches, and when we reach it, I quickly pull Derek out and lay him down on the rocky embankment.

I stand shivering in my underwear, water dripping off me.

Doctor Rod leans over Derek. She puts her ear against his chest and then nods to me. "I think he's okay. He should come around soon. But we all need to warm up, or hypothermia could set in." She puts her palm on Derek's cheek and looks at him with affection. She turns her head and looks at me. "He admires you, you know."

"I admire him. I'd be dead if it weren't for him. He's a good friend, too, you know."

"Spies aren't supposed to have friends. Your friendship is a weakness."

Derek and I have been through a lot together. We are still going through a lot. He's a great warrior, but more than that, he's a good, selfless man who tries to do what is right. "We're more than friends; we're a team. And we may have unorthodox tactics, but together we have fought our way out of some messes. We can be a powerful force—so don't try and mess with our friendship."

Doctor Rod stands up. "I wouldn't think of it. Just pointing out that trusting someone too much on your own team can be a weakness."

"Thanks," I say curtly. "But no worries, okay?"

She looks out over the water. "We have one major worry. It didn't work. The nuseum didn't activate."

I feared the same thing, but it's still hard to accept that all of our efforts failed. "I spun that barrel faster than humanly possible."

"We must have popped out of the falls too soon. We really needed to shake around underneath in that tumultuous water for a while." She points out over the water and waves her hand like she's trying to wash it all away. "There were no sparks."

"We could have missed them."

"We couldn't have missed the caramel-like sulfur smell. It would still be lingering, and it would smell horrendous."

So we've failed. Big Mac will take control. Doctor Rod was right about going to the Canadian side. I look over to America, but we are too close. Big Mac could be coming for us at this moment.

"So you think I'm a great warrior, huh?" Derek steps up behind me and puts his arms around us.

"Derek, oh thank goodness." Doctor Rod seems to melt out of her toughness and into a concerned and caring person. She gives him a hug.

"What? You were listening the whole time? We weren't even talking about you. I was talking about Archie."

"Archie my ass." Derek laughs and punches me.

Doctor Rod puts her hand over his eyes to check for concussion. "There's not enough light."

"Maybe you heard us talking about trust," she says, "as you were so sneakily eavesdropping."

Doctor Rod has removed her hand from Derek's eyes, but she still looks intently at him, almost lovingly. Is that possible?

Derek is staring back at her the same way. "I wasn't being sneaky. I could hear you, but I couldn't move, like I was in a dream . . ." He is speaking in a soft voice, and only to Doctor Rod. My God, I'm in the middle of some adventure romance.

"People," I say. "We have to go. We're in danger of succumbing to hypothermia."

"I feel warm," Derek says.

"I feel warm," Doctor Rod says.

What is happening? I look back over the river. We have come pretty far down from the Canadian falls, but the American falls are directly across from us. The colors in the sky are just starting to wake from the approaching sun. A constant rumble from both falls still encompasses all other sounds. We need to move before the daylight exposes us, but Derek and Doctor Rod seem to be falling in love right before my eyes.

"Yo. Love Ball and Dr. Cupid. When is James going to arrive?"

Derek and Doctor Rod reluctantly remove their attention from each other and look at me with irritation like, how could he be so rude?

"James?" Doctor Rod says. "I hope he is long gone by now."

I look around, exasperated. "Gone? What are we going to do? I assume you have a plan."

"The plan is to use our own resources to make our way

back," Doctor Rod says.

"Just great. So there is no plan."

"We're trained spies." Derek looks at Doctor Rod with that silly love-struck look he had just a moment ago. "And we've been trained by the best. We'll figure it out."

"I want to know how. We can't just keep looking at each other and magically save the universe."

"Eh?" a raspy voice says from behind us. "You all from Outer Space?"

Uncle Sam

FROM AMONGST THE small boulders and rocks, a person slowly stands up. It's an old, scraggly bum. He has wild, gnarled gray hair and a beard just as long to match. His skin is weathered and his clothes are in shambles. He carries a tattered old sleeping bag around his shoulders. He staggers toward us.

"Hello," I say.

"Other space creatures here," he says.

Derek looks around. "Where?"

The man points to a bridge. "The Rainbow Bridge. Space people, food, and fire." The man walks toward the bridge.

Derek and Doctor Rod start to follow.

"What are we doing?" I say.

"We need warmth," Doctor Rod says.

"We don't know who is up there," I say. "We could be

attacked."

Derek turns around and looks at me with a look that says, really? "Are you afraid of space people, CT?"

"CT, ET," the man says.

"Scotty and Karen are in danger. We have to go back and get Little Joe. He's our bargaining chip."

"And to do all that we have to escape Big Mac's eyes," Doctor Rod says. "We need to blend in. We need to disappear."

They are, of course, right, but I hate to admit it. I begrudgingly follow.

"Disappear," the man says.

Small trees and shrubs grow underneath the bridge. We climb upward, stepping around groups of sleeping people. The greenery eventually gives way to concrete, which we climb until we come close to a crossroad that passes under the bridge.

Men, women, even children are either sleeping or milling about makeshift fires. The bridge is at least four lanes wide, sufficient to provide some protection from the elements. The echoes from the falls and the cars overhead produce a peaceful, somewhat protective hum, a calming sound that creates the feeling that you are in a different and secret world.

The people are dressed in all manner of clothes, from ragtag bum outfits to designer label outdoor gear, but all of them look worn. There are American flags everywhere. It appears we have stumbled into a patriotic hobo camp.

"Welcome, friends." A tall white man with a long gray beard stands above us with his arms in the air. He holds a cane in one hand and waves an American flag in the other. He wears a tattered black tuxedo with tails and is wrapped with some type of large animal pelt for warmth. He's standing on the ledge directly under the bridge, and he looks down on us and everyone else below with an evangelical presence. "Renounce Big Mac and pledge your allegiance to a free America, and you may share our food and warmth." He smiles, and his pearly white teeth glisten pure in all the dark and gloom around us.

Derek raises his fist. "I pledge allegiance to a free America and renounce Big Mac."

"Me too," Doctor Rod says.

"I do," I say.

The man nods. "Make yourself comfortable. Each day you stay, though, you are expected to bring something to contribute: food, money, anything of value."

"Just passing through. We can only stop for a moment," I say.

Derek is rubbing his head. "I'm really tired, man."

"We need to recoup, regain our strength, and make a plan before we go," Doctor Rod says.

"I thought we had a plan," I say. "We go back and get Little Joe."

The old man who brought us here shuffles off. Uncle Sam walks down and puts an arm around Derek and me. He walks us over with Doctor Rod to a fire pit. "Make room," he bellows. We all sit down, the man's arm still around Derek and me. "I'm Uncle Sam. I'm the leader of the free north of the wall."

The fire warms us. I feel exhausted too.

"I hope you can join us in fighting the good fight against Big Mac."

"That's exactly what we want to do," Doctor Rod says.

"We fight in our own way," I say.

"Don't we all," Uncle Sam says. "But together, our ways can be powerful."

"Right on," Derek says.

"We have to be moving on," I say.

Uncle Sam stands up. "Think about it," he says.

A small girl hands us each a plastic bowl, and a woman following her dishes us out what I recognize to be Campbell's Double Noodle soup. Uncle Sam leaves us. Derek, Doctor Rod, and I eat in silence. I finish my soup. Derek has drifted off to sleep. I want to leave, but Derek was knocked out, and I admit he needs rest. I'm also having trouble keeping my eyes open. Someone must have taken my empty bowl. I slowly lean over onto the ground and fall asleep.

I'm on a fishing boat, not unlike the one in Jaws. I'm lying on a side bench out in the open, facing the stern. The sky is dark, and the boat rocks in tremendous waves. I'm wound up tightly in ropes from my shoulders down to my feet. I can't move.

I hear a maniacal laugh. Little Joe is up in the cockpit, driving the boat haphazardly.

"No."

It's Karen. She and Scotty are in the back of the boat. They are wrapped in nautical ropes, the same as me, but they are standing next to Slater. He has on a Hawaiian shirt and obscenely small gym shorts.

Slater takes a giant gatling hook with an attached line and

loops it under Karen's confining ropes. He takes a similar tackle and rigs up Scotty the same way. I struggle against my constraints, roll, and fall off the bench onto the cold, wet fiberglass floor.

Slater picks up Karen and tosses her into the sea.

I fight against my ropes and flounder like a doomed tuna. "Karen!"

"Bye, Dad. I love you."

Slater picks up Scotty.

"I love you, Scotty." I continue to flail around.

Slater tosses Scotty into the sea.

"You'll pay for this, you motherfucker."

Slater laughs. Little Joe laughs. Then Slater stands me up. Scotty and Karen are bobbing up and down, struggling for breath as the boat pulls them along. A dozen fins chase them.

"No."

A giant great white shark jumps out of the sea behind Karen, opens its wide jaws, and chomps her in half.

A fin approaches Scotty.

"Throw me in," I scream. I have no reason to live. I want to die with them.

Slater laughs. "No. You will have to watch and remember what you have done to them."

A great white lifts its head out of the water behind Scotty. I twist and thrash and try to roll in with him as it opens its jaws.

A sharp pain hits me in the side. I hear Scotty scream. Another sharp pain.

"Get off me."

I open my eyes. A bum is pounding his fist against me. "Get away. Get your own spot."

I try to move, but someone has wrapped me in a blanket, and my arms are constricted. During my nightmare, I have rolled into this fine gentleman and his territory.

I roll away and thrash around until I can free myself. I sit up, look over the Niagara River, and breathe a deep breath of the moist air.

The sun is now bright. A fine mist from the falls floats over the bridge and us. A rainbow has formed through the fine droplets and stretches over the river and into the falls. The sight fills me with hope. Scotty and Karen are still alive. I can still save them. We can still save them. We have to move. We have to make a plan.

Derek and Doctor Rod are sleeping together under one blanket, wrapped up together comfortably, like they have been a couple for years.

I shake them, and they slowly wake up.

"Let's go. We have to make a plan for how to get back."

They sit up and look at me groggily.

"We've made a plan," Derek says.

"Awesome. Lay it on me."

Doctor Rod puts her glasses on. "I'm getting old. I'm tired of this stupid game." She leans her head against Derek's shoulder. "I've finally found someone who can give me peace."

Derek smiles and kisses the top of her head. "We're in love, Chris."

"All this happened while I was asleep? Okay, okay, that's cool. We can deal with that. But what's the plan?"

Doctor Rod looks up toward Uncle Sam. He is standing, now pacing, and he looks to be proselytizing some of his wisdom to a small seated flock. "They are heading north tomorrow to start an American community in the Canadian wilderness," she says.

"Okay, so we scram tonight."

Derek stands up and puts his hand on my shoulder. "Chris, Michelle and I are going with Uncle Sam and his flock. Our fight is over. We want to live in peace."

I don't believe what I'm hearing from him.

"Uncle Sam? What about Scotty and Karen? What about the real Uncle Sam?"

"This is the real Uncle Sam," Doctor Rod says.

"What, why, how? Are you two together?"

Doctor Rod stands up and they put their arms around each other. "We were attracted to each other right from the start," she says.

"We've had our moments alone, and our attraction slowly built," Derek says. "You've just been too focused to notice."

"Yes. That's right. Because we have a job to do that you two apparently have forgotten, or have chosen to disregard, because—"

"Because we are in love," Doctor Rod says.

"And that's your excuse? Being in love absolves you of your responsibilities to your country? To your family? To your friends? Look, we need to get back to the Ile d'Orleans and the maple syrup farm. We can regroup and make a new plan."

"The election is in four days," Doctor Rod says. "Even if we do go back, we don't have enough nuseum to stop the drineys before that. I'm done playing this game for now." Doctor Rod looks at Derek. "We're both tired of it. We want a new life."

"We tried, Chris," Derek says, "but we failed. Big Mac is

too strong for just us to face right now. Uncle Sam has a plan to hide out in the Canadian wilderness, build a new American community, and return to fight Big Mac when we are better prepared."

"I'll have time to manufacture some more nuseum, or to think of a new weapon to fight with." Doctor Rod puts her head on Derek's shoulder. "And we can spend some peaceful time getting to know one another better."

"And Scotty and Karen?" I say.

"All of these people have suffered," Derek says. "You are free to go back and trade Little Joe for your family. I'm sure Slater will go for that."

"There's nothing more to do," Doctor Rod says. "Derek and I have no reason to return to the maple syrup farm. It's time to abandon ship, for everyone to do what's right for themselves."

Derek reaches out his hand to me. "I'm sorry, man."

I brush his hand away. "There's plenty to do." I turn and head up the embankment. I'm out of here.

"What are you going to do?" Derek calls.

I wave my hand like I'm pushing them away. "I'm getting some real help—some real friends. I'm calling the A-team."

"The Super Friends," someone shouts.

I continue walking. "Exactly." I look back to Doctor Rod and Derek. "Super friends."

McDonald's

I WALK INTO town. It seems every hotel and store has something to do with Niagara Falls tourism. I'm still in my underwear, but I have the blanket wrapped around me for a semblance of decency. I truly look a bum.

I notice something else. Almost every store has an American Flag with a circle and line through it. "NO JOBS FOR AMERICANS" it says. I continue on and pass more bums. The streets are filled with them: American refugees.

To keep my blanket around me, I can't help but walk awkwardly, stumbling even, completing my downtrodden persona. Normal Canadian citizens weave around me like I am a pothole. Some cast a disparaging look, as if they want to spit at me.

I see a Starbucks. Maybe some kind soul will let me use

their computer to send an email. I approach, but then I'm stopped by two large bouncers. One shoves me away. "Go back through the wall."

I thought these two were merely hanging around the entrance, but every store has a set of muscular types, assigned to keep us American bums out. And then, lo and behold, I see that oasis for Americans traveling abroad; a McDonald's.

I pick up my step and walk confidently toward the door that will lead me into the land of golden arches, efficient friendly service to all, and hopefully a kind patron who will assist me. I reach for the door, and then someone grabs my arm, and then my other arm.

"Not so fast."

Two Canadian oafs have come out of nowhere to thwart my pilgrimage into hamburger mecca. They wear black overcoats and black pants, and they sport crew cuts.

I plant my feet and try to hold my ground. "Hey. I'm going to buy coffee. I have a dollar. I'm a customer. You can't stop me."

"No wallbacks."

"This is illegal," I say. "You can't discriminate."

"We can and we will. Now go back where you came from, eh?"

They try to shove me off, but I push back. "Let me in."

My legs are kicked out from underneath me. I'm being dragged. One smiles down on me like I've made his day, like finding someone who resists is what he relishes about his job. They drag me around the side of the building and then into a deserted back alley.

"You wallbacks coming for our jobs," he says. "Lying, stealing, dishonest vermin."

"Like the Maple Leafs?" I say.

They stop walking. "Now you've done it."

Before I can respond I'm thrown against a wall. My comment struck home. A fist strikes me hard in the stomach, and I double over. The second guy is about to throw an uppercut to my face. I throw my left arm out, and with a quick jab I punch him in the side of the head. He collapses onto the ground, out cold.

The remaining oaf looks at his comrade with shock, but he is not deterred. He grits his teeth and throws a roundhouse left hook at my head. I block it with my right, and then in an instant I reach out with the bionified arm and grab his neck. I lift him off the ground, spin him around, and shove him against the wall, his feet dangling a foot from the ground. His face turns red, and he struggles to breathe.

I reach my other hand up toward him. "Cell phone."

He spits in my face and kicks at me.

I release his neck, and as he falls I give him two lightning-swift punches, one in the gut and then one in his side. I hear a crack. I tried to control my power, but I've broken some of his ribs. He falls to the ground and curls up in pain.

"Cell phone."

He reaches into his pocket and holds up his phone to me.

I clutch his arm and pull him up into a sitting position next to the wall. He groans and looks at me defiantly, and he starts to move as if he's going to stand up. I lean over and give him another quick punch, and then I squeeze his arm with a vice-like grip. "Stop. Please. Take the phone."

"You call for me." I tell him Wizkid's number. "Say these exact words: Liaison, Cannonball, in trouble. Gather help. Niagara Falls, Canada."

He calls. It seems like it takes forever, but he then says the words. "Liaison, Cannonball." And then he says, "Ow," and he holds the phone away from his ear to avoid the loud disco music that's playing. Over it, I can hear Wizkid shouting. "Thompson—that you?"

I yell into the phone. "Wizkid. It's me. Turn the music down. I need help."

I made the conscious bouncer go in and buy me twenty cheeseburgers while I waited for the other to wake up. When they both looked likely to survive, I scolded them about their bigotry toward Americans and apologized for my rough treatment of them.

I meander back to Rainbow Bridge. Everyone is up, milling about, packing bags and tents. The sun is low in the sky, and the evening's coolness has set in.

Doctor Rod and Derek sit talking with Uncle Sam by a fire. Uncle Sam looks at the McDonald's bag in my hand. "Something to contribute."

I hand the bag to Uncle Sam. "Mind if I have a word with my friends?"

"I'll pass these out." Uncle Sam takes the McDonald's bag and begins to distribute the cheeseburgers. "No Big Macs. That's good."

"We're leaving with Uncle Sam and his group in the morning," Doctor Rod says.

"We might start an American-style commune up in Saskatchewan," Derek says.

I just stare at them like a disappointed parent.

"Come join us," Doctor Rod says.

"Sometimes you just have to admit defeat," Derek says.

"Wizkid is coming," I say. "He saved us from being summarily executed outside of Atomic City, and now he can save us again."

Derek's eyes light up. "He saved us with a badass Black Hawk helicopter and a missile that sent that fat-ass Huey running." Derek laughs at the thought. "Wizkid."

Doctor Rod doesn't look impressed. "He's a chaotic misfit."

"That may be true, but with Wizkid, anything is possible. He can help us."

"Help, yes, but with what? I don't see him tearing down the wall and defeating Big Mac."

I don't know what I expect him to do, but I don't want to tell her that. "Why don't you take your obligations to your country seriously? Remember when you asked that of Derek and me? Remember?"

"I do remember, but that was when I still thought we had a chance."

"So we just give up when the odds are against us? That's your American spirit? Forget the Hail Mary? The last-second shot? The 1980 US hockey team? The . . . the—"

"Barrel over the falls," Derek says.

"A minor setback," I say.

Doctor Rod puts her hand on Derek. "Some things are more important than countries or political systems. When I saw Derek collapsed in the bottom of the barrel with water pouring in, I was scared. Love is what is most important, I realize now. I didn't want to lose Derek. I don't want to lose Derek. We want to be together, in peace, without worry or distraction."

Her mind is set. I don't know what else to say to her. "And that's what you feel, Derek, after all we've gone through?"

"That's what I feel," Derek says. "You and I have gone through a lot, I admit, but I don't think that obliges us to betray our dreams, or our pursuit of happiness."

"Pursuit of happiness," I mutter. I sit down next to them and wrap my blanket tight. "Look, Wizkid promised to meet us in the morning at some golf course called Thundering Waters. I'm going to meet him for sure." The sun has set and darkness is about us. I lie down and rest my head against some cardboard. "Think about it. Think about what's really important. Maybe you'll change your mind by morning." I close my eyes.

The morning comes, cool and gray. Uncle Sam and his group are on the move. We're walking—shuffling, more like—through the city of Niagara Falls, looking like some sort of zombie American protest.

"It's time to meet Wizkid," I say at last.

Derek and Doctor Rod don't say anything.

"So this is it?" I ask. "We're splitting up right here, in Canada, admitting defeat to Big Mac?"

"We're not admitting defeat," Doctor Rod says. "We're just regrouping."

"Taking a vacation, more like."

"Sorry, man," Derek says. "We just have to do it our way."

"Come with me to the golf course, Derek. It's just a few blocks over. At least just to say hello to Wizkid. You can catch up to this bunch later."

Doctor Rod whispers something to Derek.

"Derek?" I say. "We went through a lot with Wizkid."

Derek looks around at the slow-moving mob. "I wouldn't mind seeing Wizkid."

Derek and Doctor Rod are whispering more, almost arguing. "Ah, Michelle, it ain't like that," I hear him say.

"Fine," she says out loud. "Go say your goodbyes. No funny stuff. I'll wait for you for one hour, and then I'm catching up with Uncle Sam with or without you."

Derek and I break away and walk down Drummond Road. After a few minutes, we reach the Thunder Waters Golf Club, the scheduled meeting location.

We walk onto the golf course until we're standing between some trees on a fairway's edge. There's a small train yard, which is separated by a fence and a row of trees from the golf course. A cargo train's wheels screech as it slowly pulls to a stop behind us.

Derek looks up into the sky, searching. "Black Hawk? Apache? What do you think he'll arrive in?"

The clouds are low, and visibility is not great. "We'll hear him before we see him," I say.

We continue to search the skies.

"We can't be long," Derek says.

"A few more minutes," I say.

He doesn't seem worried. Overall, he seems more like his old self, and he's excited to see Wizkid. Perhaps he needed a day to recover from being knocked out.

"I may help you," a voice says in a Russian accent.

We turn and see a tough-looking, bald-headed man. He wears jeans and a leather jacket.

"We're just out for a walk," I say.

"The Wiz King. He see you now."

"Wizkid? You know Wizkid?"

"Wiz King. You see." He turns and walks away toward the train yard.

Derek and I look at each other, and then we follow. We climb over the fence and walk between the trees to a train full of cargo containers. The Russian stops in front of a gray container that says COSCO in blue letters. He hops up onto the train, opens the end door of the container, and motions us in. "You come. You see."

"I should really get going," Derek says.

"Real quick. Say hello and you're out of here. You should have no trouble catching up to her, anyway."

"She'll be mad if I'm late."

"Yeah, but you'll be there. She won't stay mad long."

Derek nods his head, agreeing with my logic. We both climb up onto the container.

The Russian guides us in. "Hurry. Time out."

"What?"

"Time go."

The train lurches and starts moving.

He shuts the doors.

Everything goes pitch-black.

Wiz King

DEREK PUSHES TOWARD the doors. He rattles around trying to open them. The train is moving faster. Everything is still dark.

"Locked, yes," the Russian says.

"Michelle!" Derek yells. "What's going on, Thompson?"

"I don't know. I promise. This wasn't supposed to happen." I push on the doors. We're not going anywhere other than where the train is going.

The vibrations from the train increase as it picks up even more speed.

Dubstep music suddenly pulses throughout the container. Lights flash and a disco ball turns from the ceiling. Dim LED tape lights around the perimeter walls cast a warm glow throughout. Along with our recent escort, three other identical Russian bouncers stand in the corners with their arms folded. A man in pimped-out white 1970s clothes stands in the center. Three women dance and twerk against him. We are looking at none other than the Wizkid. The music stops.

"Wizkid," I say.

All the bouncers speak at once in monotone voices. "Wiz King."

Wizkid tilts his head and raises his eyebrow as if to say, things have changed. He struts toward me with a bounce in his step and gives me a hug and manly pat on the back. He does the same to Derek, who stands and stares at Wizkid, stupefied.

"Gentlemen," Wizkid says.

"Wiz King?" I say.

"As you may or may not know, I am the mysterious founder and owner of iNuggets." He takes off his white fedora with feather and tosses it aside. His black, bushy mop of hair still pulsates as before. "Billions, Liaison. Billions, Cannonball. I had the project in the works for years, and it suddenly just exploded. My time has come."

Wow. Billions. It takes me a moment to digest this information. Wizkid is a genius, a fact that is easy to forget at times, so I guess it does make sense that he could have invented iNuggets. I admit I'm struck with a bit of awe toward the kid. "Well, that's . . . good, very good. Thank you for coming for us," I say.

"We're a team. We are friends. We save the world and live to fight another day."

Gone is the twitchy nervousness. Gone is the stutter. He's a computer genius, no doubt, but iNuggets seem to have transformed him into a jet-set Internet playboy.

Wizkid snaps his fingers, and the music and dancing resume.

A figure stands up from a box hidden in the shadows at the edge of the container. I hadn't seen him before. He's wearing blue jeans and a red T-shirt, and he looks as powerful and stoic as always.

"Land," I say, somewhat nervous, fearing some change may have come over him as well.

"Liaison. I mean, Chris, and Cannonball."

We hug affectionately, as he and Derek do also.

I nod toward Wizkid. "What's up here?"

Land slowly shakes his head. "The party circuit. The kid is nuts, I think."

"How'd you get here so fast in a train?"

"The kid's got an airplane," Land says.

Wizkid flutters his fingers in the air. "Gulfstream G-650 Aero Plane."

"Picked me up and flew to the border, where he bought this train," Land says.

Wizkid and his entourage dance around us. "Much more clandestine, don't you think? Through the border without a look."

"You own the train?" Derek cries. "Stop the train, Wizkid. I want off."

"Wiz King," the bouncers say.

"Stop the train, Wiz King, your highness," Derek says. "My lady awaits."

"It's hard to stop the party train, but if the hobo must jump, the hobo must jump. Stop the train!" he shouts to the ceiling, and sure enough, the train begins to slow down.

"Derek, please," I say. "Me, you, Wizkid—I mean, King—and Land. The core of our team. We need you."

"Michelle needs me."

"Doctor Rod can take care of herself."

The train lurches to a stop. The music stops. Derek looks defiant.

"Your lady is here?" Land asks.

"I have a new lady. She's everything I ever wanted. I'm tired of Big Mac and this mess. I want to live a normal life."

Land stands and stares, nonplussed.

"Wiz King, say something," I say.

"Man's got lady love. We got no right."

I suppose Wizkid has a point. What right do we have to convince someone to risk his life, especially someone who has risked his life and proven himself to his country before?

Land stares at Derek. "I left the reservation—left Sky, my love, and my family, whom I hadn't seen for seven years—to help Chris and his family. I was part of Emergence, part of Big Mac—as were you, Derek. We might not have known all that was going on, but you cannot tell me you didn't have your suspicions, that you didn't feel deep in your soul that what you were part of was something heinous and evil."

Derek looks to the ground. Land's comments have hit home.

Land continues: "We can't just walk away. Big Mac will always torment our conscience unless we defeat it. Whether you like it or not, our lives are part of a higher cause. We can't just stop and pretend everything will be normal. We must help Chris make it right."

Derek looks up with a tear in his eye. Wizkid puts his arm around him, as do I. Land puts his arm around me and Wizkid. We all stand so in a huddle.

"I have a plan," I say. "I have something Big Mac wants, their most-prized possession and hopes for the future. A twelve-year-old clone of Senator Joe McCarthy."

"You have Little Joe?" Wizkid says. "Where?"

"You know about Little Joe?" I say.

"Rumors." Wizkid gets a smug look on his face. "I hear a lot of things now."

"Sounds evil," Land says.

"We can bargain with Big Mac, or maybe even turn Little Joe to our side," Derek says. "When the time comes, he could bring their whole organization down."

"Where is he?" Wizkid says.

"Hidden safe on a maple syrup farm on an island outside Quebec City."

"Let's go get this clone," Land says.

"To Quebec City," Wizkid says.

"Start the train," Derek says.

"Start the train," Wizkid says.

The music starts. The lights spin. The girls and Wizkid dance.

By morning, we are in a train depot in Quebec City. We hold tight as a crane lifts our cargo container off the train and onto the flatbed of James's truck.

In no time, we are at James and Ella's maple syrup farm. Sunlight filters through the leaves and the day is warming.

Little Joe looks more relaxed, happy even. Maybe we can turn him after all. I introduce Land and Wizkid to Little Joe.

"Little Joe, my main man." Wizkid reaches out a hand and they shake, but Wizkid puts in a few more slaps, bumps, and hip finger snaps, which makes Little Joe laugh.

"Little Joe's in a good mood," Derek says.

"I think he's starting to like us," I say.

Land won't even shake Little Joe's hand. He just stares at him when introduced. Little Joe just stares back, unfazed. He finally smiles. "A real Indian—cool."

"What do you say, my little McCarthy man?" Wizkid does a little side-step dance move to music only he seems to hear. "Come check out the new bass drops on my latest dubstep creation."

"Cool," Little Joe says.

Wizkid puts his arm around Little Joe, and they walk toward the COSCO container still on the semi's flatbed. They open the door and disappear inside. Pulsing music begins to emanate from the container.

Land, Derek, and I sit down with Ella and James at the picnic table. Ella has set out breakfast for us. Pancakes and maple syrup, of course, and Derek dives right in, encouraging Land to do so as well.

"I don't think that Wizkid and his friends are providing a good environment for Little Joe," Ella says.

"Better than Big Mac brainwashing," I say.

"You worry too much about a clone," Land says. "It's not natural."

"That clone may be the key to our survival." I finish my last pancake. "He will be fine with Wizkid. We need to make plans without him hearing us, anyway."

"An abomination," Land says. "A clone is against the natural order. Sometimes nature can be cruel. Sometimes we have to be cruel to help nature."

"James and I want to adopt him," Ella says. "He can live here in secrecy and be normal."

Ella and James nod to each other, obviously they have already discussed the adoption scenario.

"We've wanted a child for a long time," James says.

If they adopt Little Joe, I won't be able to trade him for Scotty and Karen. All my options seem to be coming to a dead end.

"It'd be dangerous," I say. "As long as Big Mac is in power, they'd always be looking for him. You could never feel safe."

"Hopefully the people of the United States will vote the right way," Ella says.

"That's not going to happen with the drineys watching their every move," Derek says. "Little Joe is the only power we have over them now."

"I have to tell you something," James says. "There's something Doctor Rod didn't know. We've been making nuseum here at a much faster rate than anticipated."

"You have more nuseum?" I say. "How much? Where? Why didn't you tell us?"

"Under the right conditions, we could have enough nuseum to knock out all the drineys. We kept the information secret, even from Doctor Rod, as a precaution. It's in the United States at a secure location that only I know about. That's all I am going to say for now."

"So there's no need for Little Joe to be involved in any of this unpleasantness," Ella says. "You can defeat Big Mac with the nuseum."

"The clone is our link to Big Mac," Land says. "He has information we could find useful."

"He's an innocent child." Ella stands up and with nervous energy starts cleaning the table. "What information could he possibly have?"

"Land is right," Derek says. "Any tidbit Little Joe has on Big Mac, their locations, their power structure, could be helpful."

"The drineys are what we need to know about," James says.

Ella scoffs at him. "You, too? Can't you men figure it out on your own? Blow up the museum, simple as that."

"Knowing the proper location to blow up the museum—like where the midpoint of the whole cluster is likely to be—would increase the odds of success."

"Wouldn't that just be the center of the US population?" I ask.

"Yes," James says, "but the museum interacts with their communication too, so concentrating the explosion midway between the cluster center and the drineys' central communication hub would be ideal."

The doors to the container fly open, and we get quiet. Dubstep techno music blasts. Little Joe and Wizkid climb out and walk over to us.

"Having fun?" Ella says.

"For sure," Little Joe says.

James holds up a stack of pancakes toward Little Joe. "More pancakes?"

"Yes, sir." Little Joe takes a seat and starts working on his plate.

"You like it here, Little Joe?" I ask.

Little Joe looks around and shoves his fork filled with pieces of layered pancakes into his mouth. "This place is awesome."

"Better than living in the basement of the NSA building?" I say.

Little Joe takes another bite. "They don't have pancakes

there," he says, chewing and talking with his mouth full. We all laugh.

"They have a lot of drineys there, though," Derek says.

Little Joe shrugs. "Wouldn't know."

"You've never seen the drineys?" James says.

"Nope. Not until my helicopter ride."

"But you've heard people talking about them at the NSA, right?" I say.

"Sure, all the time."

"What do they say about them?" James says.

"All kinds of stuff."

"Do they talk about how they communicate, where the control base is, or anything like that?"

Little Joe stops eating and sets his fork down. "I don't know, maybe."

"You know, or you don't know?" Land says angrily.

Little Joe looks a little scared. "I don't know, okay? I don't know anything."

"That's fine, Little Joe," James says. "The thing is, Ms. Ella and I were wondering if you'd like to stay here and live with us for a while, or as long as you want, really. You seem to like it here, and we enjoy your company."

Ella stands behind Joe and puts her hands on his shoulders. "We could be like a family."

Little Joe's shoulders sag, and he relaxes. "That might be nice, for a while, maybe."

"Good, good," James says. "The thing is, though, it'd be a lot easier for you to stay here if we knew a lot more about the drineys."

Little Joe looks around as if he is assessing each one of us individually, as if he's trying to figure out what is really going on.

"I don't know anything about the drineys," he finally says. "Maybe I could find out, though. If I could talk to someone at Big Mac they might tell me."

I look to Derek and James. "Might be worth the risk."

Little Joe

MS. ELLA SAYS she and Mr. James want to adopt me. They'd be my mom and dad. Maybe that'd be cool.

Chris Thompson is being nice, too. There are two more people here now. Wiz King is one. I really like Wiz King. The other one is a Native American Indian who lives on a reservation. He wants to kill me. I can just tell. He used to be on Big Mac's side, Wiz King said. He's a traitor and a terrorist, then, to me. When I'm in charge, I'll get rid of all the reservations and all the Indians, so then there'll just be real Americans.

But for now, I'm making a Skype call to Big Mac. I'm supposed to find out about the drineys to make it easier for Ella and James. I know Big Mac wouldn't want them to know anything. But I'll talk to Big Mac, though, to show Ella and James I tried.

Mr. Slater came on Skype real quick. Chris Thompson and everyone else is crowded around the computer, trying to be quiet and unseen. They looked disappointed when they heard Mr. Slater's voice. They were probably hoping I'd talk to some low-level tech. They know Mr. Slater won't give anything up.

Mr. Slater is all excited to see me. We talk a bit, and then I ask him about the drineys. I can tell he knows what's up right away. He just laughs and tells me not to worry, that they'll be coming to save me soon. I tell him not to worry, that I like it where I am, and that I get lots of pancakes, so I wouldn't mind staying for a while. He says sure, whatever I like. He says he is close to finding me and we can talk more about it later.

Then I ask if I can talk to Papa McGuffin. Mr. Slater gets all serious-like and says he's very sorry, but didn't I know? Chris Thompson shot General McGuffin when he kidnapped me. General McGuffin is dead.

I look at Chris Thompson. His eyes go wide in shock, and I know right then that Mr. Slater is telling the truth. I feel like crying. Papa McGuffin is dead, and here I was having a good old time with his murderers. Chris Thompson is now shaking his head no. But why should I believe him? He's a terrorist. I believe Mr. Slater. Mr. Slater said all would be okay. He said I could be king someday. He said I was Big Mac's heart and soul. He said they were all behind me, and he was confident I would do what was right and make him proud. I could even help avenge Papa McGuffin's death.

I don't even care that the traitors are all listening. I'm tired of these people here faking their niceness with their pancakes and games. I hate them. They killed Papa and they didn't even tell me he was gone. Big Mac always tells me the truth, and that feels good. I like being Big Mac's hero.

Bond

LITTLE JOE'S SKYPE call with Slater is going horribly. I'm totally taken by surprise when Slater tells Little Joe that I shot McGuffin. I think back to our escape and how Little Joe was hidden in the crate. He just heard gunfire. He didn't know McGuffin was shot. I should have told him. Now it looks like I've been hiding the information.

The Skype call ends.

"Joe, it's not true," I say.

"Fuck you all." Little Joe looks around at us wildly. He looks like he might cry and then looks at Ella. "And you, too." He runs out of the shack and into the woods. Ella sobs.

"I'm sorry, honey," James says. "He'll come around."

"No he won't. We've lost him. Can't you see that?"

We quickly move outside, leaving Ella. Everyone talks at once.

"We have to move," I say. "You heard Slater. I think they know where we are. Big Mac will be here soon."

"Will they violate Canadian sovereignty?"

"We have to separate."

"I think they'll risk pissing Canada off."

There's a high-pitched whistle. We all look at Ella, standing outside the cabin, oddly holding a plate of cookies. "There was a message from Slater on the computer," she says. "He promises our safety, and to return Chris's wife and child, if we deliver Little Joe in twenty-four hours."

Having said this, she breaks down and cries. James puts his arm around her.

"We still need to move, and fast," Derek says.

"Where do we make the trade?" I ask.

Ella wipes her eyes. "New York. Vance Slater is speaking at the United Nations tomorrow."

"We can still explode the nuseum, though, right?" Derek says.

"Yes," James says. "We should explode it over the center of the country and hope for the best."

Wizkid looks around excitedly. "Where is it? Where's the nuseum?"

"I told you, I'm not prepared to say until we're close to it," James says.

"How about we use a hot air balloon?" I say.

James shakes his head. "The nuseum and whatever explosive device we use would be too heavy."

"Wizkid has a plane," Derek says. "Pack it tight with some military dynamite, and boom!"

"You can't blow up my G-650," Wizkid says. "Besides, Big Mac is tracking and monitoring every single vehicle in the air."

"What about the train?" I say. "We take the train to Kansas and blow it up."

"If there were some way we could send the nuseum up into the air, say about two miles, then we'd have a wide margin of error. Really, anywhere over the country would work if we could explode it that high up," James says.

"What we need to do," Wizkid says with his newfound confidence, flipping his palm over like he is making an offhand comment, "is to commandeer a nuclear submarine and shoot off the nuseum with one of the sub's ballistic missiles."

Derek, James, and I all laugh.

"Oh, I'm serious," Wizkid says.

We stop laughing.

Wizkid talks with bravado. "I got that Black Hawk for Samuel. Shouldn't be too different a hack. I doubt the Pentagon has changed their system too much, and if they have, no biggie. There's not a firewall in the world I can't break through."

The way Wizkid speaks, the crazy plan sounds almost possible.

"But, but," I say. "We had Samuel on our side to fly the Black Hawk. A nuclear sub? That takes a crew. And swiping one Black Hawk from the wee corners of some outlying military base is a tad different than sneaking some nuclear submarine from wherever they keep nuclear submarines."

"New London, Connecticut," Derek says. "High level of security there for sure."

"See? High level of security. That's what I'm saying," I say.

Wizkid stands up. "Since when has any type of security been able to stop you and Cannonball?"

"Plenty of times," I say.

"Temporary setbacks don't count," Derek says.

"I don't think we should trade Little Joe. He should be taken away from the group. Somewhere safe," James says. "Ella and I will leave with him. We can find Doctor Rod and stay with the American emigrants."

"Fuck you! I ain't staying with any emigrants." Suddenly, Little Joe is standing at the edge of the woods. "I don't want to live with you people. I want to be the king."

Land is gone in a flash. He scoops up Little Joe and throws him into the cargo container. He yells at the women and bouncers, and they groggily vacate their mobile party box. Land rushes in and reappears holding Little Joe by his shirt neck. "The pissant bit me. We're trading him."

Ella walks from the cabin with the plate of cookies fighting back tears. "You can bite on these, Little Joe."

We all look on incredulously as Ella hands Little Joe the plate of cookies.

"Thank you for all you have done, but I want to go back." Little Joe gives her a warm-hearted, endearing smile.

Land brings Little Joe back into the container. Little Joe tries to hand him a cookie.

"All he needs is love," Ella says to us.

After a moment, Wizkid walks toward his cargo container. "We've run out of time. Don't worry about the sub. I'll take care of the details."

Derek and I look at each other. I don't like this plan. It sounds too outrageous. But we have no time to argue, and sometimes outrageousness works for us. We are about to go on another mission, one that seems bigger than anything we've attempted before.

"Boohah," Derek says.

"You only live twice," I say.

"Bond?"

"Bond," I say.

Huey

WE ARE BACK on Wizkid's party train, headed for the United
States border. Ella has stayed at the farm, packing, planning to
leave in case Big Mac arrives. The bouncers and dancing girls,
much to Wizkid's disappointment, are riding with the engineer
in the locomotive. Safer for them and safer for us, I explained.
I want people around me I can trust.

Derek, Wizkid, Land, James, and I ride in Wizkid's luxury
dance hall box. Little Joe, our hostage, is here too, the one
person I do not trust. Still, I hate the thought that we are
turning a little boy over to Big Mac.

"You can change your mind," I say to Little Joe. "You can
live a good, peaceful life with Ella and James. They'd be kind,
loving parents."

Little Joe shifts his eyes toward me like a sullen junior high student who is tired of hearing my voice. "Don't be a sap. I'm going to the winning side. I'm going to be king."

"You're Big Mac's prodigy. They will always welcome you. Why don't you learn some new things? Experience life in a real family for a while."

"Learn some morals," Derek says.

If we could have some time to sway Little Joe, let him see the evil truth about Big Mac, maybe he could be an instrument for good within their system. I hate to think that Big Mac could be in power that long, but we must plan for that sad scenario. We can't ever give up. "You can have your power eventually, but be smart about it, is all I'm saying. A king needs to be wise. A king needs to understand his subjects. If you live like a real kid, you can learn invaluable lessons that will help you forever. Think smart, Little Joe."

Little Joe chuckles dismissively. "I am smart. I know exactly what I am doing. How about this? How about you and your family come over with me to Big Mac? I could live with your family. Scotty could be my brother. He and I could rule together someday. That'd be some real fun."

"Never," I say.

Little Joe looks hurt. His face turns red, and he looks away.

"May not be a bad idea," Derek says.

I guess Karen and I could try and raise Little Joe right. Maybe I shouldn't have answered so brusquely. But still, how could I raise him under Big Mac's watch? Who knows what dangers lurk in this Joe McCarthy's clone mind? Do I want to risk the possibility that he could turn on Scotty at any second?

"You killed the only person who loved me," Little Joe says, anger and resentment seething from his voice. "Uncle Slater told me. You killed Papa McGuffin."

"Slater lied to you," I tell him. "Lexi and Chip shot him."

"You lie. Mr. Slater says you can't be trusted, and I believe him. You tried to hurt me. You shot Papa McGuffin."

"General McGuffin was helping Scotty escape. He was trying to leave, too. You were in the cage. Don't you remember?"

"I had my hands over my ears. I heard the shot, though." He looks at me. "If Papa McGuffin was on your side, you would have told me by now. You would have been sad, too."

I wasn't sad, really. I didn't know McGuffin; I was just happy he decided to turn and help us when he did. I never really thought about telling Little Joe. Too much has been going on. I didn't really think he'd care anyway.

"Listen to me, Little Joe. Vance Slater was in charge of the Emergence program. Derek and Land worked for the program too. They trusted Vance Slater, just like you, but Vance Slater lied to them. Vance Slater was torturing and killing people for money. Innocent people, men and women, who were good, just like you. Isn't that right, Derek?"

"'Tis true," Derek says.

"Am I right, Land?"

Land is standing, looking reflective. "I believed in Big Mac. I believed in Emergence, but I was wrong."

"You see? It's okay to realize you're wrong. It's okay to switch sides."

"I'm not a traitor." Little Joe glares at me with malice. "I don't know about Emergence. I don't know about innocent deaths, but I do know people have to die for different reasons, and I've heard you all talking. I know what you're thinking. You've considered killing me too. So don't talk to me about who is lying and who is not. Papa McGuffin was my family. He died. Maybe you shot him, maybe you didn't, but I would want him to be proud of me no matter what."

"The wall," Wizkid says.

We all gather round the slightly open door, where he's been watching for the border, and we look out. We are in the forested wilderness heading into Vermont. It's around midnight and dark. The wall grows larger as we approach. Its massiveness, along with its searchlights and laser grid, looks futuristic against the rural landscape.

"How are we going to get through that?" Derek says.

"They have an opening for trains," Wizkid says.

"I think he means," I say, "will they let our train through?"

Wizkid smiles at me condescendingly. "Please," he says, like only a rich billionaire who doesn't have to play by the rules can.

And sure enough, the train passes through a heavily guarded narrow tunnel in the wall without incident.

We cross to the other side and see hundreds of fires. There are refugee camps and people with American flags everywhere, just like Uncle Sam's camp in Niagara Falls, but much bigger. The border has been closed, though. These unlucky emigrant want-to-bes have arrived too late.

There's a buzzing in the air. Drineys! They fly overhead, swarming. Some follow individual people, others seem to be looking for a target.

I reach for the nuseum pills Doctor Rod had left with us. I pass them out. I should have done this earlier. "Chomp on them hard," I say. "It's okay to swallow." At least that's what Doctor Rod had said.

I hear Pink Floyd music playing. People sing and chant: "Tear down the wall! Tear down the wall!"

There are screams. People are trying to get close to the wall, but the guards are mercilessly beating on them with batons. It's chaos that spills all the way up to the edge of the train tracks. One man close to us is on the ground, and a fat guard is kicking him. I look closer: it's Huey. Huey, the fat ASU campus cop turned border patrol commandant who tried to execute Derek and me on our last mission.

"Huey," I yell.

Huey turns and stares at the train. Derek leans out with his iPhone and shoots. Huey grabs his neck and looks puzzled. I lean out and wave. Huey's eyes go wide, and then he collapses.

Derek and I close the door before anybody else notices.

"Did you kill him?"

"No. Michelle gave me some tranquilizer darts to be safer under normal conditions. He'll be out for a couple hours and probably forget he ever saw us."

"That fat son of a bitch," I say.

"Yeah." Derek starts to laugh. "Yeah."

We sleep as much as we can, but I'm awake now for good. I can't see outside, but I can feel the early morning light begin to warm up the car.

Wizkid and James are speaking together in the corner. A few minutes pass, and I stand to stretch my legs.

James comes over to speak to me. "We're close to where I have hidden the extra nuseum. Wiz King and I are going to leave the train soon and go find it." He nods back to Wizkid. "He's really fascinated with the stuff, and quite smart. I could use him to help with my research."

Wizkid talks into some kind of radio device, and the train slows.

"I could really use Wizkid for the hostage exchange," I say. "I don't trust Slater, and we could use all the backup we can get."

"I'll need someone to help with the nuseum."

Wizkid joins us. "I'd love to see the nuseum. And sometimes I'm not so good under stressful situations."

Wizkid had come through for us with the old Fat Boy bomb, but during the battle he had curled up with a slight case of battle shock. Perhaps it'd be best for him not to be around if things go bad.

"Okay. You and James go for the nuseum."

The train comes to a stop. We open the back doors. In an instant, James and Wizkid are gone.

Eventually, we arrive on the Metro-North Harlem in the West Bronx.

I open the container door to look outside. Secrecy is no longer necessary, as we've alerted Big Mac to our presence in order to make the exchange. We have been granted priority clearance on the tracks. Three military helicopters pointedly mark our progress, fore, aft, and center of the train.

The train passes Harlem-125th Street Station. Vance Slater's friendly, smiling photograph and Vote Big Mac signs are ominously displayed throughout in different patriotic themes. I look over the elevated platform to the city streets below, eerily vacant of people. A few cars are on the road, drineys doggedly following them. I see an apartment building with drineys buzzing outside of windows. I think people are staying indoors or inside their cars after dodging their drineys, as if establishing any sort of barrier between the drineys and their personal space is a relief.

I see a couple walking hand in hand. They are wearing full-face motorcycle helmets. Their drineys follow close behind. One of the drineys taps intermittently on the back of one's helmet, an irritating reminder of its presence, I'm sure.

In a few minutes we are pulling into Grand Central Station, our cargo cars looking out of place among all the commuter trains. I watch the people walk along the platforms. Perhaps this isn't unusual for the normal New York City commuter, but there is an eerie sadness about these people. They walk efficiently, in straight lines, not a trace of emotion on their faces. There are no shouts, waves, friendly calls, or talk of the Yankees. They are scared. A driney follows each close behind. Nobody holds a coffee or a paper, and nobody browses in a newsstand. Only Big Mac posters decorate the station. The commuters don't look about them, up, down, or around, only ahead, like zombies, as if veering from their intended path will harm them. And perhaps it will.

Derek looks out, forlorn, missing Doctor Rod, I bet.

"I'm sorry, man. You could have bailed."

"Wouldn't miss some super-spy action with the one and only Chris Thompson."

I give a short laugh. "I really appreciate it. I couldn't fight the bad guys without you."

Derek nods. "You saved my life, man."

"You saved mine."

He laughs. "Enough said."

"Enough said. You ready?"

"Let's do this."

Quantum of Solace

A SLEEK, METALLIC black passenger train pulls in on the other side of the platform. If ever a train could look like a spy train— or even more sinister, a secret police train—this train is it. Karen and Scotty are in there, or are supposed to be in there. So much has happened that it feels like weeks rather than mere days since I've seen them, and I miss them both so much. I don't trust Slater, but I know he wants Little Joe, so I'm hoping for a smooth trade. Still, I look around for anything suspicious.

The thousands of morose Grand Central Station commuters I saw walking to and fro before are suddenly gone. No trains are moving. It seems unusually quiet for such a busy station.

A door opens on the sinister train, and about a dozen drineys fly out. They zoom up and down our train, but our nuseum must still be working, as they never hone in on us.

Out of the last car eight soldiers, looking like Nazi storm troopers dressed in all black with knee-high boots, file out and take up position. Two of them reach into the train and pull out a white podium equipped with a flat-screen LCD.

The commander of the group raises his hands to his lips to amplify his voice. "Reveal yourself, Chris Thompson."

I look at Land. He is standing in the back of the car, a controlling hand on Little Joe's shoulder. Derek stands next to me by the door, his iPhone armed and ready. He nods. It's go time.

I open and then shut the cargo door as I step out onto the platform.

The commander shouts something, and the line of troops marches toward me. The podium moves under its own power along with them. As they approach, I see Vance Slater's face on the LCD screen.

The Slater robot stops in front of me. The soldiers flank him on both sides. They have helmets with a circular Stars and Stripes logo that has the letters BM.

"Thompson," Slater bellows. "You better have Little Joe, and he better be safe."

"He's here. He's safe."

"Let's have him, then."

"My family," I say.

"Bring them out," Slater says.

Two soldiers step out of the last car. One reaches up his hand to help the next person down. Karen looks out, ignores the proffered help, and steps onto the platform. In the next instant, Scotty jumps out of the train and lands next to Karen. The soldiers walk them toward me.

I wave, and Scotty waves excitedly back. Karen and I lock eyes. She is trying to look serious, and to not smile, but she can't help herself and sends a heartwarming glance my way. Oh, how I love them both so much. I want to hug them and hold them.

Karen recovers and becomes all business. She knows this isn't over yet. But Scotty can't control his enthusiasm. He is literally bouncing down the platform, smiling broadly.

"And Little Joe?" Slater says.

I crawl back up to the cargo container and open the door. Little Joe is standing with Land ready to go. Derek is covering them slightly behind. Land removes his hand from Little Joe's shoulder.

"See ya, minority suckers," Little Joe says. "There's nothing to protect you now."

I grab Little Joe's wrist and pull him out, helping him down to the platform where we stand side-by-side.

"Trade," Slater says.

Scotty and Karen walk toward me. I let go of Little Joe, and he runs over to the Big Mac side. He passes close by Scotty. They quickly slap each other a low five, like basketball players would be introduced before a game.

I hug Scotty and help him up into the car.

"Bastards," Karen says.

I turn quickly around. Two soldiers have grabbed Karen. Two others point their guns at her.

"What the fuck?" I look at Slater.

"A boy for a boy is a fair trade."

"Not the trade we agreed. Free my wife."

Two soldiers are escorting Little Joe back down the platform toward the last car in which they came.

The remaining four soldiers raise their guns and point them at me.

"I have a trade for you, Thompson. You for your wife."

"Done," I say.

"Chris," Karen says. But the soldiers have let her go, and are circling in closer to me with their rifles.

"Shoot him," Slater yells.

And then Derek is giving me the high sign.

Before the guards can react, I turn around and grab ahold of a support with my bionified arm. With all my strength, I fling myself straight up into the air. I pass by the top of the cargo container and push off it with my legs, kicking myself into a backflip and farther up. At the same time, the doors from the cargo container fly open. Derek reaches out with his iPhone and is shooting darts before anyone can figure out what is going on. All four of the soldiers collapse.

I land on my feet next to Karen.

Derek blows on his iPhone. "Who you gonna call?"

Karen is looking at me in wonder. I hug her and lift her effortlessly up to the train like we are accomplished ballet dancers. She disappears inside.

The two soldiers with Little Joe look back at us, and at their fallen comrades. They look unsure of what to do.

On the LCD screen, Slater points at me as best as he can. "Get him."

The soldiers run at me, pointing their guns. The doors of the container fly open again, and a loud engine scream emits. Land shoots out and up, riding Ninjenna's yellow Yamaha Supersport YZF-R1 motorcycle, the same he rode while leading the Cherokee Nation against Emergence.

There's a good twenty feet to the next cargo container.

Land and the Yamaha fly over and land on the next cargo container.

The two remaining soldiers aim their guns at Land.

Derek tries to shoot his iPhone darts at them, but nothing happens. "I'm out." He hurriedly reaches into his pocket, searching for more darts.

Shots ring out, and sparks fly off of the Yamaha.

I rip the iPhone out of Derek's hand, turn, and fling it like a Japanese star with my bionified arm. It sails into the side of one soldier's helmet with a terrific clang. The force knocks him out cold.

I charge at the other soldier, hoping to reach him before he can shoot at Land again, but he doesn't shoot at Land. Instead he turns, aims right at me, and fires.

I'm hit in the shoulder, and the impact knocks me off my feet. I'm falling to the ground.

Land jumps the Yamaha off the train. He kicks out his leg and smashes it into the soldier's head, knocking him into the Big Mac train and then to the ground, out cold.

I'm on my back, but still watching Land. Smoke comes from his engine, damage from one of the bullets, but Land looks okay. I try to sit up.

"Stay down." Derek reaches me and gently lowers me back to the ground. "Where you hit?"

I touch my shoulder where the bullet hit and realize it's my bionified side. "I'm okay. The suit stopped it." I sit up, with Derek's help.

Land races the Yamaha's engine. Little Joe runs toward the last Big Mac train car. Reinforcement soldiers are starting to pile out of a car from the train's other end.

Little Joe reaches the car door, but Land whizzes by and

scoops him up, throwing him across the gas tank. Little Joe screams.

Derek and I stand up and grab the guns from the fallen soldiers.

"Chris, look out!" Karen screams from the train.

Derek and I turn. Three soldiers are on one knee, in position to shoot at us.

The motorcycle with Land and Little Joe screeches as it slides in a curve, skidding to a stop directly in front of us, blocking the soldier's aim.

Derek grabs Little Joe and lifts him up.

I put my gun into Little Joe's temple.

"Lowlife commie bastards," he shouts. "Using a kid for a shield."

My arm hurts, and it's hard to control the gun. Something is wrong with my bionified arm. I struggle to appear strong. "Guns down."

Derek points his gun at the soldiers.

"And you wanted me to trust you?" Little Joe says.

Slater has been spinning around on his podium screaming throughout, but his orders have fallen on deaf ears. "Don't hurt him. Don't hurt him," he is yelling.

We lift Little Joe off the bike.

"Chris. Careful," Karen says, her eyes intently on my gun and Little Joe. She and Scotty are looking out the back of the container. She's never seen this side of me before. Scotty, though, is taking it in with glee, like it's all a good action movie.

"Get back inside," I say sharply to them. They slowly move back inside.

Derek continues to point at the soldiers while I hold the tip of my gun into the side of Little Joe's head. I walk toward

Slater.

"This is what is going to happen, Vance," I say.

"I'll tell you what is going to happen, Thompson, because I know you don't have it in you to harm an innocent boy."

Before I can answer, Land roughly grabs Little Joe by the hair and puts a gun to the other side of his head. "I'll harm your monstrosity," he says. "I spent seven horrific years underground for your sick plans. For fifty years you sacrificed the chosen ones to protect your sins. I will destroy your mutant boy with pleasure." Land speaks with a scary edge to his voice that leaves no doubt: he means what he says.

I lower my weapon, much to my arm's relief. "Derek. Radio the engine. We're pulling out immediately."

Derek hurries inside the container. Slater starts to say something. Land jerks Little Joe's head back. "Shut up."

I tap on the forehead of Slater's image with my gun. "We're going back to Canada. If I see one driney, a helicopter, a cop at a crossing gate—any kind of surveillance—Little Joe is dead."

"Dead," Land says.

"I want a clean track all the way back to Canada. No surveillance. If all goes as planned, we will drop Little Joe off at the border with fat Huey. That is, if Little Joe wants to go back to you."

"I want to go back," Little Joe cries.

The train starts to move.

Slater is as red as a Soviet Union flag. He starts screaming orders and obscenities, but he is so upset they sound nonsensical. The soldiers do not do anything. I take his robot and kick it onto the tracks. The moving train wheels crush him.

Land throws Little Joe over his shoulder, jogs to our car, and hoists him up to Derek. Land and I jump on, we close the doors, and we are off.

Derek and Land sit next to a wall with Little Joe between them. Karen and Scotty stand and look at me with bewilderment.

"You've got to take these right away," I say, handing them each a nuseum pill.

Karen takes hers. "How did you do all that stuff?" she says.

"Dad really is a super-spy," Scotty says with pride. "I told you, Mom. I always told you." Scotty walks over and plops down next to Little Joe. "I guess my dad won that one."

"Hmph" is all Little Joe says.

I take off my shirt and pull off the bionified vest. "This helped." The bullet was stopped by one of the titanium struts. The strut is severely damaged, and I think the whole suit is now defective. It's lighter to have the suit off. My left arm feels heavy and like rubber, like I imagine an astronaut must feel returning to gravity. "And my friends helped, as usual." I look around. "Where'd the motorcycle come from?"

Land points to some tarps. "I had it back there." Land places his palm on his forehead. "The Yamaha. We left it on the train platform."

Derek laughs. "Ninjenna's going to kill you."

"That's no laughing matter," Land says.

Derek laughs some more and I join him.

"The Yamaha was done for anyway." I throw the bionified arm suit to the ground. "As is this thing."

Karen and I embrace. Scotty joins us, and we hug together as a family.

"My iPhone," Derek says. "Chris, you chucked my iPhone away."

"Saved us with your iPhone," Scotty says.

"Saved us, yes," Derek says. "But now we got no gadgets."

"And?" I say.

Derek smiles. "And boohah! That's the way we like it."

"Quantum of Solace," I say.

Little Joe

I GUESS I haven't had a real dad, except for when I lived before in Wisconsin, but I don't remember that. Maybe a real dad brainwashes you into thinking everything they do is the right way to do things. Scotty is pretty proud of his dad having outsmarted Mr. Slater at the train station. I guess it was impressive. Scotty and I got to talking about all the details, reliving every second. I had to admit, Mr. Slater with his video face and looking like a robot and screaming and spinning around and then getting smashed on the tracks was pretty damn funny. Scotty and I couldn't stop laughing about that.

Scotty says this is the best adventure yet, and I have to agree. It's a lot of fun, and it's scary too, 'cause it's real, and that makes it better than the best game ever. Scotty is really cool. He's my best friend, no matter what happens.

Did Papa McGuffin brainwash me? Is Chris Thompson a good guy and Mr. Slater bad? Scotty sure thinks so. Mr. Slater is kind of an asshole. And Papa McGuffin did help Scotty escape. He said Mr. Slater made him lose his honor, but that doesn't mean Big Mac is all bad. Maybe everyone trying to win power is an asshole. Maybe that's why I'll be such a good king. I'm smart, and I can see things clearly. That's why I should stay with Big Mac. With them I can become king and fix everything.

Chris Thompson and his friends sure like each other, that's for sure. I feel better with them than I do with the people at Big Mac. It's hard to explain. It's like they like me (except for the Indian), even though they should not. Only Papa McGuffin liked me at Big Mac, and now he is gone. I thought it'd be really nice to have a mom like Ella, but I just don't know.

But these people don't understand. The real world is not nice. They don't realize that smarter people like me are made to lead. They don't know what is good for them and they think what they are doing is right, but their way is chaos. I don't care if all the Big Mac people aren't my friends, but they respect me. Some of them look at me with awe, even. I have a destiny. My destiny is their destiny, I heard one of them say. I can do it. I can be a king. I feel it, now. This trip has shown me how smart I am. It has shown me how stupid regular people are. They need to be told what to do to live and be happy and not kill each other. I can tell them what to do. I can tell them what to think. I can make America strong. I understand. That is my destiny.

King of America

THE TRAIN HAS picked up speed, and the car shakes and wavers as it moves along the rails. A constant hiss from the passing air comes through the walls.

Karen stares at me. She shakes her head. "I never really believed you could be a spy."

"Believe it, Mom. I told you Dad was an elite secret agent," Scotty calls over from the back of the train, where he and Little Joe have been talking.

"You told me, and told me." Karen gives me the parental fatigue look, the look that says, I love my kid, but I've had enough for now. It's your turn. "Scotty and I have been in the same room for a week now."

Scotty comes over to us, and I put my arm around him. "Mom cried all the time, Dad. She wouldn't even do anything.

She wouldn't even think about trying to escape. I could have done it, though, if Mom wasn't there."

"Mom was right," I say. "Staying put and waiting was the smartest strategy."

"You wouldn't have stayed put. You would have tried to get us out of there."

I rub the top of Scotty's head. "It would have been too dangerous for you and Mom to try and escape. You saw what just happened out there. People died. This is war." I look at Derek. "Were you using the tranquilizers, or the poison darts?"

"What do you think?" Derek gives me a look that says: You just said it. This is war."

"Your parents are right," Little Joe says from the back. "Your dad has some weak philosophies on government, but he's smart otherwise. Obviously waiting it out was the best move."

"So says the Big Mac king," Scotty says.

"King of America," Little Joe says.

He and Little Joe laugh.

"You two shouldn't be talking," Karen hisses to Scotty.

"We're friends, Mom."

Karen looks to me for help.

"Having a friend who is also an enemy has its advantages," I say. "We shouldn't shelter Scotty from ideas."

Land and Karen look at me disapprovingly. I look at Derek, but he is lost in his own thoughts. I try to strike a middle ground. "Little Joe is our prisoner, Scotty. You can talk for a half hour more, but then visiting time is over."

Scotty and Little Joe immediately start talking about video games.

I introduce Karen to Land. He nods respectfully, says

nothing, and continues to watch Little Joe. I want Karen to know Derek and Land as I do, but for now, the gulf is too wide.

"So you've always been a spy?" Karen says. "Working for the customs department was always a cover. You've always held this from me?"

"No. This all just happened last month. I told you right after the president recruited me. You just chose not to believe me."

"You're telling me the president recruited you to be a spy last month, the day you landed in our front lawn on Marine One with those slutty pilots, and today you are flipping through the air, flinging guns and iPhones, all while in coordination with a stunt motorcycle?"

"I'm a quick learner."

"You should have seen some of our other capers." Derek laughs. "Though this last one sounds pretty darn good, the way you describe it."

Karen nervously intertwines and rolls her fingers over each other. "You're not the person I married. I married a person who likes to stay in and read and watch PBS and History Channel documentaries. You were a boring geek. I don't know who you are now." Karen looks me in the eyes, concerned, like she still loves me but is searching for that person she thought I was.

"Oh, he's all geek still," Derek says, trying to lighten the moment.

"Thanks," I say.

Derek is laughing. "Secret Customs Service Agent Chris Thompson. That's the dorkiest super-spy name ever."

"I just don't like the danger. I don't want you to be a spy," Karen says.

"I always wanted to be a spy, yes, but I didn't ask for it. Big Mac attacked and I—" I point to Derek and Land. "We reacted."

Derek pumps his fist. "Booyah!"

"But we're still in danger," Karen says. "What do we do now, super spies?"

"We have a plan." I stand up and walk over to Little Joe. He stares at me defiantly. "Everyone but you and Land will soon be leaving the train. You have a choice. You can remain Land's prisoner indefinitely, or you can forswear your allegiance to Big Mac and promise to stay with Ella in Canada."

"Where will Land take me?"

After the train enters the safety of Canada, Land will secretly make his way west and then back to the Cherokee reservation in Oklahoma, where he will keep Little Joe hidden. I'm not about to tell this to Little Joe. "All you need to know is that Land will keep you safe."

"What does foreswear mean?"

"It's a serious promise. It means you will not ever follow or be a part of Big Mac. You will live your life with Ella and James peacefully in Canada."

Little Joe's face softens. I think he is thinking about Ella and the maple syrup farm. "Can I think about it?"

I like the fact that he doesn't answer right away. It means he is not totally on Big Mac's side, and it also means that he is taking the decision seriously and will hopefully keep his promise if he rejects Big Mac.

"You and Land are going with the train into Canada. Once you cross the border, then you must decide."

Little Joe nods.

I walk back to Karen and Scotty.

"We're leaving the train?" Karen says.

I lower my voice so Little Joe cannot hear. "We're going to jump in a river around New London."

"That's where the subs are," Derek says.

"Subs?" Karen looks astonished and a little scared. "And then what?"

"Uh, I don't know. We have other people taking it from there."

"No, no." Karen points at the side of her head in an indication I should use my brain. "We have to go to Canada, Chris. We can be safe in Canada."

I reach up and take Karen's hands and hold them in my own. "The election is tomorrow. Big Mac will be in control for good. We have to do something." I contemplate whether I should tell Karen the details of Wizkid's nuclear sub idea, but it is just too outlandish of a plan, even for me. "We have a plan. It's a long shot, and I don't want to go into the details right now, but hopefully we'll have a chance."

"I don't see how we have a chance," Karen says.

"We've got a chance," Derek says to Karen. "Don't worry. A chance is all we need."

"Please, Chris. You've given too much. How many episodes like the last one can you survive? Can we not just go to Canada and disappear?"

I nod to Land and Derek. "My two friends have made sacrifices. They have left their loved ones, risked their lives to help me. We're too far into it now, Karen. We're among the few who can help fight Big Mac."

Her eyes look around to Land and Derek. "I don't mean to

be selfish. Wait. Yes. I don't care. I'll be selfish for my family's sake. I just want us to be safe. Is that wrong?"

"No. Not at all." I pause. "It's not wrong. I just can't do it, Karen. Derek and I could have walked away a long time ago, left Emergence and Big Mac alone and lived our own lives. And believe me, we almost did just that, several times. I don't know what keeps bringing us back, making us go on with the fight. We took an oath to the president, yes, but that doesn't really apply anymore. I don't know if it ever did. There's just this feeling that we—Derek, Land, Wizkid—have to do what is right, that we are part of some struggle that is bigger than us all, and if we don't do our part, we will have failed ourselves somehow."

"Well said, Liaison," Land says.

"Look at Little Joe," I say. "That boy back there wants to take over the world. Go talk to him for fifteen minutes and then tell me if you'll feel safe in Canada. The United States cannot contain Big Mac's ambitions."

Karen jumps up and clenches her fist. "I just want to be normal."

I stand up and try to hold her. She buries her face in her hands and turns away from me. She walks over and sits by Scotty and Little Joe.

"You could send Karen and Scotty on to Canada," Derek says. "Keep them out of the fray until it is all over."

"That would be the smartest option, but I'm not letting Karen and Scotty out of my sight." I look over to Karen. "With those drineys killing people and Big Mac soldiers doing who knows what, it's dangerous everywhere. Karen and Scotty can ride this out with me."

"If we can disable the drineys tomorrow, do you think

there's any chance the people will still vote Big Mac in?"

"Not a chance—at least, I hope not," I say. "That'd be so awesome, though, if we knocked out the drineys. Doctor Rod would sure be impressed."

Derek chuckles at the thought. "Yes indeed."

"You think she's kicking back with Uncle Sam's gang right now?"

He rubs his chin, pondering. "I've been wondering about what Michelle's been doing, and I think it more likely she's back in the game, trying to catch our trail or come up with something else to defeat Big Mac."

"That sounds more like her," I say. "I bet all that talk of giving up and living the peaceful life was just a temporary discouragement."

"Temporary discouragement. She loves me. I love her."

"I didn't mean it like that."

Derek drops his head. "I kind of just left her there."

"Cheer up. She might track us down for no other reason than to whip your ass." I laugh.

"Yeah." Derek laughs, but it doesn't sound like he thinks it's funny.

After a while, the train begins to slow. One of the Russians calls on the radio.

"Time to go," I say.

Everyone but Little Joe stands up. Derek and I grab our guns and sling them around our necks to our back. We shake hands with Land.

"If the clone decides to stay at the syrup farm, I'll drop him there and then make my way back west through Canada," Land says. "Otherwise, I'll take him with me."

"Sky is waiting for Land," Karen says. "They've waited over seven years to be together."

I smile. "Yes. Of course. Thank you for everything."

Land and I shake hands.

The train is inching along. I grab the black tarp that had covered the Yamaha, spread it out, and open the back doors. We have traveled slowly, making many stops while waiting for the tracks to be completely clear. It's night now.

"Chris, really, think about what you are doing," Karen says. "I understand you have to do what you have to do, but do you really want Scotty and me to jump into a river with you and go on some mission you won't even tell me about?"

I'm tired of Karen second-guessing me all the time. Hasn't she figured out from the fight at the train station that Derek and I know what we are doing? Doesn't she understand that it is dangerous for her to know all the details? That we have to move quickly? Does she have to have her say in everything?

"Chris, I deserve to know what is going on."

I grab Karen roughly by the elbow. "There's no time to talk," I hiss. "Just do what I say, Karen."

Karen's eyes open wide and her mouth parts, but she is silent. For the first time in my life, she looks afraid of me.

"Goodbye, Scotty," Little Joe says.

"Bye, Little Joe. It'd be cool if you were on our side."

"I hope you'll be my friend no matter what I decide," Little Joe says.

"I will," Scotty says.

"Let's move." I grab a corner of the tarp. Scotty and Derek each grab a corner as well. Karen, somewhat in a daze, reluctantly grabs the last corner. One by one, we hide ourselves under the tarp. Holding it overhead, we carefully walk outside onto the flatbed train car. We crouch together and sit on the edge, the tarp still over us like we are watching a football game in the rain.

"We could drown," Karen says. "Why are we doing this?"

"It's the plan," I say.

"The plan," Derek says.

"The plan," Scotty says.

The train is passing over a wide bridge that crosses a cove off the Thames River, right outside of New Haven Amtrak station. The train almost comes to a stop. "Now," I command.

We hop off the train and onto the bridge, holding the tarp over our heads to camouflage ourselves against the dark. So far, Slater seems to have kept his word, and I don't see any planes, but Big Mac could be using satellites to follow us. We cross over tracks and reach the railing, where we look down to the slow moving water thirty feet below us. It's not a dangerous jump, but high enough to be frightening.

The train picks up speed as it passes by the station. It will head due north from here straight to Canada.

I sit on the railing's edge and dangle my feet over the side. I hold Karen's arm, and she reluctantly joins me. Scotty and Derek quickly follow suit. Scotty sits next to me. Derek sits on the other side of Karen. We continue to hold the tarp over ourselves.

"Time?" I say.

"Ten-thirteen," Derek says.

"Ready to jump in two minutes?" I say.

"Ready," Scotty says.

I lock arms with Scotty and try to do the same with Karen, but this time, she avoids me. "Three, two, one, and—"

"Stop," Derek says, but Scotty, eager as always, has wriggled out of my arm. I try to catch him, but he is already gone, splashing into the water below.

A rumble echoes under the bridge. "A boat," Derek says. Karen screams. "No!"

A dark shape floats by underneath us, directly where Scotty had gone in. It has no running lights, or any lights for that matter. Is this the boat I'm waiting for? My mind races with other scary possibilities. But whatever their intentions, it could hit Scotty. Karen was right. I should have never involved her and Scotty in a mission. What is wrong with me? Why would I not send my family to safety? Why would I yell and scare Karen?

The shadow stops moving.

"Ka, ka, quiet up there," someone whispers. I recognize the stutter. Thank God. It's Wizkid.

"My son's in the water!" I jump into the dark.

Man Overboard

I CAN'T SEE anything as I fall. I prepare to hit the shadowy boat, but then my feet collide into someone's head and shoulders. We both tumble. I reach out to catch myself with my bionified arm, forgetting I no longer have it, and slap my hand and elbow painfully into the deck as the figure—Wizkid—and I crash. The boat is about the size of a motorhome bus. There's a metal canopy that covers rows of wooden bench seats. It's some kind of tour boat, I think.

"Man overboard!" I jump up and head for the side.

"Dad." Scotty is treading water and waving to me.

Wizkid is next to me with a boat hook. I lower it to Scotty, and with help from Wizkid, Scotty's able to climb up the side.

"Welcome aboard."

Scotty is soaking wet and shivering. "Freezing," he says with a smile that looks like he is having the best time.

"Scotty, is that you?" Karen calls.

"It's me. I'm okay."

Wizkid puts a ladder up to the bridge, helping Derek and Karen down. Immediately, Karen walks to the rail and picks up the boat hook from the holder in which I have just put it. I'm rubbing my sore elbow, and in the next instant the boat hook tip is at my throat. Karen pushes me back against an exterior cabin wall.

"Now you listen to me. Our son could have drowned. You want to save the world? You want to save our marriage? Then save us first."

I nod and struggle to talk. "Absolutely."

She lowers the hook. "And don't ever grab me rough like that again."

I've never grabbed her like that or ordered her around. There's no excuse. "You're right," I say. "I'm sorry. It's these missions, or that bionic suit I was wearing. I'm stupid and angry. I'm not myself. For now, the safest place for you is with me, here—and as soon as this is done, we'll go to Canada together and forget all of this."

Karen nods, somewhat mollified. "Thank you."

Wizkid folds the aluminum ladder. He puts it aside and takes up a position behind the wheel on the port side. "The plan has come together exactly as I wished," Wizkid says proudly. "James found us the nuseum."

"Where is James?" Derek asks.

Wizkid shrugs. "He w-went back to Canada," he says. "He f-figured you'd be sending Little Joe back, I guess, and wanted to m-meet up with him." He looks down. "Sorry I d-didn't ask you about it ahead of time. I'm sorry."

"It's fine," I say. "More importantly: Are you serious? You

have a nuclear submarine we can use? A military sub capable of launching missiles?"

"Missiles? Nuclear submarine?" Karen says.

"Cool," Scotty says.

"This is my wife, Karen, and you remember Scotty," I say.

"Ka, ka, cool," Wizkid says. "But they going to be on the sub-stealing team?"

"We have to steal it?"

"Y-yeah. You're heading in with the team to steal the sub from the submarine base just a few miles upriver."

"No. I think they will stay with you and the boat. We can rendezvous later." I look to Karen. "Okay?"

"Okay by me," she says.

"Okay, boss," Wizkid says.

"What do you mean, we're going in with the team?" Derek asks.

"We're the team." A voice I recognize comes from the boat's stern. Two figures, whom I've somehow overlooked, are sitting on the last bench in the exposed section beyond the canopy. They stand up and walk toward us.

The boat has picked up speed, and I'm surprised Wizkid can handle it so well. We come round a bend. A chilly breeze blows against our skin. Wizkid turns the running lights on, ending our blackout. An Apache helicopter races by overhead. We watch, hoping whatever it is doing has nothing to do with us.

The two figures from the back of the boat now stand before us. We know them all too well.

"Thompson," President Wright says and nods in greeting. "Mrs. Thompson. I forget your name, little guy."

"Scotty."

"That's right. Wizkid called, and Fixer and I've come to help."

"What's up, Giorgio." Fixer raises his hand to me for a high five, but I ignore him. "Family man. That's right. But on a mission."

"Temporary," I say.

Derek and I, with some help from Scotty, tell our story about what happened in New York to the others.

"We've had ka, ka, quite an adventure ourselves," Wizkid says. "James swore me to suh, secrecy, but we were in a cave and we now huh, have nuseum."

Without his entourage and guards, Wizkid has reverted back to his old nervous, stuttering self. He opens the lid from a square container underneath one of the benches. Inside are bricks of a yellowish substance, thick like cheese and packed in plastic wrap. "Nuseum." Wizkid points around to all the benches. "We're filled with it."

"We just need to blow this baby up," Derek says.

"To be sure the nuseum is effective, we have to get it up in the air. High into the air," I say.

"A blimp," Scotty says.

"Not a bad idea," I say, thinking it a much more obtainable objective than using a nuclear sub.

"Suh, suh, submarine," Wizkid says, his hair twitching and shaking. "The plan has been initiated. The submarine base is only a few miles upriver."

Karen pulls on my shoulder and whispers to me. "Is this real? Nuseum? Nuclear submarine? President Wright? Missiles? It seems so crazy."

"Somehow, it always does," I say.

USS No Name

"KILL THE DRINEYS, Big Mac loses the election tomorrow, and then the door is wide open." President Wright paces, talking seemingly to everyone, but really to no one. "I could run again." He's wearing an orange prison jumpsuit. I can't quite figure out why, but I really have no interest in asking him and starting one of his long tirades.

I'm huddled with Wizkid and Derek. "So what's the plan to get into the submarine base?"

"Do you have scuba suits?" Derek says. "We could be all Navy Seal-like, kidnap a sub captain and crew and be off."

"Or we can walk right in the front door." Fixer stands next to us dressed in a perfect Navy submarine captain's uniform. "Come over here, if you please, Mr. President." President Wright walks over and stands next to Fixer. He holds his hands out and Fixer clamps handcuffs over his wrists.

Fixer throws some clothes at Derek and me. "Put those on. You'll be guards."

Derek and I put Big Mac storm trooper jumpsuits on.

"Here's the deal," Fixer says. "The president is good friends with an admiral at the submarine base. He's against Big Mac and has agreed to facilitate your entry into the base. You'll go under the guise that you're escorting former President Wright to some secret prison."

"A plausible enough scenario," Derek says.

"The tough part will be stealing a submarine," I say.

We have motored only a short way and are close to a ferry landing. The boat is heading straight for shore. "Reverse. We're going to hit," I yell to Wizkid.

The boat slows, but does not stop. Wizkid has a smile on his face. We shudder as the boat hits, but then there is a rumble, and we are powering up a concrete launch ramp as though being pulled up the hill on an amusement park log ride.

We're on an old army duck boat that is now doing its job as a land truck.

"No need to scuh, scuba dive," Wizkid says. "We're going to drop you at the front door."

Police sirens sound, and then numerous blue and flashing lights are coming toward us.

Derek reaches for his gun and kneels down. I don't know where my gun is, but I kneel down as well.

Three military police vehicles speed by without a concern for us, and I relax. Derek puts his gun down.

"We kind of stick out in this duck boat," Karen says.

Wizkid continues driving down the road. "No worries. Buh, buh, back in the water like a regular boat right after we drop the team off."

"Do you have a license for this thing?" Karen asks, still concerned.

"There's a license plate on back," Wizkid says. "That's all I know."

We drive along the river, and soon we're in front of the Naval submarine base main gate. A guard warily approaches us.

"Special forces," Fixer shouts. He turns to the rest of the infiltration crew. "They see crazy shit like this all the time. Ready to go?"

I give Karen a long hug and we kiss. "I'm sorry," I say. "I love you."

"I love you, too."

"Be safe. I will see you soon."

Scotty and I hug. "Take care of Mom."

"I will."

"But nothing dangerous. Patience is usually the best option."

Scotty winks at me. "Got it."

Derek, Fixer, President Wright, and I exit the boat, and Wizkid drives away with my family. The duck boat motors off down the road. I watch it go with sorrow.

Fixer walks confidently in front of us. Derek and I hold on to each arm of the president.

"Prisoner delivery," Fixer barks at the approaching guard.

"You should have a record."

The guard's demeanor immediately changes when he recognizes President Wright. "One moment." He scurries back into the gatehouse.

"ID?"

A guard looks at our IDs and scans them through a computer. The gates open, and we walk on to the base. We stand around for a few moments, and then a black military police SUV pulls up next to us. Derek and I escort President Wright into the backseat. Fixer sits in front, and a military police officer drives.

I'm about to close the door when I notice a large group of lights in the sky and hear the sound of helicopters. They look to be flying in formation. I estimate they are over the river, close to the bridge we just came over. "What's with all the helicopters? War games?"

"Something about terrorists taking over a cargo train," the driver says.

Explosions sound in the distance.

"Land," I say to Derek.

Derek scowls at me.

"Yes. I think they have a land operation going as well," the driver says.

None of my team says a word. They look ahead, professional, as if nothing can faze them, and I suppose that is how I should be, too. But I'm too worried. I tell myself that it's some kind of coincidence, some different train.

The SUV pulls in next to a two-level administrative building. Two guards help us out of the vehicle and escort us inside. We walk down a brightly lit hallway past naval personnel walking to and fro. This is the evening shift, so the building is not too crowded, but we catch plenty of glances. Word that President Wright has been here will be hard to contain. We have to hurry.

The guards lead us through this building, out some doors, and into another building. This building is higher security, and there are fewer people. We are just passing through, though, and we march down a short hall and exit out the other side. We walk between a concrete wall and the river.

Fenced off next to the river is a very long, curved concrete structure. It is surrounded by a barbed wire security fence. A sign says Security Clearance Required. We stop at a guard station. They scan our credentials and then let us pass into this top secret area. The guards motion us inside the structure but do not follow.

We are in a submarine hangar. I know this because a sleek submarine is docked right in front of us. Dim lights reflect off its smooth, metallic black contours. The submarine is about 150 feet long and is impressive, but still, I know most attack submarines are twice that size, and missile submarines can be 600 feet or more.

"Whoa," I say.

"Beats stealing a school bus," Derek says.

I laugh, thinking back how we hijacked the employee bus in our failed escape from the Border Patrol indentured work crew. "Hopefully this thing is a little faster."

"We've hit the big time, CT." Derek puts his hand on my back. "We pull this off, we really are super-spies."

I look over the impressive sub again, in awe. "Indeed."

A tall man in an admiral's uniform sees us from inside a small windowed office. He steps out and walks confidently toward us. He stops and stands at attention. He salutes.

"Welcome, Mr. President."

Fixer unlocks President Wright's handcuffs.

President Wright gives an official salute, one that seems to say, damn straight. I am the true president. "How the hell are you, Stranton?" He reaches his hand out and they shake like old friends. "Meet my crew."

President Wright introduces each of us to Admiral Stranton Lee. "We're old chums from Woodford prep," the president says.

"And you're in command?" the admiral says to Fixer.

"I'm in command," the president says.

"Of course, Oscar. As always," the admiral says. "I meant the commander for the NN."

"Yes. I'll be the pilot," Fixer says.

I look at the submarine. "Having support in the air is a good idea."

"There'll be no air support," the admiral says.

Fixer cocks his head sideways and gives me a goofy look. "Come on, Giorgio. I'm flying the NN here. The submarine."

"NN?"

"Top secret. A ballistic mini-sub to counter the Russians' Piranha."

"So secret it has no name," the president says.

"He said it was the NN," Derek says.

"NN." The president says. "No Name." He laughs. "Get it?"

Everyone is laughing but me. I'm starting to understand what is going on here, and I don't like it. "There'll be a qualified crew on board, right? A real pilot, I hope to God?"

"You're the only crew," the admiral says.

"What!"

Fixer slaps me in the chest. "There you go again, Giorgio, complaining about my piloting skills. How many times have I told you I'm the best pilot in the world?"

"Of airplanes. And how many times have I told you I'm never riding with you again?"

"In an airplane. A submarine is much easier."

"Don't worry," the admiral says. "This thing has so many robotic, computer, automatic things it practically sails itself."

"Time to go," President Wright says. "No more dillydallying."

"Fixer does not know how to pilot a submarine," I say.

"Or is it just dallying?" the president says.

"You're right," Admiral Lee says. "Time to go. It's almost midnight. The election starts in seven hours."

"I hope I win."

"You're not on the ballot, Oscar."

"But if we take out the drineys. Then I win."

The admiral speaks with gravity. "I can't help you. I have no crew to give you. The drineys are controlling everybody." He pops a pill into his mouth. "I've only got a few nuseum pills left. But yes, we can win if you take out the drineys. Big Mac will lose the election, and the military will step in and retake control."

"And then I win."

"And then we all win."

"What if Big Mac wins the election?" Derek says.

The admiral looks at us like a man losing patience. "Just take out the drineys."

Free Bird

"I FELT BETTER about going over Niagara Falls in a barrel." I look around at the control room of the secret USS NN.

Fixer sits in a chair like he's controlling the Starship Enterprise. Flat-screens surround him. He has a joystick in his hand. "Nothing to it, Giorgio. I figured it all out on the interweb yesterday."

"Interweb of what?" Derek says.

"The interweb of flying any-ass thing that moves." Fixer presses some buttons. "Prepare to dive."

"We're in a river." I quickly move toward Fixer, thinking I can stop him from bottoming us out, but then I stop. Fixer is laughing.

"Think I'm stupid, Giorgio? Tug's got us now. Why don't you go up top and see how things are going?"

"You're certifiably crazy," I say. "And to let you control anything is stupid in my book." I climb up a ladder, open up a hatch, and climb farther up to another hatch. I open it and stick my head out of the tower. Two small pilot boats lead us fore and aft. A tugboat is attached to our port side, motoring us along the Thames. We both have our lights out.

We have just passed under the highway and train bridges. I can see flames and helicopters swarming somewhere out to the east. I hope, again, that it's not Land's train, and I hope Wizkid has had the sense not to take Karen and Scotty anywhere near the fire. I try to reassure myself of Wizkid's genius mind and resourcefulness. But then again, he's not so good under pressure. He's better behind a computer screen, or during the planning stages. When it comes to action in real life . . . ah, shit. What can I do?

I continue to look out, watching out for Big Mac to discover us, or hoping to see some sign that will assure me Karen and Scotty are safe. In twenty minutes we reach the mouth of the river. It's hard to detect, but I think the NN is now under its own power. Sure enough, the tug detaches. The pilot boats turn away. The NN starts going down. We are submerging.

I duck down, close the hatch, and hurriedly descend the ladder. Down here, Fixer is engrossed with his joystick and screens. He has a look of utter bliss on his face. I must admit he is a good pilot, and he actually seems to know what he is doing with the NN. He releases his hands from the joystick, looks at me, and laughs.

"Water rising up scare you?"

"Pay attention."

The president sits in the seat next to Fixer, his mind

somewhere else. Derek stands uncertainly with his hand on the periscope.

Fixer retakes the controls and levels the sub off. "I bet I could roll this thing." He presses a button and then jumps up to look out the periscope.

I grab Fixer's arm and hiss into his ear. "Just get us to the rendezvous point. No funny shit."

He rotates his arm to avoid my grip. "Relax. We'll skim under the water nice and easy around Fishers Island, and then we'll autopilot her out to the rendezvous point." Fixer scoots around me back to the commander's chair. "After we fire that missile, though, I'm a free bird."

It's one in the morning now. We plan to shoot the missile at five a.m. Admiral Lee and the military will then take control. I want to be back on that duck boat as soon as possible with Scotty and Karen. Fixer and whoever else is crazy enough to stay with him can do whatever they want with this submarine then.

Fixer maneuvers us around the island without event, as he has promised. Derek has taken up monitoring the periscope. President Wright mumbles to himself, practicing a speech he plans to use when he retakes power.

I familiarize myself with the submarine. It may be a mini-sub, but it seems giant and lonely without any people on board. And as it's mostly an autonomous submarine, without all the sleeping quarters and other crew facilities, I feel like I'm in the center of a living machine.

I check out the ballistic missile the admiral has had

prepared for us. The NN has room for four missiles, but we have only one. It is big, probably five feet in diameter and forty-five feet long. A special wrench has been left to open up the warhead, and I use it to do just that. There's a ten foot empty space for the nuseum, more than we need.

Derek comes up behind me. "That's our hope?"

"Rendezvous with Wizkid and his duck boat, fill this baby up with nuseum, shoot it off toward middle America where it explodes and takes out the drineys. Easy, right?"

"The Wizkid part makes me nervous," Derek says.

"Yeah. Me, too."

I close the warhead lid, and suddenly everything moves. I feel like I'm on a skateboard that is getting away from me. I try to grab on to something for support, but am in vain. I fall to the ground.

We are diving.

Hand in Hand

I PULL MYSELF up to a standing position and have to lean back to balance out the diving sub. Slowly, the sub levels out, and everything feels normal.

Derek and I make our way back to the command center. I walk through the final doorway, and I'm rocked backward again. This time we are rising. I'm able to hold on to the door hatch and steady myself.

"Giorgio." Fixer is in his element, piloting a machine and aggravating me.

I give him a venomous look, but I don't do anything to disturb his piloting.

"What?" he says. The sub levels out. "There was a fishing boat I had to avoid."

President Wright is flailing his hands in the air, giving the speech of his life. "I didn't ask to return to the office of the presidency. I was chosen. Chosen by the fine, the free, the fabulous citizens of these United States."

We reach the rendezvous point, five miles off the coast of Long Island, straight out from East Hampton.

I pace. Derek is on watch with the periscope. "Still nothing," he says to me.

Fixer is tapping his thighs with his hands. "Sitting still is no fun. Sitting still is good for the enemy's gun."

"How's the weather?"

"Good." Derek takes another look. "The seas are calm. Wizkid, Karen, and Scotty should have no problem motoring out here in the duck boat."

The president is mumbling again. "The McCarthy era is over forever."

"I've got something. Coming right at us." Derek is all concentration. A minute passes in silence. "It's the duck. It's them. They're safe."

I clench my hands in namaste fashion. "Yes."

"Dive," Fixer says. The sub leans, and we all hold on.

"What are you doing?"

"Practicing evasive action. And we can't let them ram us." Fixer levels the sub off and brings her in a tight, arcing circle until we are behind the duck. "Now for the big surprise," he says.

"You have a right to your private thoughts," the president says.

Derek and I look at each other. The president's seemingly obvious statement is probably the most astute and forward thing either of us has ever heard him say.

"Surfacing," Fixer barks. We break the surface and level

off. "Go, Giorgio. You're the tower man."

I quickly put on a life jacket. I scamper up the ladder and through the hatches, sticking my head out into the night air.

"Whooh, Dad." Scotty has his arms in the air, waving to me and taking in the NN. "Awesome."

Karen is at the wheel of the duck boat. Wizkid is curled up on a bench—is he seasick? Karen moves the boat closer to us. I connect myself to the sub with a safety line and then climb out onto the deck. Scotty throws me some lines, and I tie them up. I slowly pull the duck boat in. Scotty lowers some bumpers. I keep tightening the slack until the duck boat and the USS NN submarine are together, and then I hitch the lines fast.

The deck of the NN is higher than the duck boat. Scotty unfolds the ladder and hands it up to me. He throws me some lines, and I fasten the top of the ladder to the sub deck. The bottom rests on the duck's open-door gangway.

I climb into the duck boat. "Why are you driving, Karen?"

"You know I can drive a boat. And Wizkid is curled up sucking his thumb on a bench. That's why I'm driving the boat."

"I could've drove," Scotty says.

Scotty and I touch our temples and point at each other. I kiss Karen on the cheek. "I'm so glad you're both safe."

Derek appears atop the sub's tower. "Everybody okay?"

Karen gives me the eye. "Scotty, Wizkid, and I are mostly okay. Thank you for asking, Derek."

"It's s-scary." Wizkid is standing, looking frazzled. "I, I, kind of—"

I remember how Wizkid was shell-shocked after our helicopter crash into Emergence. There were those explosions earlier; maybe the stress has gotten to him. "Don't worry about it, kid. We've got work to do and we have to hurry."

We make an assembly line. Wizkid has no interest in going into the submarine, so he stays on the boat. He hands the nuseum to Derek on the ladder, who carries it to Karen in the hatch. She passes the nuseum to Scotty and Fixer, who run back and forth to the torpedo room, where I neatly pack the cheese-like bricks of nuseum into the warhead. To any observer, we would appear to be drug runners transferring cocaine.

President Wright continues to practice his speech; which is fine. If he helped us, he'd goof up something anyway.

Twilight has started, and the black sky is giving way to an orange-and-blue glow. At five a.m., we finally finish. I'm exhausted; we all are. But the missile, though we are slightly behind schedule, is about to launch, and the tension is palpable.

Before we dive, Wizkid pulls the duck away. I'm the last on the conning tower. I wave to him. "See you soon."

Wizkid looks away. He hasn't heard me, or maybe he's just concentrating too hard on piloting the boat to acknowledge me. The duck boat turns and motors off toward the place where he will wait in safety a half mile away.

The sub dives. We make some last-minute checks. Launch time is now set for five-thirty, which will still leave plenty of time before the election begins. Except for Wizkid, we are all on board the NN.

Nobody is even thinking of sleeping.

"Go time," The president says.

"Hooyah," Derek says.

"You ready?" I ask Fixer.

"Always."

Fixer controls the missile from his command post. I watch on a screen a piston push the missile into the launch chamber. Fixer has programmed the missile to detonate over Iowa.

A camera on the periscope monitors the calm waters above the sub, displaying the image on the screens around us in the command room. Everyone is nervous, except for Scotty. He is thrilled, excited to be on a submarine, and confident that all will work out. I guess you could say he embodies that true American spirit: that through persistence we will prevail no matter what the odds.

"Launch sequence initiated." Fixer lifts his hands from his control panel. "Out of my hands."

One of the screens has a countdown timer. It's at twelve seconds. Nobody says a word. Scotty grabs my hand, and then Karen's. I hold Derek's hand, and he holds President Wright's. Fixer joins hands with Karen and the president. We all stand hand in hand in a circle, not saying a word, a silent vigil to propel our hopes with this rocket to free America.

"Ten, nine, eight," Scotty says.

The rest of us join as we stare at the screens. "Five, four, three, two, one—" and then silence.

Godspeed

A QUICK, DEEP sound vibrates through the submarine. "The
rocket has left the building," Fixer says.

"Elvis," the president says.

We stare at the screens. There is nothing but a pale, blue
sky and a calm, dark ocean. And then the missile breaks the
surface, awash in a foamy circle of its own making. It moves
slowly, and then, once it's completely out of the water, it seems
to float in the air for a brief instant. It tilts on an angle. Flames
pour out from the engine. And then the missile shoots into the
sky.

"Godspeed, John Glenn," the president says.

The missile picks up speed and is then gone, only a thin,
arcing contrail left as evidence of its existence.

Fixer sits at his control panel and puts on headphones. He

listens intently. "Pentagon's detected it."

"What if they blow it up?" Scotty says.

"They sure caught it quick," Derek says.

"They're going to try and bring it down," Fixer says.

"But that's okay." The president taps on Fixer's shoulder. "You said that was okay."

"Yes. yes." Fixer shoos the president away and tries to listen. Two minutes go by.

Everyone looks at Fixer, expectantly.

"Boom," Fixer says. "They got it." He whips his headphones off. "Taken out. Blown up over western Pennsylvania."

"Over two miles up, though, right?" I say.

Fixer gives me a thumb up. "We're good."

Scotty punches a fist into the air. "Yes."

Karen and I hug. Derek and I shake hands and then hug. Everyone congratulates each other. Good feelings abound.

"Time to go work," President Wright says. "Regardless of the election. Drineys are down. We have to hit Big Mac hard and retake control."

Fixer puts his headphone back on. "Contacting Admiral Lee and General Moore."

"We are now on Submarine One. Official command and control for the liberation of the United States." The president looks to Derek and me. "I want you two to take the duck boat with Wizkid into New York City to capture Vance Slater."

"A support team will meet you at Ellis Island," Fixer says. "Surfacing now."

"I'm not doing it," I say.

The president's face contorts and his lips gyrate until the words escape. "Say what?"

"I'm not going to capture Vance Slater. I'm done. I quit. I'm staying with Scotty and Karen."

"Loser," Fixer says.

"Order Admiral Stranton, or Lee, or whatever his name is," I say. "Or somebody else."

"But not me," Derek says. "I'm done, too. I'm going to find Doctor Rod, my true love, and be with her for a while."

The president is pointing his finger back and forth at us. "We'll . . . we'll . . . you . . . and you—"

"Double losers," Fixer says. "We are now on the surface."

"We'll talk about this later," the president says.

Wizkid returns with the duck boat, and we tie her off to the sub again. Wizkid is pale, like he is seasick and about to throw up. "Are you okay?" I ask.

"Huh, huh, hurry up," he says.

Derek, Karen, Scotty, and I climb aboard the duck boat. Wizkid nervously scampers around untying the lines. Fixer watches from the control tower, staring at Wizkid.

Finally, Wizkid pushes us away with his legs. "We're off."

Karen is at the controls. She gently eases the duck boat away from the sub.

We all wave and salute to Fixer and President Wright, who has joined him in the tower. I have just refused an order from the most powerful man in the world. Well, he should thank my compatriots and me for the fact that he's in charge again, although I'm sure he doesn't think of it that way. Still, I think we've gone through too much for him to stay angry with me. So I salute the president, and he salutes me back. Respect.

And then Wizkid scurries over to the wheel and brusquely takes control from Karen. He guns the engines, and we all stumble. Suddenly he's taking us away from land, directly east, out to sea at full throttle.

A panicked look overcomes Fixer's face. He pushes President Wright down, and then he hurriedly follows himself and closes the hatch. Shortly after, the submarine disappears below the water.

"Where are we going?" asks Derek.

I run over to Wizkid. "What's going on?"

He's crying. He holds on to the wheel and doesn't respond.

I grab him and pull him away from the wheel. "What have you done?"

A huge explosion erupts in the water behind us.

Muenster

WATER AND METAL fall from the sky. Waves from the explosion rock us.

Derek grabs Wizkid with both hands and throws him to the ground. Wizkid is still crying. "What the fuck did you do?"

"I, I saved you."

"You knew the sub was going to blow?"

Wizkid nods. "You all were supposed to be on it. I saved you."

Derek looks at me. "We have a traitor."

I try to search into Wizkid's scared, rapidly moving eyes for an answer. I can't believe he'd be disloyal without some good reason. He's just a college kid, really, possibly confused, easily manipulated. He must have been threatened. Why didn't he say anything, ask us for help, trust us? I want to strangle him and hug him at the same time.

While I'm thinking, Derek lifts Wizkid above his head as easily as a drum major flipping around a fake rifle.

Karen screams. Derek's going to throw Wizkid overboard.

I jump in front of them. Derek is furious. He's not joking around. "Derek. Wait."

"Out of my way, Chris. No discussion."

"He might have information we need. Think like a spy. Interrogate him first." I have no intention of killing Wizkid, but Derek is in no mood to hear any pleas for mercy. I have to appeal to his sense of logic.

"Fine." Derek throws Wizkid roughly into a bench seat. "Interrogation begins now."

Wizkid's eyes are wildly looking around. His breathing is erratic. He might pass out or go into shock.

"Please. Let me handle this," I say to Derek.

Derek just breathes, looking ready to kill. I take that as a yes.

I hold one of Wizkid's hands with both of mine. "Wizkid— Randall Linquist. Look at me." He settles down and his eyes focus on mine. "Everything will be all right. Tell us what happened."

"They knew the whole time."

"Big Mac."

"Yeh, yes. Since you first contacted me in Canada."

Derek kicks a bench. "A freakin' Big Mac agent the whole time. We're as good as dead."

"You are dead," Wizkid says.

Derek slaps Wizkid in the face. "Don't you taunt me."

I see Scotty staring in shock. Derek's not fooling around. This is real.

Wizkid was one of us, part of our team. We took down Emergence, and Big Mac for a while. An emptiness fills my core. We fought together, risked our lives. He saved me more than once. "I still don't understand."

"I, I, iNuggets," Wizkid says. "Big Mac manipulated the iNugget market for me. They gave me a monopoly. I'm a buh, buh, billionaire. Girls like me now. I just couldn't give that up. I thought I could do it without you guys getting hurt."

Derek and I look at each other. He rolls his eyes. "Girls."

"I saved you," he says defiantly.

"What about the people who died?" Derek says. "President Wright, Fixer."

"James," I say, suddenly realizing.

Wizkid nods. "After he led me to the nuseum, they took him out."

"You're lying," Scotty says. "If Big Mac knew where the nuseum was, why did they let us shoot it off?"

And then I remember. The missile went off. The nuseum has activated. The president and Fixer are dead, but we can still defeat Big Mac.

"That's right," Derek says. "The nuseum went off. We can still win."

"That wasn't nuseum," Wizkid says. "You shot off Muenster cheese."

"Shit." Derek grabs Wizkid. "That's it. You're going over."

I hit at Derek's arms until he lets go. "Just wait." I look at Wizkid. "Why are we here? Why did we shoot cheese? It doesn't make sense."

"They wanted you dead," Wizkid explained. "So now the media can say Big Mac shot down a missile fired by rebels led by President Wright. A per, perfect excuse to kill him and look like heroes themselves. Plus, when you started the plot to retake power, it revealed those in the military and elsewhere disloyal to Big Mac. They're probably being rounded up now. And if you were following the plan I came up with—which wouldn't work—then, then they knew you weren't following some other plan that might have worked. Be, because you trusted me."

Derek is breathing like a bull. "The kid goes. Then we haul ass to Bermuda or something."

"They're coming for me," Wizkid says suddenly. "Please, you all have to leave. They'll be here soon in a helicopter to take me back. If you're all here, we all die."

"I'll take my chances," Derek says. "Now you're going over."

"No, no," Wizkid says. "I've got a plan."

Little Joe

I'M ON THE train. I'm the Indian's prisoner, but I don't have to be. I can live with Ella and James on the maple syrup farm in Canada if I want. That seems really nice. I really don't want to be a prisoner. I'm afraid the Indian could kill me if he gets angry. Where is he going to take me? Will I be able to talk to anybody? I like talking to Ella, and all those people—except the Indian—who are against Big Mac. They're good people, I suppose, just messed up a little on what is best for America.

I wish I could just stay with Ella and James for a while and then go to Big Mac, but Chris Thompson says I have to forsake Big Mac forever. I don't know. I'll have to think about it. I have until Canada to decide.

But then, explosions go off everywhere. All hell is breaking loose. The train stops. The Indian grabs me roughly by the neck and drags me off the train and into the bushes. Train cars are exploding, all of them but the one we were in. Helicopters fly overhead and men are landing from ropes on top of our car. They bust in, but we are gone.

I try to fight the Indian, and he hits me. I go limp on purpose, and he has to carry me. He runs through the woods, and branches hit me everywhere. And then we are tackled by a bunch of men. I can't see them at all. They punch the Indian and pull me free. The men are in all black and have night vision goggles on. Very cool. I'm special. They came for me.

Somehow the Indian breaks free. He jumps over a log and runs in and out of trees really fast, and then he is gone. The men holding him can't tell which way he has gone so they don't chase him.

I go back to Big Mac. I tell Mr. Slater everything that has happened, and he praises me for not forsaking Big Mac. And even better—Mr. Slater says I can visit Ella for vacations and holidays and stuff like that. It'll be really cool. I can eat pancakes and drive the four-wheeler through the woods and hang out with Ms. Ella. So, really, I get the best of both worlds.

Mr. Slater says Scotty and his family, Derek, Doctor Rod, and James are all dead. That makes me really sad. Mr. Slater says if I'm to be a good king, I have to learn to accept sadness sometimes and deal with it. He says lots of people are going to die, and sometimes that is what is best for everyone else. Sometimes America has to kill to be strong, to be free.

Big Mac won the free election and is now the only political party allowed. Mr. Carlson is now president, but Mr. Slater is really in charge. He says I will be king someday, but he will take care of things for now. Mr. Slater said he was sorry I had to live such a boring life so far, but it was necessary for my education to be king.

I live in the White House now. I have a room just for water balloons. I have all the balloons I want, and I can throw them at whomever I want, too, people I don't like or who make me mad. Sometimes if a character on a TV show does something stupid, they bring the actor into the balloon room, and I can pelt them real good until I'm not mad at them anymore. Other times they just bring in Big Mac traitors, and I throw balloons at them before they go off to prison or wherever they go next. So you can see it is lots of fun.

I have like a million friends, too. Girls even. They like me. A lot.

America is a great place. A place where even a clone like me can live out his destiny. I love America. I love that I'm going to be king. I will fulfill my destiny. I will be king of America.

Culebra or Bust

I BREATHE IN and out, concentrating to remain calm. I'm three feet underwater, in a circle holding hands with Scotty, Karen, and Derek. We all are in scuba gear and have been hovering under here for about twenty minutes.

The sound was muffled, but I think a helicopter flew over ten minutes ago. Perhaps Wizkid is on his way back to the United States of Big Mac. Who knows what they did with the duck boat?

It was difficult to persuade Derek to let Wizkid live. I explained that if Wizkid was missing, it might appear suspicious, and they might continue to search for him, possibly finding us. I asked Derek to remember when he was young and did stupid things, and that girls and billions of dollars would be a tough thing for any college boy to give up. In the end, though, I think he was only persuaded by the fact that Wizkid was responsible for Doctor Rod coming to our rescue.

Doctor Rod didn't go with Uncle Sam after we disappeared. She returned to the maple syrup farm, and Wizkid was able to contact her there, trying to think of a plan to rescue us from whoever had abducted us. The thought of reuniting with Doctor Rod diffused Derek's anger.

It's cool in the water, quiet, peaceful, comforting. We all relax more. We can't talk to each other, but we don't need to. Just being together, safe, with the ones we love is enough. Isn't that what we are really striving for, why we have fought against Big Mac? So that we, or anyone, can be together, happy, without worry or fear of being taken away for no reason? So that we can think and say what we feel about anything at all and not be harmed for it?

Yes, we have lost, but I don't feel sad. I feel relieved. I'm done fighting, and my family is safe. The battle is over, but maybe, just maybe, Little Joe has seen and understands a little of our truth. Maybe the war someday can still be won. That will be someone else's fight, though.

Derek taps on my shoulder and points to my watch. I hold up my finger to him. One minute left.

On my signal, we ascend and break through the surface. The morning sun is bright. White clouds are far in the distance and high in the blue sky. The sea has picked up a bit, and we bounce in the waves.

We all look anxiously around. Wizkid said we would be picked up, and we trusted him. We've tried to stay in one spot so as not to move too far from the coordinates he gave us.

Scotty kicks with his fins and propels himself high above the water, spinning around like a dolphin. He does it again. He points. "A sail."

We all turn and look, kicking ourselves higher. A sailboat is headed directly toward us. We wave our arms and shout.

A forty-foot double-masted cutter comes around into the wind right next to us. "Ahoy." Doctor Rod stands on the deck and throws out a life ring and line.

It's evening now. The sun is about to set. A warm breeze blows over the port bow. Karen and I sit arm in arm across from Derek. Doctor Rod stands behind the wheel. Scotty lies out on the bow deck, dangling his feet over the gunwale.

The salt air smells good, and the scene looks idyllic, like we are on a luxury Caribbean cruise, a glass full of red wine in each adult's hand.

"I'm not too happy you boys lost my bionic suit and iPhone dart gun," Doctor Rod says.

Derek stands up and puts his arms around Doctor Rod's waist. "I wasn't so happy about a lot of things, but I'm happy now." They kiss.

Karen and I hold hands. We look at each other and smile. Scotty sees us and waves. We wave back. "I'm happy, too," I say.

We don't even talk about Big Mac. The loss is total. What we will do in the future, I have no idea. But for now, at this moment and for a while longer, all I want to do is be with my family and relax.

"Where to, Captain?" Derek says.

"I thought you knew," Doctor Rod says.

Derek smiles. "I didn't forget. Culebra Island, Puerto

Rico."

I hold my glass up. "Culebra or bust."

We all clink glasses. Here we go.

ACKNOWLEDGEMENTS

FOREMEOST, I WOULD like to thank all of my readers, especially those who so graciously complimented my first book, *Happy Utopia Day, Joe McCarthy*, and then requested I write a sequel. Your kind words encouraged me to no end.

A special thanks goes out to my Editor, Jeanne Thornton. Jeanne's work on both the books in the "Chris Thompson" series has been indispensible.

Thank you Shannon Hewson, Nath Jones, and Alan Larson.

And finally to all of my family, friends, and fellow writers. Your help and advice was greatly appreciated.

ABOUT THE AUTHOR

J.T. LUNDY lives in Naperville, Illinois where he writes novels and screenplays. He likes to read , write, travel, and eat good food. A graduate of Indiana University, he also holds an MFA from Spalding University and an MBA from the University of Chicago. Learn more at JTLundy.com.

www.ingramcontent.com/pod-product-compliance
Lightning Source LLC
Chambersburg PA
CBHW070628260626
47161CB00007B/2627